WOLF'S KISS

WØLVES OF ODIN
BOOK ONE

MADELYN LAYNE

WOLF'S KISS (Wølves Of Odin, book 1)

ISBN (ebook) : 978-0-9950890-6-8

ISBN (paperback) : 978-0-9950890-7-5

Copyedit by Cole-Hearted Editing (Kari Cole)

FREE BOOKS!

**Sign up for Madelyn Layne's
Newsletter and get access to
free books, bonus material, and
exclusive content.**

Madelyn's Newsletter:
www.madelynlayne.com

**Note to Reader: Originally, I published a different book as book 1 in Wølves Of Odin. That book was called First Kyss, and it was written in third person POV.

I have changed the covers, titles, POV, and book order in the series. Wolf's Kiss is now book 1, and Wolf's Reign (formerly First Kyss) is now book 2. Both books are written in first person POV.

For my family—always and forever.

CHAPTER 1

Missoula County, Montana

<u>*Britta*</u>

THE DRIVING BEAT OF THE MUSIC—*BOOM, BOOM, BOOM*— reverberated deep within the cells of my body. I had this nagging fear I'd shake apart from the inside out—and reshape into something else entirely. And it wasn't hard to guess what that new form would be.

Fur, claws, a tail, and sharpened canines.

Closing my eyes, I took a moment to center myself and the agitation inside me settled. But then a scantily-clad woman, gyrating close to me on the edge of the dance floor, bumped into my arm and jostled the drinks I carried. My lips pulled back from my teeth and I almost snapped at her.

She turned, giggling, her cheeks flushed and her eyes glassy, pawing my arm in apology.

I forced my mouth closed and twisted my lips into some kind of smile. Then I counted to ten.

I would get through this night without biting someone even if it killed me.

Unless, of course, that *someone* was built like a brick house and intent on annoying me. Then I couldn't be held responsible.

Lifting my gaze, I scanned the shadowy mass of bodies on the dance floor. Robbie—mister annoying, himself—wouldn't be hard to spot among the humans. Even in a group of Valdyr he was usually the biggest male.

Not that I was looking for him.

Okay… maybe I was, but only to prevent a murder. If he gave me one more knowing look tonight, I might just burst into a killing rage. And really, who could blame me? A female could only put up with so much *understanding* before she lost her non-wolfy shit.

I re-balanced the tray of drinks that rested on the palm of my hand and puffed out an irritated breath, blowing back the strands of hair that had fallen free of the tight bun pinned at the nape of my neck. The tension from the last week swirled within me, and I tried to push it down and find myself again. My real self.

Britta Larssen. College student, dancer, city dweller.

Not wolf. Not warrior of Odin.

Definitely not that.

Soon, I'd be done with college and hopefully have offers from dance companies all over the country…maybe even from around the world.

I could get away from this town, these mountains, and my pack.

The Varda.

The first pack created by Odin eons ago to hold the line against Hati and Skoll and keep their father, Fenrir, imprisoned.

Basically, to stop *Ragnarök*.

Whatever.

It's not that I didn't believe in that. I did. I'd seen the warrior wolves battered and torn after a fight, and I'd gone to many Valdyr funerals and seen the bodies burned in Odin's fire.

I knew what was at stake.

But even if my wolf rose for the first time tonight, there's no way Odin would want me. What could I possibly do to help the Varda? Have a dance-off with Hati and Skoll?

Bring it on, ass-hats. Then prepare to lose because baby's got some moves.

I snorted as I pictured Hati and Skoll breaking it down on the dance floor. I'd never seen Loki's twin grandsons, but I'd heard they were beautiful—in a scary, psychopathic kind of way.

A growl rumbled up from the depths of my body, and I lost my smile.

Clamping my jaw together, I tried once again to breathe away the weird feeling inside—which I told myself was hunger pangs. I'd had a spicy burrito for lunch and hadn't had any dinner yet.

Maybe I was just hangry.

Besides, the whole wolf thing had probably passed me by. I was well past the age when most females joined with their she-wolves. My mom had celebrated her ulf-risa on her nineteenth birthday. I was almost twenty-three.

But then my mom, Magna, had always known she'd fight beside my dad in the war against Hati and Skoll.

Me? I'd taken dance classes and then applied for college in Missoula.

Not a wolf...even if I wanted to bite someone tonight.

I scanned the dance floor again, thinking of Robbie. When I didn't see him, I spun quickly toward a stairwell that rose along the wall, intent on taking the drinks up to my Alpha, Erik, and the other Valdyr gathered on the balcony. Instead, I stepped straight into a wall of muscle. My drink tray tipped precariously and an arm shot out to steady it. The sleeve of the black T-shirt I stared at strained over the bulging bicep.

"Whoa. I got you," Robbie said.

Something inside of me softened and I almost sighed, but then an irritated snarl surfaced and broke through my lips.

Any normal guy wouldn't have heard it, especially in a darkened night club with music pounding and people shouting to be heard.

But Robbie wasn't normal. Or a guy.

Even for a Valdyr, he was just a little bit taller, faster, stronger. And those freaking muscles bulged out just a little bit farther.

Very annoying.

He quirked an eyebrow and grinned. "You still mad?"

I clenched my teeth and then forced my own smile, albeit a frosty one. "I wasn't mad. Quit analyzing me, Robbie. I'm beginning to think you've chosen the wrong career path. Ever consider psychiatry, Dr. Helvig?"

"Nope. And being a rekkr isn't a career choice. Odin called me to fight. You know how it is…warrior wolf, saving the world, that kind of thing." He said it with just a hint of laughter. Nice to know one of us was amused.

I pushed his arm out of the way and stepped past him toward the stairs, my long legs taking them two at a time. He followed— tight on my heels. His breath stirred the loose strands of hair at my nape.

It made me shiver.

"Actually," I said, tossing the word back over my shoulder, "I don't know how it is. No wolf. Remember? I don't expect I'll be around the Varda much longer. One way or another, I'll be gone from this town soon."

Missoula, Montana, was technically a city, but with the mountains and forests all around it and the rivers cutting through it, it felt like a small mountain town. Everyone else I knew loved it here—and there was lots to love—but I dreamed of crowded, noisy streets, people who minded their own business, and buildings that rose so high they blocked the sun.

And preferably a city much farther away from Wolf Ridge—the den where I grew up—than just a few hours' drive.

But a pang of uncertainty, one I'd been plagued with lately, filled my chest. I ignored it. Life in the Varda was for other Valdyr—like my mom and dad. My brother, Tyr.

Like Robbie.

Not for me.

College student, dancer, city dweller.

I reached the top step and then inhaled in surprise as Robbie grasped my arm and gently pulled me around to face him. The drinks swayed again, and I tilted the tray to compensate.

He stood two steps down from me, his normally neat brown hair ruffled. The intense shine of his hazel eyes shot into mine—two golden rays of light. For the first time in what felt like weeks, something settled within me.

Stilled.

My breath filled my lungs, and I suddenly found myself on the edge of tears—my throat tightening, my eyes pricking. Robbie rubbed his thumb up and down the skin at the crease of my elbow. Another shiver ran up my spine, and goosebumps broke out all over my body.

I quickly blinked and shifted my gaze over his shoulder, gathering myself before taking a mental and physical step backward.

Away from him.

His hand dropped. "I'm sorry, Britta. I spoke without thinking. I know it must be difficult for you to be without your wolf… to be missing that part of yourself."

I met his gaze again—guarded, this time, against my own vulnerability. "Nope. Not missing anything at all." I pointed at him. "Rekkr. Fights for Odin against killer, monster-shifters." I pointed at myself. "Dancer. Leaps across the stage in front of an adoring audience." Back to him. "Needs a vicious wolf." Back to me. "Needs a good sense of balance. I'm kinda okay just being human."

"Human?" a voice from behind me scraped along my nerves. "What the fuck, Brit? Have you told Mom and Dad that you're adopted?"

I turned and glared at my brother, Tyr, his pale green eyes—the exact color of mine—a sharp contrast to the electric blue of his shaggy, dyed hair. "Ha ha. Quit listening in on people's private conversations, meinfretr." The old Norse slur, which literally meant stinkfart, escaped my lips before I could stop it. Nothing like being around my loud, obnoxious, older brother to make me feel like an eight-year-old again.

Tyr had called me worse—much worse—over the years. And Robbie had heard it all—he'd lived with our family for four years after his dad had died fighting Hati. Sadly, his mom had passed in a car accident three years before that, so Robbie had been orphaned at fourteen.

I'd been ten. And I'd adored him.

But then Robbie's wolf had risen on his eighteenth birthday, and he'd howled to join the Varda. Odin had accepted him right away—no surprise there—and he'd gone to live in the vast caverns beneath the den at Wolf Ridge.

Six months later, my brother's wolf had risen, and he'd also howled to join the pack—something a wolf had to do if they wanted to stay.

Which I didn't. My time at Wolf Ridge was limited.

If my wolf *did* rise—and my mom insisted she would—I either had to ask to stay and be bonded to the pack—if Odin accepted me—or head out into the big, wide world.

A lone wolf.

I shivered at the thought of leaving, of being cut off from the pack, but I knew it was my destiny. Hel, I'd planned for it. I'd sent in audition tapes and letters of recommendation to worldwide dance companies. I *wanted* to leave.

And it's not like I couldn't come back and see my family again —see Robbie. For a few days, anyway. My wolf wouldn't be comfortable staying longer than that. And the pack, who had raised me, loved me—even if I'd doubted it over the years—wouldn't want me to stay.

That hurt, but I'd seen it happen.

Aren, my Alpha's younger brother, had howled to join the Varda, and Odin hadn't accepted him. And another wolf, a friend of Tyr and Robbie's had been rejected too. Aren still worked for the Varda in the fight against Hati and Skoll, but not as part of the pack.

And sometimes, it worked in the opposite way. My friend, Dahlia, as unlikely a candidate as me to get into the Varda, had howled right away—or her wolf had—and been accepted within seconds, leaving everyone, especially our Alpha, Erik, who was Dahlia's much-loved cousin, shocked.

The small, sweet Valdyr seemed as much an outsider as me. But Odin had a plan for her, and he didn't share it.

Maybe it had something to do with her magic—the magic Freyja gave to all female Valdyr when their wolves rose. A magic that most of them kept secret.

If they chose to share it with you, that was a privilege.

My brother snapped his fingers in my face. "Earth to Britta. Come in, Britta. Where in Hel are you?"

I jumped, and inside of me, something lunged forward. My body actually jerked from the force of it, causing the drinks to sway.

Robbie inhaled sharply behind me. I whipped my head around and gazed at him. Had he sensed that?

"What?" I asked him, holding my breath.

He'd moved up a step and now crowded behind me, his big body looming over mine in the tight space. A muscle jumped in his cheek as he stared at me. Then he shook his head. "Nothing."

Reaching out, he grabbed the tray I carried and stepped past me. The weight lifted from my palm.

"Hey, what are you doing?" I felt vulnerable, somehow,

without my platter of drinks, like I'd lost my ticket backstage. Technically, I was still a Valdyr and part of the pack, but I was also the way-too-old freak without her wolf.

"It's okay. I got it," Robbie said. He shouldered Tyr away from me with a growl. "Quit bugging her."

It was a command—and one Tyr couldn't refuse. If I'd ever doubted who was more dominant between them, I now knew.

"I wasn't bugging her. I was trying to get her attention." He frowned at me over Robbie's shoulder but kept backpedalling into the lounge. "She spaced out, like she always does."

Irritation shot up my spine at my brother's familiar grating tone and his *isn't-she-an-idiot* look. A look I knew well, and one I gave back to him several times a day. Or I had before I'd moved to Missoula.

Ignoring him, I glued my eyes to Robbie's retreating back, mesmerized for a moment by his massive shoulders barely contained beneath his black T-shirt, and his long legs and muscled butt encased in faded jeans. Even the slight wave in his light brown hair made me sigh. It looked soft. Touchable. Then I caught sight of the drinks sloshing over the rims of the glasses.

"Robbie, you're spilling them!"

"I said I got it. Take a breather, Brit."

He headed toward some booths against the wall where a number of Valdyr sat, and he started handing out drinks, sliding the glasses across the tabletops like they were shuffleboard weights—fast and smooth.

A round of Old Norse curses filled the air as the various recipients caught their drinks, making me snort. I'd be surprised if half the liquid remained in the glasses. Good thing the Valdyr always drank for free at Savage.

Releasing a tired sigh, I willed my shoulders to drop. Maybe Robbie was right. I'd been on my feet all day—first at class, then at rehearsal, then waiting tables. A breather would be welcome.

I scanned the Valdyr around me. Many of them were rekkrs—

the Varda's warrior wolves like Robbie and my brother—and all of them were tall, strong, and deadly. Some were dressed in jeans and sweats, while others wore more club-appropriate clothes, like me. Which wasn't hard—most of my tight, stretchy dancewear could pass as clubwear. All I needed was a little bling, a short skirt, and a push-up bra, and I could end up with hundreds of dollars in tips a night.

Not bad for a college student.

Other Valdyr stood at the edge of the balcony, overlooking the dancers, including Dahlia.

I grinned when I saw her, looking so out of place squashed between two huge Valdyr—one male, one female—her head not even hitting their shoulders. I was considered slender for a Valdyr, but I was just as tall and fast. And strong. Maybe even stronger in some ways because my body was so highly trained in a different way than theirs. I'd often thought it would benefit the rekkrs to incorporate some of my dance training into what they did.

I'd mentioned it once to my brother and Robbie, and Tyr had laughed for days until I'd beaten him in a complicated strength test that Robbie had set up for us. As usual, Robbie had known my physical capabilities better than my family did.

Or I did.

That was a few years ago. And I still lorded it over my brother.

Grinning again and with renewed energy, I hurried toward Dahlia. She was standing next to our new Fyrsta, the Alpha-female, Linnea, who appeared to be giving her some sort of lecture. Dahlia's head was lowered in deference and continued to droop further by the second, her shoulder-length brown hair falling forward to cover her face.

A frisson of anger shot through me toward the dominant female beside her, and Linnea suddenly directed her gaze at me. One of the benefits of not having my wolf yet is I more easily stood my ground—her wolf couldn't dominate mine in the same way she did others through the pack bond.

But it was hard—our Fyrsta was powerful and intimidating. And every inch the hard-ass. Literally and figuratively.

She wore the stretchy workout gear that she favored, shaping her bountiful chest and muscles, and her glorious red hair tumbled halfway down her back.

Drop dead gorgeous—whether she knew it or not—and scary as hel.

Our old Alpha female, Inga, had been the pack's healer—a calm, gentle older woman who had nursed us back toward emotional health and stability after our Alpha, Erik, had lifted a curse from the pack that had leeched its way into the hearts of every member—including me.

Erik held the curse tightly within himself now, and I knew it weighed heavily upon him. Some part of me, deep in my soul, sensed it—like I sensed the emotional damage the curse had done to the other members of the pack—whether my wolf had risen yet or not.

"Fyrsta," I greeted Linnea, meeting her eyes. She stared me down, and I stared back. I shouldn't have, but I could see Dahlia's lip trembling, and my anger boiled to the surface. I reached out and squeezed my friend's fingers, who squeezed tightly in return.

Linnea frowned at me. "How old are you?" she asked abruptly. "Why can't I sense your wolf?"

My back straightened, and silence fell beneath the booming music. Every wolf here was listening. From the corner of my eye, I saw Robbie step toward us, but I lifted my hand to stop him.

I could handle this.

"I'll be twenty-three next month, Fyrsta. And my wolf is…on vacation?" I shrugged, like I didn't care, and continued to hold her gaze—a challenge to her wolf and ultimately to her authority.

Her hands fisted on her hips, and she seemed to grow taller, more dominant. Pressure built within my head, but I resisted.

She may think that because I wasn't a fighter, I was weak, but she hadn't seen me put on pointe shoes over bloody toes or practice the same move a hundred times every day until I had it just right.

Or perform while injured.

She may have been accepted by Odin to lead the pack alongside Erik, but nobody liked her. She hadn't grown up here or made any real friends. And no one else had challenged her for the position.

But I also knew that she hadn't wanted the job, and I kinda felt sorry for her—or I had until now. Erik had picked her for her fighting skills when no other female had stepped forward to lead the pack after Inga had died peacefully in her sleep last fall.

Gods, I missed her.

"My wolf rose at seventeen," Linnea said, jarring me from my reverie. "She's never gone on vacation."

I raised my brow and spoke before I had enough sense to stop myself. "Well, maybe she should. Go have a Mai Tai and swing on a hammock. It might do everyone some good."

Linnea advanced on me quickly, but I was quicker. I'd always been the fastest in any race at school—wolf or no wolf. Jumping back, I pulled Dahlia behind me...just as Robbie stepped in front of me.

Tyr also stepped up beside me, and for some reason, that brought tears to my eyes. It wasn't often my brother and I stood together.

Then I heard a voice say my name—in a tone that set my heart pounding.

"Britta."

That's all it took. That's all it ever took. My defiance crumbled, and my stomach sank.

I glanced toward the other side of the lounge and saw my Alpha, Erik, standing in an open doorway to the club's office. His arms hung loosely by his side, making him look relaxed, but I wasn't fooled. Unlike Linnea, Erik had had to fight to lead us.

Brutal battles for dominance in the domr six years ago after his father and mother—our previous Alphas—had died.

He was our youngest leader ever—our strongest leader ever—and he'd saved us not only from Hati and Skoll but also from ourselves when he'd sucked the curse that had poisoned us through the Alpha bond and into himself.

Erik put the dom in dominant without even trying. And now he was staring straight at me.

"Fudge balls," Dahlia whispered behind me. "Okay, don't panic."

"I'm not panicking," I whispered back, aware he could probably hear us.

"Then how come you're shaking?"

"I'm not. I'm…hyperventilating."

Erik's lips twitched before he turned back to the office. "Come and see me. Now."

He disappeared inside, and after a little shove from Dahlia, I followed him. At the door, I glanced back and caught Robbie's gaze. He was frowning at me fiercely, and his lips had pulled back from his teeth. Dahlia gripped one arm while Tyr gripped the other—as if holding him back.

Linnea had disappeared.

What was going on?

Then Gunn, Erik's second-in-command, stepped between us and blocked my view with his massive shoulders.

"He's waiting," he said before nudging me inside and closing the door behind me.

CHAPTER 2

Britta

"Take a seat," Erik said to me as he sat behind a desk situated at the back of the small, dark office, which obviously doubled as a storage room. Boxes were piled neatly in the corners, and bar stools had been stacked along one wall. I even spotted some cleaning supplies on top of a metal shelf.

Nothing at all like Erik's pristine office back at Wolf Ridge.

My eyes fell on a wooden chair near the door. I grasped the rickety back and dragged it forward. It was heavier than it looked, and the legs scraped loudly against the floor.

I darted my gaze to him before lowering it. "Sorry, Fyrstr."

"Don't be. The floor's already scratched. Relax, Britta."

I glanced back at him, and he smiled. The air gusted from my lungs in relief. This was Erik, who'd done nothing but support me over the years, who'd saved all of us over and over again. "I thought I was in trouble for getting snarky with Linnea."

"Your Fyrsta doesn't need me to fight her battles. Although it wouldn't hurt to be a little more respectful when dealing with her. Just…talk to her like you would to me."

I raised my brow. "It's not the same. Besides, she was dominating Dahlia—the nicest person in the world who just wants to make everyone happy. Was I supposed to let that go?"

Erik's eyes changed from his usual chocolate brown to a shining golden brown, and I almost smirked. His wolf was mad—and not at me.

He adored his cousin, and he knew as well as I did that there were better ways to get your point across with the sweet, submissive wolf.

"I'll talk to Linnea. But in the meantime, give her some space. Odin chose her as Fyrsta for a reason. She just needs to find her way."

I shrugged and bit my tongue, so I wouldn't remind him that Odin hadn't had a choice. No other female had challenged her for the position. But it was as if Erik had read my mind.

"She stepped up when I asked her to. No one else did. She's a strong wolf and rekkr, and she puts the fight against Hati and Skoll first, no matter what. The Varda needs her." He shrugged. "I can work with her on the other stuff. The interpersonal stuff."

I wanted to argue with him, but who was I to question pack leadership? Erik always knew best—I trusted that down to my core. And it's not like I'd be here for much longer. As soon as my wolf rose, I'd be out. Because why would the Varda need a dancer? An interior designer, maybe.

I glanced around the room again, letting go of my annoyance toward Linnea. "You could do with some decorating in here, Frystr. And proper lighting. Although then you'd see all the dirt and grime, and be forced to...you know...clean."

Erik snorted. "We don't use it as an office very often. Mostly for storage. I did get the door sealed, though."

I knew what he meant—magically sealed so no one could hear what was going on inside. A piece of wood and some drywall couldn't keep hyper-sensitive Valdyr ears from listening in. Although that was less of a worry than our enemies listening in—either with their own sharp hearing or electronic surveillance.

I made a show of brushing the dirt off the chair before sitting down. "Did you call me in here for a reason? Or just to break up the fight that was brewing out there. My brother and Robbie didn't take kindly to Linnea coming after me for no reason."

Okay, maybe I hadn't let it go.

Erik raised his brow, and I grinned. "I know, I know. She had reasons. But seriously, you have to talk to her soon. Who's she going to try and dominate next? Kat? That's all we need—a healer who is too scared to actually heal."

Erik sighed and shoved his hand through his chocolate brown hair—an exact match to his gorgeous brown eyes. I knew many females in the pack who drooled over him, but Erik never looked at them twice—at least not since he'd become Alpha and siphoned the curse out of everyone's hearts and minds and into himself.

He took his responsibilities seriously.

"Kat can hold her own," he said. "And Linnea understands Kat's place in the pack. She doesn't know what to do with Dahlia."

"Well, she can start by leaving her alone. Let Dahlia find her own place in the Varda instead of picking on her—the weakest wolf. She's already insecure enough."

Erik growled, and I stilled, the hair rising on the back of my neck. Gods, why did I have to keep pushing it? I dared a quick peek at him.

His hands had fisted, and his eyes shined golden again—his wolf even more agitated this time. But at me or Linnea?

"Dahlia is not weak. My cousin fits into Odin's plans. How she fits just hasn't been revealed yet."

"I know." I struggled to hold his gaze. "I'm sorry, Fyrstr. I'm… out of sorts and edgy. I have been for a while. I'm not sure, but I think…maybe…"

His face softened, and the compassion that was such a big part of him came through. "…that your wolf is close. I know. She is close, Britta. Very close."

Heat pricked all over my body, and I inhaled sharply. "Are you sure?"

"Yes. I sense her. And my wolf is excited. He can't wait to meet her." He smiled again, but sadness lurked beneath it. Erik covered his heart with his hand in an unconscious gesture. "But I don't want to lose another packmate, to lose you. It kills me every time."

I knew what he meant. Once my wolf came through, I'd have to leave—my pack gone in an instant. Odin wouldn't want me.

For a moment, my own sorrow welled, and then I shoved it back down.

My destiny was out in the wide world somewhere. Not with the Varda. I'd planned for this all year—dancing whenever I wanted, going wherever I wanted, doing whatever I wanted. I'd even moved away from Wolf Ridge.

A lone wolf.

"Who knows, maybe Odin will choose me. But if not, it's okay. It's not like I'll never see you again."

He nodded, and a heavy silence grew. "He picked Dahlia."

"Yeah. That was a surprise." I somehow summoned a grin. "When I found out, I told her to buy a lottery ticket."

He grinned too. "And did she?"

I shrugged.

Then he cleared his throat and folded his hands on the desk in front of him. "That's what I wanted to talk to you about."

"Winning the lottery?"

"No."

"Being a lone wolf?"

"No."

"Going to—"

"Britta!"

I laughed out loud, this time. I loved being able to exasperate my Alpha. Sometimes Dahlia and I did it on purpose, ganging up on him until he dropped his head into his hands. Totally. Whipped.

Boo-yah!

A folder sat on the desk, and he opened it then handed a sheath of papers to me.

"What's this?" I asked as I took them from him. The top sheet was a deed of sale for a building and property here in Missoula. I flipped through several pages of legalese before coming to a blueprint. I turned it sideways and squinted, trying to read the small print.

"I purchased an old theater near the University that was scheduled to be torn down to make way for a strip mall. And some adjoining property too."

I raised my eyes from the blueprint, confused. "Why would Wolf Ridge purchase a theater in Missoula?" The pack owned Savage, but the nightclub had a purpose—it was a place the Valdyr could relax and blow off some steam. Or find someone to hook up with if that's what they wanted.

"Because I'm planning to build a new one there—a performance venue for every artistic endeavor. Acting, singing, painting, film—all of it." He leaned forward, excited. "And I want you to be the Artistic Director and head administrator."

Shock hit me like a punch to the gut. All I could do was stare at him, my eyes wide, and my jaw dropped open. "Artistic Director?"

"And dancer and choreographer as well, of course. I want it to be a true artistic center with classes and performances where our pups can fully express themselves, if that's what they desire."

"Like I did."

"Yes. But it'll be easier for them to learn than it was for you. A place the pack, especially the pups, can develop more than just their fighting or tech skills. Obviously, keeping Fenrir imprisoned and winning the battle against Hati and Skoll is still our primary objective, but so many wolves who aren't chosen by the Allfather feel lost and unworthy afterward, and nothing could be further from the truth. Odin just hasn't called on them yet. I want them to pursue all avenues of development and expression, to build confidence, and widen their scope, whether it leads to them being picked or not. Because none of us know what Odin's plans are and how we fit into them."

I looked back at the blueprint, seeing several performance spaces and multiple rehearsal rooms. Unbelievable. A tingle of excitement started to work its way through my shock. "So...a center just for Valdyr?"

"Not always, but sometimes, yes. We'll need to find more teachers, obviously, and technical people to run the shows. But think of it, Britta. Can you imagine a performance solely for a Valdyr audience—where you won't have to hold back?"

I sucked in a breath. Always, when I danced, I had to pull back on my ability, or I would look exactly like what I was—supernatural. My leaps would span the stage, my strength and balance would outperform the other dancers, and my speed would shock the audience, leaving them dizzy and confused.

But dance wasn't all about power and technical ability. It was about evoking emotion, and I felt everything when I danced. That was my real superpower. That's how I touched people.

"No, I can't imagine it." I looked back up at him, tears filling my eyes as the enormity of what he was doing for our community, for our pups, and for our pack hit me. "Erik, this is amazing. If I'd had access to classes like this when I was young...if my parents had been more supportive instead of training me to fight day after day, everything would have been so different. I would have been happy and energized rather than feeling trapped and misunderstood all the time."

He reached out and squeezed my hand. "They didn't understand, Britta. And because you were so fast and agile—and strong in your own way—they thought you were meant to be a rekkr."

"Like they were."

"Yes." He sighed and sat back again. "You're probably too young to remember, but by the time I became Alpha, the curse had eaten away at most of the pack and family bonds within the Varda. It had twisted our emotions, perverted them. We were slowly being torn apart, and nobody even knew it was there. It was a terrible time."

I lowered my eyes. It had been terrible, and I *did* remember. Everything. I'd felt the anguish throughout the pack—deep down in my soul.

Then Erik had funneled the curse out of the Varda and into himself, guarding it night and day in that mystical plane of existence where our wolves resided—where we resided when our wolves were present in this world.

The Hjarta.

"You did," I whispered.

"I did what?"

"You knew that the curse was there. What it had done to us."

He closed his eyes for a moment. Shook his head. "Only because of what my dad did to my mom. He felt the curse at the end—after she died—and he warned me. The force of it, rebounding into me after he passed, was like being hit by a semi-truck of seething rage and violence."

His lips twisted in what some might think was a wry smile, but I knew better.

"It still is," he added.

"Can the others help—"

"No, it's manageable." He pulled back from me, reining in his emotion. "I didn't intend to worry you, Britta, I just wanted you to understand—about your parents."

I nodded, remembering those early teenage years when I was

drowning in their disapproval, their anger, and their frustration. Before Erik had become Alpha, and intervened. Finally, I'd been allowed to take one ballet class a week in Missoula, but that meant they had to drive me there. Almost an hour both ways…if they weren't working.

Not that I could blame them for putting me last. When Odin called, you answered. Missing a ballet class or recital couldn't compare to saving the world.

But then I almost died one night after I'd stolen our car and driven myself to my end-of-year performance—without my license and in an unexpected spring snowstorm.

The performance had gone well, and I had been transformed. I had found my calling. I knew what I wanted to do with my life, and I would go to almost any length to do it—to be it!

A dancer.

But first, I had to survive the drive home in a snowstorm. I didn't make it. Instead, I spent seven freezing hours stuck on the edge of the mountain still wearing my costume—because I was young and dumb and thought I was invincible. I hadn't even taken a jacket with me.

Luckily, the pack had found me in time. Unluckily, I was banned from any more dance classes.

But Erik knew. He could see the determination in my eyes, feel my outrage down the Alpha bond.

"If you hadn't insisted on flying me to classes in Missoula, they never would have conceded."

"You would have found a way."

"Yes. Even if it meant running away to Missoula or somewhere else. So, thank you for saving me."

"It was nothing. I just offered you a lift."

"It was everything. My parents could hardly say no when I was helicoptering into the city and back again every day with their Fyrstr."

He shrugged. "I liked having you there. Except for the talking. Non-stop gibberish over the headset."

"Hey! I've never gibbered in my life. Just be glad Dahlia wasn't there too."

A pained expression crossed his face, and I laughed.

"So, you'll do it then?" he asked, nodding toward the papers I still held in my hand.

I looked down at them, my thoughts swirling. "I...I don't know, Erik. I have to think about it."

He tapped his thumb on the desk. "Okay... Is it because of Robbie?"

I jerked up my gaze. "Robbie? No. Why would it be about him? It's about me and my future—away from Wolf Ridge. I've applied to dance companies all over the world. I've sent in audition tapes. They may...want me."

My voice cracked at the end, emotion bubbling through the words, and heat filled my face.

Erik's eyes softened. "We want you too, Britta. We need you. Even if Odin says no."

I nodded, my throat too tight to speak. They may need me and my wolf once she rose, but only from a distance. Even my parents would get antsy if I was in their home for too long. It was the reality of being a lone wolf.

And it sucked.

"Just think about it, ulf-ungr."

Young wolf.

He hadn't called me that in a while.

"I will. I promise."

He reached across the desk for the file he'd given me, and I laid my hand over his. "Thank you, Erik. It means more than you know."

He squeezed back. "Don't lose faith, Britta. He may still choose you."

Something defiant rose within me, coming from a hurt, painful place. "And what if *I* don't choose *him?*"

Erik took a moment before answering. I waited on pins and needles, my breath held tightly in my lungs.

"I'm sorry to say, it doesn't work that way. Your wolf will follow her instinct and trust in Odin's decision. So will you." He raised his hand to a medallion he wore around his neck—a tiny Viking longship with a dragon head and a square sail—and squeezed it. His gaze grew distant. "You've yet to be a part of the Handsal ceremony, to see the sky light up when a wolf howls the yla, to hear the pack pick up the notes and sing in harmony. And then, if Odin accepts the wolf, and bonds it to the pack, the sound as the notes rise to a crescendo, and the colors burst across the sky… It's…divine."

"Divine?"

"Yes. Literally, divine." He focused his gaze on me again and smiled.

"And if I send out the yla, and Odin rejects me? Is it divine then?"

His smile faded. "Yes, it's divine. Divinely sorrowful. For everyone."

A pit, dark and bottomless, opened in my stomach. "Then I won't call. I won't send out the yla." But it was my wolf's choice. Not mine. And I knew it.

And we would be rejected.

I rose with a sigh and straightened to my full height—just over six feet. My dreams of dancing the *pas de deux* had faded years ago. I'd never had a partner fully able to support me. Not tall enough, not strong enough, not fast enough.

My eyes dropped back down to the papers on the desk. But maybe that could change for some other Valdyr female and her partner. Maybe I could teach them.

"I'll let you know in a few days. I'm…waiting on a few things."

Like my wolf rising and whether or not my position in the pack would change.

Britta Larssen. College student, dancer, city dweller. *And lone wolf.*

Turning, I headed to the door. When my hand grasped the knob, Erik called out to me. "Britta?"

I looked back at him. "Yeah?"

"You resisted it more than others."

"Resisted what?"

"The curse."

I turned all the way to face him. Something inside me moved —an acknowledgment, somehow. But it didn't feel like my wolf. "What do you mean?"

"I know you think you had it bad—you did have it bad—but your family came out of it relatively unscathed. Not everyone was so lucky."

"Lucky?" That was the last word that came to mind when I thought about my childhood.

He nodded. "In the year before my father died, before I became Alpha and funneled the curse out of the pack, seven Valdyr were murdered. And not by Hati or Skoll. They were killed by parents and siblings, ulf-verrs and ulf-vifs, friends and…Alphas."

"Alphas?"

"Yes."

"But…how could the Alpha…?" I couldn't even say the words, couldn't wrap my mind around what he was implying. The Alpha protected the pack.

"How could a parent hurt a child? Or an ulf-verr hurt an ulf-vif?" he asked. "We are bonded. It should have been impossible. The curse did that to us—to packmates and to families."

I knew things had been bad—I'd sensed the loss of connection between friends and loved ones, and the rage within us—but murder? "It's been six years. Are things still like that?"

"No. The curse is gone, and the pack is healing…just not fast enough." His hand went to the file again. "I thought this might help. That *you* could help—whether Odin chooses you or not.

"Think hard, Britta. Please. I know it's asking a lot, but we need you."

CHAPTER 3

"Calm down, Rob," Gunn commanded me from where he stood in front of Erik's closed, office door.

His words were more than sounds, hitting my ears. They also felt like a powerful body slam by his wolf or a bite to the jugular through our pack bond.

But my wolf wasn't listening, no matter how strong the order.

I couldn't answer Gunn—my second-in-command in pack hierarchy after Erik—I couldn't respond in any way. All my energy was focused on controlling that other part of myself, which was a hair's breadth away from shifting and charging through Gunn, as impossible as that seemed, to get to our Alpha.

And tear him apart.

"Yeah, good luck with that," Gunn growled as he walked toward me. His wolf's eyes shone brightly in his gaze, an unbelievable green against Gunn's dusky skin.

Shit. Gunn was as connected to me through the Alpha bond right now as Erik was. He knew exactly what my wolf wanted to do.

And why.

Britta.

Which shouldn't be a surprise. Wasn't it always about Britta?

No. It couldn't be. I wouldn't let it be. Britta was empathetic and creative—an artist—like my mom. Not a warrior like me. Like my dad.

Her place was out in the world pursuing her dreams—not being tied down by Odin at Wolf Ridge.

Or tied down by me—like my mom was by my dad.

But my wolf didn't care. And this past week, especially tonight, he'd been crawling right beneath my skin, pushing to get to her.

He sensed her wolf. He knew the female was coming through.

And we were going to leave her the fuck alone.

Calm down! I yelled at him.

Mate! He howled back.

She's with our Alpha. She's safe.

That incensed him even more, and he lunged forward, almost bursting through my skin. Hands tightened on each of my biceps, holding me back, and I knew Tyr and Dahlia were still beside me, trying to help. Not that Dahlia had the physical power to keep me in place, but her gentle presence and the fear I had that I might hurt her, lowered my wolf's aggression just enough that I stayed in control.

Then a vision came to me down the Alpha bond—Erik showing me Britta through his eyes. She sat opposite him, smiling and at ease, teasing him. I felt his wolf's affection for her as he also watched her, curious and happy to greet the wolf of a female he'd known since she was a pup—and nothing more.

Then my Alpha turned and snapped at us through the bond— so fricking dominant and strong my wolf stumbled back a few steps and whined in submission, his head and shoulders lowered.

I'd just been told off, or rather my wolf had, and he'd submitted.

But there was pride and joy in that submission, too, because the power that crushed me was my Fyrstr—my leader in this apocalyptic fight against Hati and Skoll, the sons of Fenrir and grandsons of Loki—who fought by my side to keep Fenrir imprisoned and the world safe from Ragnarök.

He was Odin's champion.

And he was stronger than all of us.

I relaxed as my wolf receded, and a gust of air escaped my lungs. Beside me, both Dahlia and Tyr released their hold.

Gunn stood directly in front of me, just as big as me, and shook his head. "Idiot," he said. Then he punched me in the shoulder—hard.

Wincing at the burst of pain, I raised a hand to rub my throbbing arm. I'd been lucky—I knew it, and my wolf knew it. Erik could have torn me to shreds, and no one would have raised a finger to stop him. Not even Tyr.

That was meant for you. Happy now? I asked my wolf.

The male sat in that mystical place we called the Hjarta with his back to me. I saw him in my mind's eye, felt him in my heart and body. Then he slumped forward and laid his muzzle on his paws, almost as if he was embarrassed, although I knew that emotion wasn't one my wolf ever felt—or shame, or guilt.

No, those emotions were reserved for me.

Embarrassed? he asked, still refusing to look at me. Maybe he did feel a little embarrassment.

It's a...Valdyr emotion. One of the ones you don't understand. I sent him the image of when I was a rekkr-in-training, and I'd failed an exercise set up to test my leadership ability—and to stay open to all possibilities during a fight rather than focusing on only one outcome. In doing so, I'd closed myself off to other potential threats, and my team had paid for it.

It didn't matter that almost everyone failed that test the first time; I had been crushed. And embarrassed.

My wolf grunted in understanding and then rolled to his side, quickly drifting off to sleep.

I straightened to my full height with a frustrated sigh and reached out to Dahlia to make sure she wasn't hurt. "I'm so sorry. Are you okay?"

"I'm fine," she said with a quick smile.

"What's with you, bro?" Tyr asked as he flexed his hand—the one he'd used to hold me back.

I shrugged, not wanting to say that my wolf had gone crazy because of his sister. Whatever that meant. I couldn't meet his gaze.

He stared at me for a moment, then shook his head. "Well, fuck. I'm gonna need another drink."

Tyr stepped past us and weaved his way between the other Valdyr toward the stairs, his electric blue hair shining brightly whenever it caught the dim light.

I turned back to Dahlia and Gunn, feeling the heat in my cheeks. Dahlia watched me with curious concern. Gunn just looked amused, in a let's-torture-him-a-little-more kind of way.

"What's going on?" she asked. "I've never seen you like that before—your wolf fighting you." Then panic filled her eyes, and she darted her gaze up to Gunn, who towered over her—we both did. "Oh, my gods, is it the curse? Is Erik okay?"

She stepped quickly toward the office, but Gunn put his arm out to stop her. "It's not the curse. He's okay, Dahlia. I would know."

"Are you sure? What if it's broken out of Hjarta? What if it's in Erik?"

"It's not. This was all on Robbie. His wolf was freaking out about something."

She turned back to me, still looking unsure.

I sighed and nodded. "My wolf senses—" I stopped. It wasn't my place to tell her that Britta's wolf was rising, especially with everyone around. Secrets were hard to keep in the Varda, and news traveled fast. The last thing Britta needed right now was more pressure.

I tried again. "My wolf has been agitated lately, and he's been testing me." That was definitely true. "He's...feeling caged-in. I need to let him out for a long, hard run. Seriously, it has nothing to do with the curse. Erik has control of it, as always."

Gunn's amused smile turned into a worried frown, and he huffed out a breath. More of a growl, really. I knew he wanted Erik to share some of the burden of guarding the curse with a few strong rekkrs—myself included—but Erik wouldn't pass on that responsibility to anyone.

Dahlia let out a sigh of relief and squeezed my forearm. "Okay. Is there anything I can do to help you? Or your wolf?"

"You can bake him some more of those cookies you made last time," Gunn said. "Lots of them. That'll make Rob feel tons better —and calm his wolf."

Fucker. The last time Dahlia had made me cookies—on my birthday—I hadn't gotten any of them. All the other rekkrs had scarfed them down—including Gunn.

"But before you bring them down, let's talk about the recipe," I said. "Maybe add a little something extra in there."

"Like what?" she asked.

"Like chocolate chips," Gunn said. "Or more chocolate chips."

"Or something else..." I added, putting an ominous tone in my voice.

Dahlia looked back and forth between us, her brow furrowed, trying to figure out what we were talking about.

"Is this a rekkr thing?" she asked.

"Yes," I said, at the same time as Gunn said, "No."

Then Gunn's gaze focused on something behind Dahlia, and his jaw hardened. "Well, fuck. What's this all about?"

Dahlia and I turned, following his gaze, and I caught sight of another massive Valdyr, wearing lots of leather, torn jeans, and shit kickers. Dark sunglasses covered Dane's eyes despite being in the dim nightclub, and his short, blond hair spiked upward.

But he wasn't part of the pack.

Beside me, Dahlia inhaled sharply, and all kinds of contradictory scents poured off of her—fear and admiration, nervousness and anticipation, dread and...desire? I sniffed again. Yep, definitely desire.

That wasn't good. Dane was a real badass. A lone wolf who fought against Hati and Skoll on his own, sharing his intel with the Varda only when it served him. I'd seen him fight—hel, I'd fought beside him on a few occasions—and he left bodies strewn behind him on the battlefield, intent on only one thing... inflicting as much damage as he could against the sons of Fenrir and their Jotun brethren.

More damage than I was comfortable with. I was a warrior of Odin, fighting to keep Fenrir imprisoned and prevent Ragnarök —thereby saving the world.

Dane was fighting for revenge—and the more pain and bloodshed doled out against Hati, Skoll, and anyone who worked for them, the happier he was.

Revenge for what, I didn't know, but my wolf was wary of his. Something had happened to him years ago, and it hadn't been pretty.

He was the last wolf a sweet, submissive Valdyr like Dahlia should be getting involved with. I prayed to Freyja that she never did.

Rumor had it that Dane was as dominant in bed as he was on the battlefield. And he left just as many worked-over bodies behind.

I did not want my friend to be one of them.

Dane made his way toward us through the crowd—the Valdyr in his way, stepping back just enough to allow him through. Inside, my wolf rose to his feet and faced him, watching the lone wolf through my eyes. As always, when in Dane's presence, my wolf was prepared for anything and flexed his muscles in dominance.

I did the same and noted that Gunn seemed to grow a little bigger and taller too. We both shifted to stand in front of Dahlia.

Dane stopped a few feet away, assessing all of us, including Dahlia—for longer than I was comfortable with—before his gaze settled on Gunn.

"Gunnar Lang," he greeted Gunn formally, a hint of insolence underlying the words—a ballsy thing to do in the middle of a bunch of rekkrs loyal to Gunn, who trained daily to take out much bigger and deadlier wolves than him.

Hati and Skoll were descendants of the Jotun, and they were literally giants.

Gunn took a moment to answer, and I felt a slight buzz on the edge of my mind. He was talking to Erik, of course, letting him know that Dane was here.

Then Gunn replied with the exact same amount of formality and insolence. "Dane Madsen. The Fyrstr comes."

Erik's office door opened behind us, and I knew my Alpha led the way, with Britta right behind him. I was hyper-aware of her, and even though I couldn't see her, I could smell and hear her. And I definitely knew she was curious about Dane—she always was about rekkr business. Her interest caused my wolf to growl, and it rumbled up loudly from my throat. He was ready to kill the interloper that threatened us.

But then Erik's hand landed on my arm, and his wolf pushed into my head. And I felt Britta squeeze in beside Dahlia as if she, too, protected her friend.

My wolf notched down his aggression just a little.

"Vel finna, ulf-einn," Erik said to him, reciting the ritual words for greeting a lone wolf—one who had never howled to join the Varda. Or been rejected by Odin because of that. "Is the yla within your heart and upon your tongue? Do you ask Odin's blessing to join the pack?"

"Vel finna, Fyrstr," Dane replied just as formally. "The yla is not within. I choose to wander."

No shit.

"Are you here on business?" Erik asked, the formal greeting over.

"No. I have information. Let's talk. Privately." Dane jerked his head toward Erik's office.

Erik nodded and led the way, with Gunn bringing up the rear. Dane knew as well as I did that a private meeting would always include Erik's second-in-command.

At the very last second, Dane glanced back over his shoulder as if scanning the room for unseen danger, but his gaze landed on Dahlia just a millisecond longer than anywhere else.

Maybe I was imagining it. Gods, I hoped so.

Dahlia didn't seem to notice, and when the office door shut behind Gunn with the others inside, she half sighed, half groaned. "He is so hot."

Britta spun toward her—her brow raised in alarm. "He is not hot. Get that out of your head, Dahls. He is bad. As bad as they come."

"Yeah. Like I said. Hot." Dahlia fanned herself with her hand.

I groaned. "Dahlia…"

"What? I can dream. It's not like he's ever going to look at me twice."

"Of course he would!" Britta exclaimed, looking and sounding offended that her friend would think so little of herself.

I shoved my hand through my hair. "You don't want that male to look at you twice, Dahlia. Seriously, if he ever does, run for the hills. Or better yet, run straight to Erik. He'll protect you."

Dahlia gave me a look. "From what? The best sex of my life?"

"Oh, my gods!" Britta grasped Dahlia's arm. "How do you know that? Has he—"

"No! Unfortunately. That's part of the whole not looking at me twice, part. Weren't you listening to me? Or to any other females in the pack? He's hot, Britta. All the females think so. Except you, apparently. And he's made an impression...if you know what I mean. Word has gotten around."

"Yeah, because *he's* gotten around," Britta added, then she squeezed Dahlia's hand. "You've got such a big heart, Dahlia. Don't let him break it."

Dahlia rolled her eyes. "How exactly could that happen when he doesn't even see me? I'm like...a freak of Valdyr nature. I still look like I'm fourteen years old, for Odin's sake. No Valdyr male is going to look at me in that way."

"That's not true. You'll get more than a second glance when it's the right male. And seriously, who cares how tall you are? It doesn't affect a thing." Britta pinned me with her gaze as if wanting me to back her up. "Right, Robbie?"

I nodded in agreement, but deep down, I knew both females were right. Yes, when Dahlia met her mate, nothing about her physical appearance would stand in the way, but right now, all the males I knew looked at her like a little sister. And who could blame them? She was sweet, loving, and adorable...and unable to protect herself in our harsh, high-stakes world of life and death.

Dahlia needed a whole pack of *brothers* to look after her.

She crossed her arms over her chest stubbornly. "Well, if the right male will come along for me, no matter what, then the right female can come along and tame Dane too." She held up her hand to stop Britta from protesting. "And I'm not saying that that female is me. I'm just *saying*."

Britta gave me another look. Did she want me to add something? I was treading on quicksand here.

"Um...technically, I guess you could be right..." Britta's frown darkened, and I swerved as the sand started shifting. "...but, ah, maybe you should still be careful...and, um, find someone else who's just as good at the, you know...sex part."

Now they were both glaring at me. I had just made things

worse. Inside, my wolf lifted his head and grunted, almost as if he was laughing at me.

And what would you have said? I asked him.

He flopped back down again, and I felt his commiseration. *Females.*

Then Erik's office door opened again, and Gunn stuck out his head. "Robbie!" he called.

Relief flooded through me. Just in time. A battle with Hati and Skoll would be more enjoyable—and winnable—than this fight.

And more understandable.

"Gotta go," I said. "Why don't you get Tyr up here to referee for you? He's great at giving advice. I'll give him a call."

I turned and hightailed it towards Erik's office, a grin creasing my cheeks as Britta's curses filled the air behind me. When I passed Gunn, I knew something was up by the intent look on his face, and my smile faded. I honed in on Erik and Dane hunched over a city map on Erik's desk.

Erik looked up as I crossed toward them, my heavy boots clomping on the floor. "Can you stay in the city overnight?" he asked. "I need you to check on some suspicious activity with Dane."

"Of course." I scanned the map, noting several red circles drawn on it. "Where?"

Dane pulled out a folded piece of paper from inside his leather jacket and handed it to me. An address was written on the inside.

"It's toward the airport," the lone wolf said. "A complex of warehouses. Do you know it?"

"Yeah. I've been in the area several times."

"Good. Meet me there around three. I've got something to do first." He glanced down at my boots. "And change your shoes. I don't want them to know we're there."

Irritation shot up my spine—I could be as quiet as a mouse

when I needed to be—but I let the annoyance go and shoved the address inside my jeans pocket. "They won't hear a thing."

Erik laid his hand on my arm. "Don't go in on your own. No matter what you hear or see. And if Dane doesn't show up, you stay put and call me."

I nodded. "Got it. Surveillance only. Do you want me to wolf in?"

"Use your own judgement. Park about a mile out, and let me know when you're going in. And Robbie?"

"Yes, Fyrstr?"

"If it all turns to shit, I want you to follow your instinct. And if it's telling you to get the fuck out of there—with or without the lone wolf—then do it."

Erik turned and looked Dane straight in the eye. "He's not pack."

CHAPTER 4

Britta

I stared at Erik's closed office door, unable to look away. And even though he'd told me it was magically sealed, I still strained to hear what was happening inside—nervous about all those dominant, dangerous wolves in there with Robbie.

Which made no sense. He was just as dominant and dangerous as they were. And he was with our Alpha.

But I couldn't calm my agitation. Or stop myself from trying to listen in—even as Dahlia prattled on beside me.

And something inside me listened too—waiting, as I waited, for the door to open.

A shiver ran over my skin as I made that connection.

My wolf. Waiting for Robbie's wolf.

She was near, moving beneath my skin, agitating me, filling me with a need and longing I didn't understand. Did she want to escape and run free? Take over my body? My soul?

Enough, already! I shouted silently at her. *Come on out. Please! You're driving me crazy.*

I held my breath, hoping for some kind of response. Anything.

Disappointment filled me, and I sighed, but then someone—or something—looked at me from inside my body, pinning me in place. I felt the weight of her stare.

An excited breath rasped through my lungs. *Is that you? Are you in there?*

I concentrated as hard as I could, wishing desperately to connect to the she-wolf. *I'm right here! Whether you like it or not. And I'm assuming not, or you would have come out years ago, but I promise it's going to be okay. Yes, our lives will be disrupted, but we'll manage. Come on out! We'll learn to live with each other. Please! I want to meet you.*

A strange sound resonated through me as I rested in the sun-kissed glade, the air sweet from the new blooms. Curious, I rose to my paws and cocked my head, swiveling my ears as I tried to understand where the sound was coming from.

Above me, the wind rustled the leaves and then blew across my fur. I sniffed, but I couldn't smell any danger.

And then something moved within me, something I'd sensed before. It felt natural to me. A part of me. Images flitted through my mind—shadowy and perplexing—and my ruff raised a little as I assessed them. Is that where the other wolf was?

I wanted to see him again.

With a gasp, I jolted back to my own reality—*Britta's reality.*

They weren't my ears...they were *her* ears. It wasn't my fur or ruff or paws...it was *her* fur, *her* ruff, *her* paws! A burst of joy spread through my veins—through our veins—like the sweetest champagne, and I laughed.

I'm here! I shouted.

"Britta?"

My head jerked up, pulling me from my awareness of my wolf, and our connection was lost.

Dahlia stared at me with concern. "What's so funny?" she asked.

I stared back at her blankly, still reeling and unable to form words. Had I laughed out loud?

"It's…uh…nothing. Just a…a thing I was…thinking." I don't know why I lied, especially to Dahlia, who'd been with me through every hiccup in my life. But the connection with my wolf seemed too private and ephemeral to put into words—like speaking about it would disintegrate it.

My wolf and I had taken our first step together, communed for the first time in that way together. I felt what she felt. I thought and saw what she thought and saw.

Amazing!

Dahlia's brow furrowed as she watched me, unconvinced. "A thing you were thinking?" Then she pointed to Erik's closed door. "I'm pretty sure I know what you were thinking about. And whom."

"Whom?" I huffed out a laugh. "Please, tell me you didn't just say that."

"I did…stalker."

"Stalker?"

"Uh huh."

I rolled my eyes. "I'm not the one who goes into stalker mode every time a certain someone walks into the room. A very bad someone."

"He's not bad…" she said.

I snorted, and then we finished the sentence together, "…he's just misunderstood," before bursting into laughter.

We'd been telling each other that since we were thirteen years old—about all the no-good boys we were crushing on, humans and Valdyr. And how they weren't bad. They were just misunderstood.

Somehow it never got old, whether it was true or not.

In Dane's case, it definitely was *not* true. He was as bad as they came.

I was about to tell her that and to be careful when Erik's office door opened behind me. My heart jumped, and I spun around to see Dane stepping over the threshold and into the dimly lit lounge. Robbie followed behind him. His gaze found me immediately. Relief flooded my body, and my knees weakened.

It was all I could do to stay standing. What was wrong with me? Did this have anything to do with my wolf rising?

I huffed out a breath and looked toward Dahlia. Her head was lowered, but I could see her watching Dane through her lashes. He didn't seem to notice as he walked past us without a second glance. A faint blue light glowed behind his dark glasses.

What was that all about?

Beside me, Dahlia let out a tiny, high-pitched squeak, and Dane suddenly stared at her. That blue light behind his glasses flared brightly for a moment before he turned his head away and kept moving through the lounge toward the stairs.

Hopefully, the complicated lone wolf wouldn't be back anytime soon.

When he reached the top step, Tyr appeared from below. Dane started down, and my brother pressed his body to the wall, so the dominant wolf could pass by.

It made me wonder who would have stepped aside if that had been Robbie.

Dahlia sighed when Dane disappeared from sight, and I gave her a look. She shrugged. "Maybe he's misunderstood."

"Maybe," I said, humoring her.

And then I smelled Robbie right before he stepped up beside

me, those broad shoulders nudging mine. A shiver ran through me.

Chill. This is Robbie.

"What time are you off tonight?" he asked.

I shivered again. Definitely not chilling.

Glancing down at my thin, gold watch, I noted it was just past midnight. "Now. Unless they want me to stay longer, but it's a slow night. Everyone's prepping for finals."

Tyr joined us, a drink in one hand and a grumpy look on his face. "What was he doing here?" he asked, jerking his head toward the stairs where I'd last seen Dane.

"He had a meeting with Erik," Robbie said.

I waited for him to elaborate, to say he'd been in the meeting, too, but he kept quiet.

"What about?" Tyr asked.

Robbie didn't answer straight away, and I glanced at him. His mouth opened and then closed as if uncertain what to say. Or not to say.

What *had* gone on behind those closed doors?

I turned to my brother, wanting to ease the pressure on Robbie. "The door's sealed. We couldn't hear anything."

Not a lie.

"Something's going down. He wouldn't be here otherwise." Tyr sipped his drink. Whisky by the smell of it.

Valdyr could get drunk—and some did—but it was a rare occurrence. Their wolves didn't understand it. To them, it was poison, and it made them uneasy.

And whatever buzz the Valdyr got from the alcohol disappeared as soon as they shifted into their wolves—going through a non-corporeal, energized state between bodies called the helmingr. The poisons flushed from their cells in the same way any tattoo ink did. Or hair dye—much to Tyr's dismay.

Anything the wolf considered unnatural.

But it also meant Tyr could change up his style as often as he wanted—which was a lot—and never damage his hair.

He groused about it, but he'd be sporting a fantastic, new color the next day.

Too much work for me.

I blew at the strands of brown hair that framed my face, making them dance. Maybe I should get some purple streaks before my wolf came through.

No, not purple. Magenta!

I wasn't totally without some badassery. A few years ago, I got a small tattoo of a pointe shoe—its silky ribbons floating around a wolf's head and twining the two images together. It flowed gracefully over my hip. That marking wouldn't stay with me once I'd gone through my ulf-risa—only changes that occurred to my body on a cellular level would remain, like the faint scars on my right fingers after I got frostbite when I was stranded in the mountains as a teenager.

I looked down at my hand and rubbed the pads of my fingers together. I'd been lucky. The feeling returned to them after several months, and the scars had mostly faded.

It was a good reminder to always stay safe in winter and pack extra clothes and blankets in the car. Although once my wolf rose, that wouldn't be a problem.

I stilled as I realized what I'd said, and a thrill shot through me. *Once my wolf rose.*

She was inside me, and I was inside her. I'd communicated with her!

All those years of feeling unwanted and somehow "less than" began to fade. My wolf was with me. Maybe she hadn't been ready to come out yet because I hadn't been ready. But now, just knowing that she was there and that either way—accepted by Odin or not—we'd be moving into our future together made me feel less afraid.

My mother had always said, and now I understood, that I would never be alone once my wolf became a part of me.

And I became a part of her.

Odin may not want me. The Varda may not want me. But my wolf would always be by my side.

Tyr tipped back his drink, finished it, and then shot me a look. "Are you ready to go?"

"Go where?" I asked, but I had a good idea what he was talking about, and my shoulders and jaw tightened in anticipation of the fight I knew was coming.

"Home. Tomorrow's Húsl." He gave me that you're-such-an-idiot look, and I almost growled, even though my wolf had completely disappeared.

Húsl was our biggest holiday and celebrated Odin's creation of the Valdyr and the sacrifice made by his favorite wolf pack so the Valdyr could be born, bursting fully grown from the wolves' bodies and killing them in the process.

Hence the sacrifice.

"Mom's been working like a dog to get the house decorated," Tyr continued, "and dad's been elbow-deep in meat and blood, making the sausages and preparing the organ meats and venison pies for the feast. The kitchen looks like a crime scene."

My mouth watered as I thought about the traditional blóð sausage, dýr pies, and the marinated meats that were central to the traditional Húsl feast.

And the rice pudding with cranberry sauce for dessert. Yum.

Although if I thought about what the dessert represented and what it actually consisted of back in the days of the first pack, I wouldn't be able to eat it.

Legend said that Odin killed an evil Jotuness—who was both witch and wolf—mixed her blood with his semen, and fed the concoction to his wolves, basically impregnating them. When the first Valdyr were born, they burst from the wolves' stomachs, fully grown, killing their hosts in the process.

Nice.

"Did dad make Smalahove, like he's been threatening all year to do?" I shuddered at the thought. Maybe once my wolf rose, I would like the dish better, but right now, the idea of staring at a cooked sheep's head on my plate, beside my cauliflower, potato dumplings, and tomato salad, made me gag.

I'd had to endure it a few times as a child when my grandmother visited, and it had horrified me. Tyr, on the other hand, had chowed down.

"No. But the house looks like a barber pole with all the red and white. Mom's going all out. She wants to make this the best Húsl ever. You have to be there."

Red and white. Blood and semen. So primal and mythological.

And so gross.

It's not that I didn't want to celebrate with my pack and family—although for years I had dreaded the holidays, especially when the curse was still poisoning the pack—it's just that I had a rehearsal tomorrow morning that I couldn't miss. And ever since I'd been stranded in that snowstorm when I was a teenager, I'd been afraid to drive the mountain road if there was even a hint of snow.

Not that I could tell Tyr that. It would be another weapon in his arsenal against me. Sad really, that my relationship with my brother had become so contentious. Or had it always been that way?

We'd certainly fought a lot growing up. And I remember being afraid of him sometimes when the curse still infested the pack—and of my parents too. They could be volatile and unpredictable.

I'd learned to tread carefully, to read the room and the energy. When I found myself in a tense situation—with my family or other pack members—I would close my eyes and breathe deeply, ask Freyja to spread love in the room and Odin to bring clarity and wisdom to every heart and mind. And I would imagine a wind blowing the negative energy away.

Thank the gods, it seemed to help—for my family, at least.

It made me think about what Erik had said—that my family had been one of the lucky ones in the pack. We hadn't suffered the same violence that other families had suffered as the curse twisted our emotions and disintegrated our bonds. But we had suffered—every one of us. I could still feel it resonating in the family—and the pack.

Seven murders.

Sadness welled within me. I laid my hand on my brother's arm and squeezed gently. "I want to be there, Tyr. I will be there. I just can't come tonight. I have a rehearsal tomorrow morning."

He tensed, and I squeezed my fingers a little more firmly, imagining that cleansing wind blowing through us and expelling the negative feelings. Just like I'd done when I was a kid.

Suddenly, he huffed out a breath. "Okay. I'll crash here tonight and wait for you. I know you don't like driving through the mountains when there's snow on the road, and there's still some at Wolf's Pass."

My brow rose. "You know about that?"

"That you're a big frickin' scaredy wolf? Of course. It takes you three hours to make an hour-long drive—I don't have to be Freud to work out why. You're the granny-driver who holds up everyone else on the road."

Beside me, Dahlia snorted. I glared at her, and she pulled her T-shirt up to cover her face. "Sorry," she said, her apology smothered by the thick cotton—and her muffled laughter.

"Don't wait," I told my brother, miffed. "I'll find another way home." When I realized I was still holding his arm, I snatched my hand back. And then called him another one of my favorite names from childhood. "Fúinn fiskr."

Dahlia burst out laughing and tugged her T-shirt down from her face. "What does that mean?"

I bit my cheek, trying to stop myself from laughing too. I'd loved learning Old Norse when I was younger, and then applying it where appropriate. And calling my brother names he didn't understand was very appropriate.

"Who the fuck cares," Tyr said.

Robbie's brow furrowed. "Rotten something or other. It's on the tip of my tongue."

"Rotten breath?" Dahlia suggested.

"No."

"Rotten vegetables?"

"No!"

"Rotten crotch?"

"Oh, my gods, Dahls," I groaned. "Rotten crotch? I was nine when I made up those words."

"Well, I don't know. I was just guessing."

"And that's where your brain went? Nine-year-old me thinking up names like rotten crotch?"

"Fish! It's rotten fish," Robbie said triumphantly. "I knew I knew it."

Tyr turned to me and raised his brow. "That's what you've been calling me all these years? Rotten fish?"

I shrugged. No way would I admit to anything.

My brother rolled his eyes. "I like rotten crotch better."

"No surprise there," I said.

Dahlia burst out laughing again.

"Erik asked me to stay over tonight," Robbie said. "I can pick up Britta when she's done tomorrow and drive her back home."

Tyr looked at him, and a short silence fell. I knew they were talking privately to each other through their bond. Tyr probably wanted to know why Erik had asked him to stay. So did I.

"Fine," My brother finally said. He spun around and started heading for the stairs, shouting over his shoulder. "Just don't be late and break our mother's heart!"

"She won't!" Robbie said. "I'll make sure of it."

I watched Tyr until his blue head disappeared down the stairs. Then I turned to Robbie. "You don't have to drive me. I'll make it…eventually. Or I can see if Erik can fly me in tomorrow. Maybe he's staying overnight too."

"He's not," Dahlia said. "I'm flying home with him tonight. He has to get back to prepare. We're leaving in about an hour."

"It's not a big deal, Britta," Robbie said. "I'm here anyway, and the Range Rover's a lot safer on those roads than your Kia—and faster…with me driving."

I smacked him playfully across the stomach with the back of my hand. He let out an exaggerated 'oof'.

I don't know why I was hesitating. Maybe because I wanted to prove my brother wrong. I was so used to fighting for everything I wanted and expecting to be left out that relying on someone else made me uneasy, like I'd be hurt if I let my guard down.

But it was also about Robbie. I'd be leaving soon—for good—and I didn't want to get any closer to him than I was now. Sitting together in a car for a couple of hours—okay, one hour—would only draw us closer. And that connection we'd always had would only make it harder for me to leave when the time came.

Things were changing between us…no, not changing…evolving. It was apparent to me that my wolf was always watching for him, and I was too. I wanted to be with him.

And where would that lead?

Nowhere. I'd still be out of the pack as soon as my wolf came through, and then Robbie would be left between two worlds. Pack and non-pack. Not a comfortable place to be.

But I still needed a ride. I forced myself to smile. "Okay. Thank you. I'll pack a bag, and we can leave after my rehearsal—around two."

He nodded. "I should be done by then."

I wanted to ask, *done with what?* Instead, I bit my tongue. I just hoped it wasn't dangerous.

A yawn caught me unaware, and I quickly covered my mouth

to hide it. "Sorry. It's been a long day." With a tired sigh, I smoothed the strands of loose hair back from my face. "I think I'm going to call it a night. I have to be up early, and I still have to cash out."

It had been a trying few weeks, but at least now I knew why.

My wolf was coming.

"I can cash out for you," Dahlia said. "I have some time to kill before Erik wants to leave. I can stop by tomorrow afternoon and drop off your tips."

"That would be amazing. Are you sure?"

"Yes." She turned to Robbie. "Can you drive her home?"

My eyes flew to Robbie's. "Oh, no. That's not—"

He grabbed my hand. "Shut up, Brit. Let's go." Then he tugged me behind him through the half-empty lounge.

And suddenly, my wolf was back, just beneath the surface, pacing and sniffing…

For Robbie.

He slowed at the top of the stairs to let someone else go first, and I bumped up behind him. Gods, he smelled good. A lethargy invaded my limbs. My face pressed into his shoulder, and I closed my eyes and opened my mouth to scent him better, letting the pheromones waft over my tongue. Waves of need rolled through my body.

It felt like heavy, thick liquid pouring into every cell, heating them, filling them. My skin sizzled, and my heartbeat thudded heavily in my ears.

I was here but not here.

He stepped down, pulling away from me, and I squeezed his hand in protest. My wolf growled—a deep and throaty rumble that filled my throat.

Robbie froze and turned to me, his eyes widening as they met mine. "Britta."

It sounded like a plea and a protest all at once.

A song played around us, a favorite of mine. I closed my eyes and listened to it. The music drummed through my veins, slow and languorous. My body swayed to the sensual beat as my wolf twined through tall grass…searching.

I opened my eyes to half-mast, my lids heavy. Robbie stared at me, his wolf in his gaze, his chest rising and falling like he'd sprinted a couple of miles.

"Britta," he said again. But this time, it sounded like surrender.

I closed the gap between us, moving my body against his as the music wove around us. It was almost an out-of-body experience, yet I felt more energized and grounded in my body than ever before. "I love this song. Let's dance."

The air gushed from his lungs. "I don't know if that's a good—"

My wolf nipped him, and he jumped.

"She's here," he said.

I smiled—slowly, sensuously—then I pulled him behind me. "I said let's dance, Robbie."

CHAPTER 5

DON'T DO IT. DON'T DO IT. DON'T DO IT.

I trailed behind Britta, a willing captive even if my brain urged restraint. The music thrummed around us, deep and dark, as she led me onto the dance floor. Or maybe her wolf led me—led my wolf. I wasn't sure.

I couldn't keep my eyes off her, the way her hips swayed hypnotically with each step, and her top rose to reveal a sliver of skin around her waist. The sight of our fingers twined together caused my chest to expand almost painfully.

I wanted her. I couldn't deny it any longer, but was she even in her body right now? Aware of what was going on?

Of course she was. Our wolves couldn't take over and direct us like some possessing demon, but they could influence us— how we felt, what we wanted.

And her wolf wanted mine right now.

I stopped abruptly, and our arms stretched out until she felt the tug of resistance and turned to me, our fingers still clasped together, her eyes shining a lush green in the dimly lit club. The other dancers swayed around us.

Gods, she was beautiful. So slender and graceful, yet as strong as a warrior—in her heart and body. The structure of her face was delicate and powerful at the same time—her lips perfectly arched, her nose small, her cheeks and brow sculpted by Freyja herself.

Thick lashes framed hypnotic eyes that were so familiar to me but different now too. Her wolf may not have fully risen, but she was there, watching me, assessing me.

Seducing me.

Britta smiled, and it was as sweet and sinful as honey, her lips filled with the promise of a long, dark kiss.

She reached up and pulled out the pins that held back her hair, dropping them one by one to the floor until the light brown strands tumbled around her shoulders and down her chest. My eyes, almost with a will of their own, followed downward and traced the shapes of her breasts, tight and high beneath the thin, stretchy shirt, her nipples outlined against the cotton.

Then she began to move to the music, and I all but lost my mind.

She danced like other people fucked: her body undulating, her hips rocking and rolling, her muscles contracting and releasing—every beat elongated, every note a ripple across her skin.

She stepped toward me, shifting her hand so our fingers laced together and our palms joined. Then she pressed her body to mine.

I groaned, long and hard, my wolf moving within me just below the surface of my skin as Britta rocked to the music. She was so soft, yet there was strength in her form, which excited me.

Excited my wolf.

The blood pounded through my body and pooled in my groin until my cock swelled so tightly that it pushed almost painfully against my jeans—bigger and more engorged than ever before. I anticipated every stroke of her hips against me, every caress of her breasts across my chest.

Releasing her hand, I found that sliver of skin at her waist. I slipped beneath her shirt and spread my palm and fingers across her back, pulling us even closer together. The music and darkness enclosed us in our own little bubble as we danced in perfect alignment.

"Robbie," she whispered, her arms wrapping around me.

I dug the fingers of my other hand into her hair, cupped the back of her head, and held her in place.

Captive.

My wolf growled his approval.

Her lips parted on a soft sigh, and the tip of her tongue touched her bottom lip. My gaze narrowed on it, and I lowered my head, inch by inch until her breath mingled with mine.

She tilted her head to the side, and her hair fell back, exposing her neck and shoulder, and my canines lengthened in anticipation.

I would mark her. Claim her. Fuck her.

My wolf howled triumphantly inside me. Now!

And then the music stopped. Bright lights filled the club like a shower of freezing rain, and the other dancers groaned in protest.

I yanked my head back from her, the air rasping through my lungs and my heart racing at what had almost happened. She opened her eyes, looking dazed, the lush green light from before fading to her softer, more natural green.

The green I loved—my friend's eyes, my best friend's little sister's eyes.

Almost family.

The points of my canines receded, and I drew in a labored breath, dragging my hands away from her hair and body. She slumped against me as if she couldn't stand on her own. Her breath puffed, warm and shallow, on my collarbone.

I stood stock still, my arms held stiffly by my side, and willed my cock to do just the opposite—to turn small and limp.

Thor's balls, what a thing to wish for. But this was Britta!

The female I'd lived with like an older brother when my dad had died, the daughter of my adopted parents and mentors. The pup I'd watched grow into a strong, amazing, caring female.

She meant the world to me—her friendship meant the world to me—no matter what my wolf said. I wanted the best for her, which was away from Wolf Ridge and this fight against Hati and Skoll so that she could pursue her dreams.

Be the dancer—the artist—she was born to be.

Just like my mother.

She pushed against my chest and took a wobbly step backward. My hands formed into fists as I resisted the urge to reach out and steady her.

Gods, what I wouldn't give to touch her.

Inside, my wolf huffed—grumpy and annoyed.

This is your fault, I accused him.

Mate, he said simply, then laid down and rolled to his side. In minutes he'd be twitching in his sleep.

Maybe that would help my desire ease—to retreat and never come back.

This was Britta! I repeated it as if that would cement it into my head and take back everything that had just happened.

But my wolf's words reverberated in my head. *Mate*.

My lips tightened, and I took an abrupt step away from her. Britta's hands fell from my chest. She swayed unsteadily, looking bemused, and pink tinged her cheeks with embarrassment.

Gods, I didn't want that. This was my fault, not hers. I should have been stronger. Directed her away from the dance floor and the intoxicating music.

Instead, I'd let her wolf drag me around by the dick.

"Britta," I said.

Just as she said, "Robbie."

An awkward silence grew between us. Great. That had never happened before.

I shoved a hand through my hair. "We should go."

She nodded and then spun around and headed for the door, giving me another view of her ass and long bare legs in that short, stretchy skirt. I forced my eyes upward and stepped past her as we reached the stairs leading to the door.

A young rekkr manned the exit. He reached into his pocket when he saw me and tossed me a set of keys. "The Rover's around the corner." Obviously, orders had come down for my mission tonight.

"Thanks, Eddie."

When his eyes fell on Britta, his smile turned adoring. He reached into a cupboard, grabbed her keys and phone, and handed them to her. "Night, Britta."

"Night, Eddie. See you tomorrow at the feast."

"Can't wait. Happy Húsl."

"Happy Húsl to you too." She laid her hand on his arm and flashed him a warm smile.

Suddenly my wolf was wide awake. He jumped up, fur puffed out, and let out a possessive growl.

Eddie's eyes widened—he'd heard my dominant wolf, felt him through our bond.

"Sorry, Rob," he said, dropping his gaze and lowering his chin just enough to appease my wolf.

I darted my eyes to Britta. Thankfully she'd already stepped outside and hadn't seen or heard our exchange.

I shook my head. "Don't be. It's not what you think."

He straightened, his eyes wide and brow raised, but he didn't say anything. He didn't have to. His expression said it all: *Keep telling yourself that, dude.*

Now *I* wanted to growl, even though he hadn't uttered a word. Inside, my wolf laid back down, satisfied.

I may have nudged Eddie with my shoulder just a little too

hard as I stepped over the threshold and into the cool night air. He huffed out a laugh behind me.

Britta waited on the sidewalk with her arms crossed tightly over her chest. Goosebumps covered her bare skin, and I almost wrapped my arm around her shoulders to keep her warm. Instead, I shoved my hands in my pockets.

"Do you have a jacket? You'll freeze. I can go back and get you one." We always had spare clothes at the club, and anywhere else we congregated—like the den at Wolf Ridge and Wolf Tower downtown. Often, we ended up shifting back into our Valdyr form in a different place than where we started, and we needed clothes.

Britta uncrossed her arms and dropped them by her side. "I'm okay. It's not cold."

She was lying—I'd seen the goosebumps—and my teeth clenched.

I was tempted to strip off my shirt and pull it over her body. My wolf liked that idea. He wanted our scent all over her. But I knew if I did, she would think I'd lost my mind.

"Which way?" she asked, shooting me a quick glance.

"Over here." I started toward the corner, making sure I walked slowly enough for her to keep up.

When I saw the big, black Range Rover, I breathed a sigh of relief. I'd have her warmed up in no time.

Pointing the remote at the vehicle, I unlocked it with a beep. I was tempted to open the door for her, but I knew if I did, she would give me that look—the I-can-kick-your-ass-anytime-I-want-to look. But she didn't understand that opening her door wasn't about chivalry or thinking she was weak; it was about looking out for her and keeping her safe.

I must have telegraphed my thoughts because she said, "I can open my own door, thank you very much."

And I got the look.

Whatever.

Still, I kept a sharp eye out. I fought evil every day, and if Hati chose to attack tonight, I would be ready to protect Britta.

I waited until she sat down and closed the door behind her, before I walked around, climbed inside, and started the car. The powerful engine roared to life, and I cranked the heat. "It won't take long to warm up."

She stretched her hands toward the vents as the air gushed out. I glanced into the back seat, hoping to find a jacket for her, but the seat was empty.

"How are you not cold?" she asked, almost accusingly.

"I run hot."

"That's for damn sure."

My lips quirked, but I made sure not to break into a full smile. She was agitated and wouldn't appreciate me laughing. And I was way too pleased that she thought I was hot.

Damn.

I quickly pulled onto the empty street and made my way across the Clark Fork River and toward the University District. It wasn't a long drive—maybe ten minutes—and the traffic was light, but the silence that stretched between us made it seem longer.

It didn't help that her scent filled the enclosed space, intoxicating me with every breath and bringing to mind the smell of her hair as we'd danced together, the feel of her body against mine.

My blood surged hot again, and I gritted my teeth.

Think about Hati and Skoll. Think about the disgusting taste after biting one of those mother fuckers. Or the pain after one of them bit me.

My blood cooled a little.

Turning off the main road, I entered a residential neighborhood and stopped in front of a renovated, pale pink bungalow from the nineteen-forties. A light shone on the porch, revealing a black arched doorway, a black mailbox, and a swinging, wicker egg chair. Inside, the house was dark. Either Britta's roommates were asleep, or they hadn't come home yet.

Maybe I should walk her to the door and apologize? Make things right between us. I loved her—I always had—just...not in that way.

I couldn't. She was destined for a life outside of the Varda.

"I'm sorry," she blurted out suddenly, and I whipped my head toward her. Her hands were fisted in her lap, and she stared through the front windshield. "Apparently, my wolf is coming through, and I'm doing all kinds of things I wouldn't usually do...like...on the dance floor. With you." She cleared her throat. "It was my wolf, I think. And the music. I love that song. I'm so sorry."

Like an idiot, irritation shot up my spine, and I clenched my jaw. Why in Odin's name would I be annoyed by that? She was only saying what I'd been telling myself for the last half hour. This was good. She was doing what I wanted to do—making it right between us.

She tucked her hair behind her ears and continued. "I take complete responsibility for the, um, dancing. It was my fault. Completely my fault. It'll never happen again. I promise. I'm really sorry."

"Yeah, you said that. Three times," I ground out.

Fuck. Why did I sound so pissed?

She turned to me—finally—her eyes flashing and her chin set stubbornly.

I knew that look, that attitude. My shoulders squared almost mulishly as I faced her in the confined space.

"Look, I'm just trying to apologize," she said. "Do you have to make it more difficult? I've known you my whole life, Robbie. We have to get past this. You're like a brother to me."

My wolf growled in denial, and I leaned forward, teeth clenched. "I am not your brother, Britta. Don't ever forget it."

Her throat worked as she swallowed. "Fine. But it still shouldn't have happened."

"I agree. But you don't need to take all the blame upon your shoulders. And you sure as hel don't need to blame the music…or your wolf. Come on, Britta, let's be honest here."

Shit. No. What was I saying?

"Honest? What the hel, Robbie. Do you want me to be honest about wanting to crawl up your body and rub myself all over you? Or how we almost kissed? Newsflash, there are some things better left unsaid."

My breath stuttered out of my lungs at the images she'd brought to life in my head. I tried to think about fighting Hati and Skoll again, but it didn't work. All I saw was Britta swaying to the music as her eyes glowed with her wolf. Inside, my wolf moaned.

"I just meant…I thought maybe we should…"

"We should what?" she asked, rounding on me again.

I shoved my hand through my hair. "I don't know. I'm just saying that it wasn't only your fault. That's all. I was there too." I reached for the door handle and pushed it open. "Come on, I'll walk you to the door."

She started to protest, but I ignored her and stepped out of the car, automatically scanning for danger. By the time I reached her side, she'd already gotten out. We walked together up the long pathway, the silence deafening, before stopping awkwardly at her door.

She fumbled with her keys, and I noticed a letter poking out of her mailbox. I handed it to her. "Here."

She took it, distracted, but then stilled as she focused on the letter. I followed her gaze and saw the return address printed on the envelope. It read Complexions Contemporary Ballet, New York City.

Dread filled the pit of my stomach.

"What's that?" I asked, but I already knew—an acceptance letter.

She pressed it to her chest. "It's…ah…nothing."

"Open it," I insisted.

"Robbie, I don't—"

I snatched it from her and tore it open. I couldn't help myself. The envelope fell to the porch as I extracted the letter.

"Hey!" She tried to snatch it back, but not before I'd read the first few lines and saw… Britta was leaving.

"Congratulations," I said as I handed it back to her, feeling like a boulder had lodged in my chest.

She glanced briefly at the letter and then re-folded it. When she lifted her gaze, she glared at me. "Jackass."

I couldn't argue with her. That was indeed a jackass move. And illegal.

So sue me.

"Hey, you guys!"

My gaze swiveled toward the street. Two humans turned onto the walkway toward the house—a man and a woman. Britta waved, and I relaxed. I'd never met her roommates before, but this must be them. She quickly tucked the letter in her pocket.

The woman was short, even shorter than Dahlia, with bleached blond hair and dark roots pulled back into low pigtails just behind her ears. She was staring at me with wide eyes and an open mouth. The man beside her, his hair and skin darker, wasn't much taller, and he stared at me in the exact same way as the woman. Then he grabbed her hand and exclaimed, "Lord have mercy, Esmeralda, what am I seeing?"

I realized I must look like a giant to them and shifted uncomfortably.

Britta snorted. "Esme, Benni, this is Robbie."

Benni held out his hand as they drew closer and then pretended to swoon when I grasped it. "That's Benni with an 'i,'" he said. "Like Bennifer."

Esme giggled beside him and gazed up at me, her eyes glassy and cheeks flushed. They smelled of alcohol and sex—but with different partners.

I drew back my hand. "Nice to meet you, Benni. I'm Robbie with an 'ie'. Like Robbie."

Esme broke into a trill of laughter and laid her palm on my chest. "I always thought Britta was too choosy when it came to men, but now I can see why. Are you an old one or a new one?"

"A new what?" I asked, just as Britta said, "Esme, shut up."

"A new love monkey, of course," her friend said.

I raised my brow. "I don't like monkeys. They freak me out—especially when people put clothes on them. If I had to pick an animal, it definitely wouldn't be a monkey."

"Oooh, what would it be then?"

"A wolf," Britta said. "A big, bad wolf." Then she fit her key in the lock and opened the door, motioning for her friends to go inside.

Esme stepped slowly over the threshold, her fingers trailing over my chest and her eyes glued to my face—until Britta gave her a tiny shove forward. The blonde let out a squeak as she stumbled into the house.

"Sorry," Britta said, but I could hear a subsonic growl beneath her words. "I slipped."

My wolf perked his ears, and a feeling of satisfaction from him washed over me. I tried to catch Britta's eye, but she refused to look at me, her cheeks slightly pink under the porch light.

"I'm okay," Esme said, slouching dramatically against the wall. "I may never be able to dance again, but I'm okay."

Benni looked at Britta, eyes wide, and stepped dramatically away from me, his hands raising in front of him. "No touchy, touchy. No feely, feely. No shovey, shovey."

Britta let out an exasperated laugh and shook her head. Obviously, she'd seen her friends drunk before.

Then Benni crouched down, looking like he was going to

crawl into the house, when he suddenly spotted the empty envelope I'd dropped to the porch floor.

"Sweet heavenly mercy. Is that what I think it is?" He picked up the envelope, straightened, and waved it at Britta. "Did you hear from them?"

"Hear from who?" Esme asked, stumbling back outside. She looked at the return address on the envelope and let out an excited squeal. "Where's the letter?"

Britta tried to school her features, but then she broke into a wide, excited smile…and my heart fell.

"It's here." She pulled the letter from her pocket and showed it to her friends, who crowded around her to read it, blocking me out.

"They said yes! They said yes!" Benni yelled after a moment.

Esme jumped up and down. "Oh, my God! You're moving to New York!"

"Unless she gets accepted to the Norwegian National Ballet or that one in Australia."

"Oh, my God!" Esme yelled again. "You're moving to New York or Oslo or Down Under!"

I felt like I couldn't breathe, that boulder crushing me again. Britta was leaving me. No, not me. She was just leaving—exactly as I wanted her to do. She was going out into the wide world to live her dream. This was fantastic news.

Then why did I feel like I was dying inside? My wolf let out a long, mournful howl.

Britta glanced at me over her friends' heads, and we locked gazes. So much was said yet left unsaid. It had to be.

I forced a smile. "I'll pick you up tomorrow." Then I turned and walked away.

CHAPTER 6

I PACED UP AND DOWN THE GRAVEL ROAD BESIDE THE RANGE Rover, straining to hear any sound or see any headlights in the distance. Unfortunately, all I heard were crickets, and all I saw were the pinpricks of shining stars in the darkened sky.

Dane was late. He was supposed to meet me here almost an hour ago so we could surveil the warehouse, but I'd sensed neither hide nor hair of him since I'd arrived. Literally.

I stopped abruptly and let out a frustrated sigh, rubbing my thumb and finger into my eyelids. I should contact Erik, but I didn't want to disturb him if I didn't have to—especially on Húsl.

Inside, my wolf prowled restlessly, as disquieted as I was, and my instinct buzzed a constant warning that something was wrong. I looked at my watch again and waited for the last sixty seconds to tick down—4:30 am, one hour past our meeting time.

Erik had told me not to go in alone, but I had a growing urge to do exactly that.

Fuck it. I'd have to wake him.

I reached out to him through our bond. *Fyrstr. You told me to call if Dane didn't show up. It's been an hour, and he's not here. What do you want me to do? Instinct's telling me to go in alone.*

I waited impatiently, agitated by the growing sense of urgency that I knew came from that instinctual part of my wolf—from me —that alerted us to danger and sometimes even signaled us where to go and what to do.

When Erik didn't respond, I pushed a little harder. *Fyrstr?*

And then shock rippled through me as I realized the bond that connected me to the pack was dead, like I'd picked up a phone, expecting a dial tone, but instead got flat, empty air.

Erik hadn't answered because he couldn't hear me.

Fyrstr! I yelled. *Are you there? Tyr! Gunn! Is anyone there?*

Holy Thor! How had I not sensed the disconnection immediately? Now that I was reaching for it, the absence of it sliced through me. Gutted me. My wolf paced in tight circles, growling and barking—as if calling out to the pack. Then he howled long and loud.

I waited expectantly, hoping he could break through, but when he finally stopped, no one was there.

How could I have missed it? I swore profusely as I reached into my pocket for my cell phone, berating myself for not noticing sooner that the bond had been severed. I'd been in my head, preoccupied about the mission, preoccupied with Britta— always, it seemed lately, about Britta.

I tapped Erik's number on my cell and waited…and waited, but the call didn't go through, just like my call down the bond.

Shivers raced up my spine. I knew this area was within range of a cell tower, and my battery was fully charged, which meant the signal must be jammed—it was too much of a coincidence.

Someone didn't want me—or anyone else—calling out. I was completely cut off.

I breathed deeply, and the calmness and clarity that always overtook me before a mission settled in. Hyper-focused. Alert.

Go! my wolf urged.

I was already running—driven by instinct to fight against Hati and Skoll, to keep their father, Fenrir, imprisoned and prevent Ragnarök.

To keep Odin, the Allfather, safe.

To keep my pack and the rest of the world safe.

Neither my wolf nor I questioned what form to run in. We just knew…me now, him later.

I didn't have to squint in the dark to see. My eyesight was highly developed, as were my other senses, enabling me to navigate the gravel road and then across the field and parking lot toward the warehouse at full speed. I easily leapt the nine-foot fence around the property. Then I quietly headed toward a single light that shone above the door at the far end of the steel building, stepping carefully as I kept an eye out for physical and electronic surveillance.

The yard was strewn with overturned crates and tools. I'd just crouched behind a mound of gravel when a familiar scent hit my nose—and an almost imperceptible growl hit my ears.

I stared toward a forklift that had tilted over onto its side and saw twin points of blue light.

Dane.

This is why he hadn't shown up. He was already here.

The lights disappeared, and I knew he'd slipped his sunglasses back on. I'd never seen him without them—no matter what time of day.

I methodically checked for cameras, listening for the energetic hum that always accompanied electronic devices. One was visible above the door, but another was hidden in the metal eaves of the roof. A laser trip wire also extended across the front of the building.

Dane was hunkered down just out of camera range, and I moved toward him.

"Why didn't you wait for me?" I asked when I got there. The words whispered so softly only he could hear them.

"I saw Hati drive by on the main road. I recognized his bike." He pointed to a sleek, black motorcycle parked by the door. "I took the same route you did and got here first—barely. Luckily, I got upwind of him."

That *was* lucky. No Valdyr wanted to face Hati Hróðvitnisson on their own—or his brother Skoll. Even a Valdyr as strong as Dane or I would most likely be killed. Together we might stand a chance to maim him…before he used his magic to ride out on a moonbeam, leaving our jaws snapping together on empty air.

"Where's your car?" I asked. "I didn't see it."

"In town. I wolfed in."

Dane wore jeans and sunglasses. Nothing else. I knew his wolf must have carried his jeans, but I'd seen his sunglasses reappear on their own every time he shifted back into his Valdyr form after a fight—like magic.

"Did you park where I told you to?" he asked, still whispering.

"Yeah. Off the main road. He won't see the Rover unless he goes looking."

Dane nodded and returned his gaze to the door. "I wasn't expecting you."

My brow rose. "Why not?"

"Didn't Daddy Erik tell you not to come?"

Anger sparked within me, especially when I saw his smirk. I wanted to wipe it away with my fist. I was just as big as Dane, as fast and powerful. It would be an even match.

But if Hati *was* inside, we would need to fight together to take him down.

I reached for my previous focus and calm. "The Fyrstr didn't tell me anything. For your information, my connection to him and the pack has been blocked, and the cell signal has been jammed. I can't get through."

He turned to me slowly. "Since when?"

"Since now. I came here as soon as I found out—led by instinct."

The blue light behind his sunglasses flared. "Does that happen often—the disconnection?"

"Never." The weight and worry of being cut off, and what that might mean for the rest of the pack, pressed down on me. "It would make it a hel of a lot easier to defeat the Varda and get Fenrir out of prison if Odin's rekkrs can't communicate."

"Fukja," Dane cursed in Old Norse. He returned his gaze to the door, and I could see a muscle jumping in his cheek. "It's magic. Bought and paid for."

"What do you mean?"

"Hati was met at the door by two Dvergar. I heard more of them inside and smelled chemicals or something. I think it's a workshop or a lab of some kind—a magical one."

The Dvergar weren't our enemy, but they couldn't be trusted. They had their own home world—Nidavellir—but some of them had relocated here and resided in and around the mountains of Earth. They were magical alchemists, and they knew how to imbue objects, often gems and earthly elements, with magic to create supernatural devices. In the past, they'd worked for the gods, but if the price was right, anyone could hire them—like Hati and Skoll.

"We raided a Dverg lab the first year I was a rekkr. The… potions….can be volatile. A vial was broken in the process, and we lost a rekkr after she inhaled the fumes. A horrific way to die."

"Got it. No breathing."

"Or touching. Someone else got a bad burn from picking up the wrong object."

I looked at my watch and then up to the sky. Hati was tied to the moon, and Skoll was connected to the sun. Literally. We had about an hour left before the moon set and tugged Hati to the other side of the world. Then it would be Skoll's turn here.

"Hati will be pulled away soon," I said, trying to remember if there was any crossover with the sun and the moon today, enabling Hati and Skoll to be in the same place at once—double the threat. Usually, I would check my cell phone for the information, but that obviously wasn't an option right now. I should know better than to rely on technology. "Skoll could show up at any time after that. Or before, depending on crossover."

He gave me a look. "There's no crossover today. How can you not know that? I've seen the big board in your den, counting down to all the astronomical events. Forget to check?" Sarcasm laced his words. He really was an acerbic asshole, and he sure as hel didn't like me.

Or maybe he didn't like anyone.

But he wasn't wrong. It was a stupid mistake, and I tried to ignore the dig. "Yes. I forgot to check." I scanned the building, seeing if there was another way in. Nothing. "How do you want to play this? We could ambush Hati once he's out of the lab and then bring in reinforcements to raid the workshop. We don't know what they've got set up in there."

"No time for that. And no ambush. I'm gonna follow Hati and find his hiding place before he moonbeams out. He's bound to have one. You can do whatever the hel you want—go back to daddy if that's safer, or just sit back and keep observing. Get yourself some fucking popcorn. Me, I'd be in that lab trying to blow this place the fuck up before they know you're here."

I ground my teeth, resisting the urge to take out a few of the lone wolf's teeth. "You're such a dick."

He grinned. The fucking maniac liked that I was riled. But he had a point about sneaking in. My instinct was urging me to do exactly that.

The door opened partway, and I immediately scented a mix of things that raised both the hairs on the back of my neck and my wolf's ruff—Hati, Dvergar, chemicals, and something else that roiled my stomach. What the hel was that? It pierced my sinuses and shot hot darts of pain behind my eyes. Was it some kind of chemical weapon to use on the Varda? Or something the Dvergar used in their magic?

I glanced at Dane to see his brow furrowed and his jaw tight. So he was feeling it too. If Hati were to use that against us when we were fighting him, we'd be severely compromised.

"Go in now," he muttered to me, "before it's too late."

"I'm planning on it." My instinct was screaming at me to get in there and destroy everything.

Dane turned without another word and quickly disappeared into the darkness. Seconds later, Hati appeared in the doorway dressed all in black leather. A female Dverg followed him, wearing a lab coat. Her red hair was pulled back into a braided top knot.

I made sure to stay still. Any movement would draw Hati's attention, and the Dvergar, who preferred to be underground during the day, had excellent night vision.

Like his father, Hati was a wolf shifter but also magical, like his witch mother. And he was even bigger than me—over seven feet tall. His Jotun blood made sure of that.

The Dverg standing next to him looked about half his size. Generally, Dvergar were shorter than the average human female —under five feet tall—but they had tremendous strength and a fierce nature. And they were hella smart.

I made sure to keep low and stay hidden, peering at them from between the wheels of the overturned forklift I crouched behind.

My wolf got a bead on them, too, and let out a low, rumbling growl.

Don't let them see or hear us, I chastised, worried my eyes would start shining in the dark or my vocal cords would vibrate due to his agitation.

Not a pup, he replied, annoyed at my unnecessary rebuke. *Find us a way in.*

I swallowed my own annoyance. *As soon as I can.*

Despite my heightened senses, I couldn't hear the conversation between the female Dverg and Hati, which was animated—

the Dverg waved her arms angrily. The building must be sound-proofed like Erik's office at Savage. And most likely shielded too. Damn, that would make getting in even more difficult.

For now, all I could do was wait for Hati to leave. I couldn't survive a battle with him, but I *could* survive a fight against several Dvergar.

Hati turned and quickly descended the few stairs to the ground, stepping past the laser trip wire at the bottom. Suddenly I could hear his boots crunching on the gravel—he'd crossed the sound shield.

He glanced up at the predawn sky, his eyes as black as the night he dwelled in, and then he leapt onto his bike in one great bound, gunned it, and took off, his long white hair and skin shining with a luminescence that rivaled the moonbeams he rode in and out on.

When all I could see were dwindling red taillights, I turned back and was surprised to see the female Dverg hunched over with her hands covering her ears and a pained expression on her face. Holy Thor! They must have forgotten to turn off the alarm, and Hati had tripped it when he stepped across the beam. I couldn't hear the siren because the shield was still in place.

Lucky for me. Unlucky for them.

I barely thought, just reacted, and threw two large stones at the cameras above the Dverg, smashing them. She glanced upward as glass and pieces of the camera casing rained down upon her. Then I leapt forward, the siren Hati had set off blaring in my ears as soon as I passed through the barrier and tackled her. She flew backward, breaking through the top wooden railing and falling to the ground with me on top of her.

It took less than four seconds from the time I threw the first rock to get there.

I quickly immobilized her and pressed my forearm into her throat so she couldn't breathe. Still, she struggled beneath me like a thousand-pound crocodile, strong and wily, and I had a hard time holding her down. Eventually, she weakened and went limp. I waited another ten seconds and then slowly let up, hoping I hadn't killed her.

Yanking off my shirt, I tore it into strips and quickly tied her up, gagged her, and shoved her into an empty hollow beneath the stairs, along with the broken wood from the railing. Hopefully, no one would notice that the top board was missing.

The alarm suddenly cut out, and I could hear yelling and the sound of pounding feet from inside the building. I scrambled back onto the top step and leapt into the eaves above as the door banged open.

Below me, Dvergar poured out, at least eight of them, carrying weapons that resembled human rifles but with glowing, magical-looking attachments. They spoke Dvergish, and I cursed my incompetence with languages—I understood some of what they said, but not all of it—they were speaking too fast for my brain to keep up.

The Dvergar spread out into the yard, and I quickly swung down from the eaves and into the dimly lit warehouse. I darted to the side behind a concrete pillar and let my eyes adjust, reminding myself that as good as I could see in the dark, the Dvergar could see better. They may be short and slow compared to me, but they were still powerful opponents.

More security forces ran past me to the door, carrying their magical-looking rifles. I made a mental note to try to snag one of them before I destroyed the place.

Lifting my gaze, I spotted a metal walkway about forty feet up around the perimeter. It looked nearly deserted—most of the guards must be outside by now or in different parts of the warehouse.

Claws, I said to my wolf.

My fingertips dissolved into the helmingr, and long, sharp-as-knives claws solidified there. I leapt vertically as high as I could and grabbed hold of the pillar, digging my claws into the concrete. Every muscle strained, and my fingers burned as gravity tried to pull me back down.

Fuck. My wolf would be pissed if any claws ripped out. Not to mention it would hurt like hel—for both of us.

In my head, my wolf growled a warning even though I hadn't lost a claw yet. I was tempted to hang there a little longer to tick him off.

Whatever. Big fucking puppy.

He bit my ass—hard—and didn't let up until I'd pushed off from the pillar and jumped to the walkway. I landed silently—not that anyone would have heard me over all the commotion.

Rolling to the wall, I listened for any further uproar that might indicate they'd seen me. Nothing. Then I took a moment to harass my wolf...*Payback's a bitch.*

I sent him an image of me waking him every time he curled up for a nap.

He growled back and gnashed his teeth at me, but his heart wasn't in it. His claws dissolved into the helmingr, and my fingertips reappeared. Blood scented the air from a ripped nail, and I quickly licked it clean.

Valdyr could differentiate between species and animals just by smelling their blood. I didn't want to chance it that the Dvergar could do the same.

I crawled to the edge of the walkway, my fingers and ass still stinging, and looked over.

From my perch, I could see the entire warehouse. Makeshift offices and storage areas lined the edges of the walls, and multiple lab stations had been built in concentric circles around a larger station in the middle.

My gaze sharpened on the strange objects in the center of each station. A crystal, about the size of my fist, pulsed with a luminous amber light in the middle of a wide, shallow bowl. Turquoise liquid filled the bowl halfway, and Old Norse runes—

both those given by Odin to the gods and by Dvalinn to the Dvergar—were inscribed on the silver-lined surface.

Each bowl was connected to the vessel in front and beside it with what looked like brass clamps and wires until the larger center basin was reached. The clamps dipped a few inches into the turquoise liquid.

Was it a type of magical battery?

I pulled my cell phone from my back pocket, covering it so no light escaped, and checked again for service. The signal was still jammed.

But that didn't mean the camera wouldn't work, especially with the upgrades made to every rekkr's phone by Valdyr engineers—upgrades that would allow me to snap well-lit photos in the dark…silently.

I made sure the flash was off and then took several pictures from as many different angles as I could, zooming in close and then pulling wide, panning the warehouse, and getting close-ups of every Dverg for our intelligence files—especially the scientists. Then I sent them to Erik, hoping they'd transmit as soon as I destroyed whatever was jamming my cell phone—and my connection to the pack.

I put my phone back in my pocket and studied the "battery" below. Most of the guards had left the building, which would make moving around down there easier, but it could make getting out of the building more difficult.

And I *was* getting out. I'd promised to pick up Britta from her rehearsal and drive her home for Húsl. It might be our last time alone together. Ever.

A lump tried to force its way up my throat from that boulder still in my chest. I forced it back down.

Focus, Helvig. I chastised myself. My wolf grunted in agreement—but I could also feel his sorrow about Britta leaving.

You and me both, buddy.

Below, several Dvergar crowded around the central lab

station, looking nervous. One of them bumped the table when he was jostled by someone else, and the turquoise liquid in the bowl moved like gelatin that had just started to set, almost slopping over the rim of the bowl.

Immediately, the other scientists started yelling at him and then at each other. No longer just nervous; they were scared now too. I listened hard, trying to make out the words, even closing my eyes to concentrate better.

I understood several phrases, but the puzzle didn't fall into place until I recognized the word for "explosion".

Thor's balls! The fluid wasn't stable.

That could work for me if I didn't get blown all the way to Asgard first.

I scanned the area for any other signs of a blast and spotted black, sooty spots in several places on the floor and one against the far wall, which looked like it had been repaired—but nothing around the battery's hub.

Three Dvergs broke off from the group and hurried toward another exit at the back of the warehouse. They bunched around it in a tight circle, talking animatedly to each other and then yelling back and forth to the main group. A fourth Dverg drifted toward them, looking back uncertainly.

Were they trying to escape in the chaos? Or worried the building would blow?

Somebody pushed the door open, and another alarm went off, ripping through the silence. He shut the door, but the alarm kept blaring. More yelling erupted between the two groups. The door was pushed open again, and one Dverg dashed outside. I could still see him. He'd stopped just a few feet away and looked back into the warehouse, gesturing for the others to come stand with him.

What the hel good would that do? If the warehouse blew, he'd have to be farther back than that to be safe. Unless…

I squinted but I still couldn't see well enough to discern

details, so I brought my camera out again and used it to zoom in on the Dverg outside. Yup. There it was—a red laser.

The Dverg had crossed it and then turned back to the others inside.

Maybe the warehouse was shielded for more than just sound. Maybe it was shielded to suppress a blast too? If the "battery" was *that* unstable, they would need to prepare for all possibilities—specifically a way to contain and conceal it. They wouldn't want to alert the Montanan authorities or the Varda to what they were doing.

Too fucking late.

I quickly started formulating a plan. It had two steps: get some of the blue liquid, drop it, and get the hel out of there before the warehouse blew.

Okay. Three steps. And if I could grab one of those crystals and a magical rifle as well, that would be the cranberry on top of the Húsl pudding.

They'd give me a bloody medal. Or at least keep their grubby fingers off my birthday cookies.

I scanned the warehouse floor again, wondering where the blue liquid came from. Was it stored somewhere?

Danger, my wolf warned.

He could sense things—magical things—that I couldn't sometimes. *Magical or chemical?* I asked.

Both.

Is it the liquid that's giving me a headache?

It took him a moment to answer. *Yes.*

Then we definitely need to take some back and analyze it. They must have it stored somewhere safe.

Maybe. Maybe not. Guards returning.

Fuck.

More of the Dverg scientists had moved toward the door, and now two of them stood outside on the other side of the red laser. The sun's rays had begun to shine over the horizon, and the sky was lightening. Good for me because it meant that if I had to fight them outside, their eyesight would be compromised, and Dvergar did not do well when things weren't going according to plan. They tended to run for the hills.

Or tunnels.

But it was also bad for me because it meant that Skoll could show up at any time after sunrise—and then *I'd* need to run for the hills.

I had to get down there and search the stations, see if I could find any of the stored liquid. And I'd have to clear that doorway. If I intended to beat the blast, I'd need my exit unclogged.

I backed away from the walkway's edge and ran in a crouch toward a large support beam that spanned the roof. I was almost there when I heard a guard race up the stairs ahead of me, his heavy boots telegraphing his position.

With no time to hide, I put on a burst of speed and clocked him hard in the face with my fist as he appeared in front of me, knocking him out cold. I caught him before he fell backward and yanked him the rest of the way onto the walkway.

Odin Almighty, he was heavy.

I shoved him behind a support brace and then clocked him again to make sure he stayed down. Then I grabbed all his weapons, including one of those magical rifles, and hooked it over my shoulder.

One down.

Jumping onto the transverse beam, I yelled, "Fire!" in dvergish as I ran, hoping they could hear me over the din of the still ringing alarm. "Run! Run! It's the Varda!"

It worked. The scientists at the door panicked and darted outside, shielding their eyes as they hit the light. Several more left the central station and ran for the exit. And they didn't stick around. As I suspected, they had their own bolt holes for when things got tough.

Only one scientist stayed put, looking upward toward the

sound of my voice. He yelled at someone I couldn't see—a guard, maybe?—and pointed upward.

Then a shot ricocheted next to me—and not just a regular, human bullet. This was a bright green, glowing projectile that singed my arm and hurt like hell.

Bite it out! my wolf snarled immediately.

I didn't hesitate, chomping down on my bicep with my wolf's teeth and spitting out the chunk of poisoned flesh. It would heal.

Got it.

Then another shot bounced off the roof near my head, punching a hold in the ceiling and causing green sparks to rain down upon the warehouse floor. The beam I stood on trembled, and I caught hold of a steel truss to stay standing as one of the support brackets loosened.

Taking the roof down would be one way to make the building go boom.

The scientist below screamed at the guard to stop shooting as he waved away the sparks and debris that floated down from the roof. One of the sparks landed on the rim of a bowl in the outermost ring and slowly slid off the side. The Dverg let out a frightened squeak and ran for the door. The guard followed after him.

I crawled along the network of beams toward the center and then leapt to the floor. It was a long drop, even for me, and I sent a quick prayer to the Allfather that my landing would be soft.

I timed it exactly—my body limp like a rag doll, my knees bending like Silly Putty, my roll onto the floor easy and controlled. When I rose, I stood at the center of the maze of wires right in front of the middle station. For a moment, I was awestruck. The bowl that housed the battery was lined with silver and engraved with runes inside and out. An eerie mist drifted upward from the turquoise liquid, and the amber crystal shined so brightly I could see my reflection.

How could I transport everything safely?

No touch, my wolf said.

Yeah, I guessed as much.

I crouched down and opened the cupboard beneath the workstation, hoping to find something to use to move at least the crystal, and hit the jackpot.

I reached underneath and pulled out a specialized, square bag with a zippered top. A symbol was marked on the outside of the bag that reminded me of a hazard sign. Farther back in the cupboard, silver stoppered vials engraved with runes stood neatly in test tube racks. Next to them lay tongs and thick, medical-grade gloves—everything I would need to stay alive.

Except I suddenly smelled Skoll…and my chances of surviving diminished—with or without the gloves.

He's coming, my wolf said at the same time.

Be ready to get us out of here. And take this bag and the gun, if you can. They have straps.

I didn't delay, unzipping the bag and grabbing the tongs, gloves, and vials. I dropped my phone and the extra vial in the bag, which I hooked around my neck, and then shoved my hand in the glove, thankful for the loud alarm that drowned out any noise.

"I know you're here," Skoll said, his voice as thick and rich as honey. "I can smell you."

I peeked around the edge of the workstation and through the brass wires that weaved between the batteries. Skoll stood at the edge of the room where I'd first entered, looking up at the walkway. He would jump to the top, the same as I had, and when he did, he would spot me on the floor below.

My mind spun out my options, none of which were great. I needed more time—just a few seconds—and then I needed speed.

And a big, fucking explosion.

Slowly, he turned his head toward me, his golden skin and long, golden hair shining like the sunbeam he rode in on, his eyes as bright and blue as a summer sky.

Other than those differences, he and Hati were identical—

both as resplendent as the sun and the moon, both as cruel as they were beautiful.

"But where, oh where, are you? The fumes from the liquid are dispersing your scent." He sniffed the air like he would fine wine, his eyes closed and his hand wafting the air toward his nose, savoring it. "Two scents outside. One in here. Did you separate? Is the widdle Valdyr all alone? Not even a female nearby to use her magic. That would make this more fun. But I have a busy day, so let's do this."

Suddenly he spun and jumped to the walkway above him. I rose just as quickly and sprayed him in the back with the green bullets from the magical rifle that had hurt so badly when they'd grazed me. He let out an agonized roar as he fell forward out of sight.

Then I hooked the rifle over my neck, grabbed the crystal with the tongs, and dipped a vial in the turquoise liquid using my gloved hand. I dropped the crystal in the bag, stoppered and shook off the vial for extra drips, and dropped it in, too, then zippered the bag closed—all in under two seconds.

Two seconds too long.

The ground shook as Skoll landed in front of me on the other side of the station, his skin smoking, his eyes burning a rage-filled, acid blue.

Jumping in the air, I kicked the bowl with the liquid at him, then loosed my wolf, who shifted forms with me instantly and sprinted over the workstations toward the door, kicking the other bowls back at Skoll as he went.

Skoll was only a wolf-length behind us when I felt the first drops hit the floor, and the powerful surge of magical and chemical energy began to blow outward. Skoll cursed, but instead of grabbing hold of my wolf, he shoved him out of the way and reached through the door for a sunbeam, disappearing as soon as the light hit his fingertips.

My wolf crashed into the doorframe and hit the ground hard,

still sliding forward. He was almost over the red line when the blast hit us, and we were shoved forward at explosive speed into the empty yard, moving up through the air. The silence behind us told me the barrier had held.

Then we landed—hard—in the scrub-filled field beyond the fence I'd crossed earlier, battered and broken. With a pain-filled yip, my wolf retreated back into Hjarta.

I groaned in agony when I reformed, naked, lying on top of the hazardous material bag and the rifle. At least I'd done that right.

I tried to focus, to call out to the pack through the bond, but it felt like I'd been through a meat grinder. I couldn't move, barely staying conscious, but I could feel a difference in the bond. It wasn't entirely back, but I was aware of it, and relief flooded me.

Until Skoll's almost imperceptible scent drifted up my nose again.

Down, my wolf urged, his thoughts barely a whisper in my mind.

Not...going...anywhere, I whispered back.

In the distance, I heard metal smashing together and then an enraged roar. I tried to lift my head to look toward the warehouse, but I couldn't even lift my eyelids. Thankfully, I must be upwind of him.

I prayed to the Allfather that Skoll wouldn't widen his search.

And then I couldn't hold on anymore. The last thing I saw in my mind's eye was Britta's eyes popping open and panic scoring every line of her face. Then everything slowly went blank.

CHAPTER 7

Britta

I'D BEEN IN A DEEP SLEEP, LOST TO FORGETTABLE DREAMS WHEN I suddenly saw Robbie, as real as the pillow beneath my head, lying naked on his side in a scrubby field. He was bloody and battered, and he looked dead.

"Robbie!" I screamed, instantly awake, my eyes popping open as I sat up straight in my bed.

The terrified sound echoed in my room and ricocheted through my body, causing my heart to race and my spine to prickle. Every little hair on my skin stood straight out.

I pressed my hand over my mouth, trying to contain the sobs that punched up from my chest. They hurt!

"Robbie," I said again, softly, brokenly.

Had that been real? It couldn't be real.

Still, panic invaded every cell of my body, overwhelming me until I couldn't think straight. I pushed back the quilt and pressed my feet into the soft, circular rug beside my bed, trying to orientate myself to my surroundings—the old rocking chair in the corner that used to belong to my grandmother, the purple dresser I'd excitedly bought from the secondhand store and repainted when I moved to Missoula, my first ever pair of pointe shoes hanging by their soft pink ribbons over a pin in the wall.

On the bedside table sat an antique vase filled with dried white roses that Robbie had given me when he'd first seen me dance. I'd been sixteen, and I'd cherished them.

I still did.

I took long, steady breaths to calm myself—in through my nose, out through my lips. It was only a dream. It couldn't be real.

Fated mates were connected to each other and knew when their other half was in trouble, but I wasn't Robbie's fated mate—I didn't even have my wolf yet. It wasn't possible.

It must have been a nightmare—maybe caused by the uncertainty I'd been feeling lately over my wolf rising and leaving the pack.

Still…I picked up my cell phone and checked for messages. Nothing. Which made sense. Why would he call or text me so late? Or so early? He wouldn't. He'd be either working or asleep.

I scrolled down and found his number—I couldn't help myself—and then hovered my thumb over it. *Stop, Britta. He's asleep!*

I tapped it anyway and then brought the phone to my ear. I was hard-pressed not to cry as it rang. And rang. My arms wrapped closely around my body, and my eyes squeezed shut.

"Pick up," I whispered, uncaring now that I might wake him. I dug my toes into the carpet as I waited.

When the phone stopped ringing, I jumped up from the bed and paced in a tight circle.

Suddenly, I stopped and yelled, *Robbie!* in my head as loud as I could, trying to project my voice into Hjarta. But we had no connection—I wasn't connected that way to anyone in the pack outside of my immediate family. The pack bond wouldn't happen until my wolf rose, and I was accepted into the Varda, which wasn't going to happen. Ever.

I sat back down on the side of the bed and dropped my head

into my hands. So many thoughts were circling around in there, always coming back to Robbie.

Where was he?

I could call my mom and ask, but then she'd want to know why I was so concerned. She'd start digging, analyze everything I said and did, and convince herself that I was fated to be with Robbie when I just needed to know that my friend was okay.

My destiny lay elsewhere—I knew it, Robbie knew it, and Odin most definitely knew it.

Needing to move, I crossed to the bedroom door, and stepped into the hallway.

The house was quiet despite my scream, and I closed my eyes and said a quick prayer of thanks that I hadn't woken Esme or Benni. The drama would have been epic, ending with me calming them instead of the other way around.

The morning light was bright in the rest of the house, pouring through the glass in the front door and the uncovered windows in the kitchen and living room. I wore a soft, oversized T-shirt that fell below my butt and off one shoulder. Looking down at it, I froze, seeing the name of Robbie's favorite band—it was his shirt. I'd had it for years. It was too small for him now, and he'd never asked for it back.

I suddenly hugged the material around me as if that would hold him close to me. A lump formed in my throat.

Stop it! It was just a dream. You are not connected to him.

My eyes fell on my phone again. It was too early to call without making my mom suspicious, but...I could pretend. I didn't like lying to her, but if I didn't want her scrutinizing my friendship with Robbie for the next ten years, I had good reason.

I strode into the living room, fell into an over-stuffed armchair, and then called her. It rang twice before I hung up.

My phone rang seconds later, and I picked up on the second ring. "Hello?"

"Britta, what's wrong?" my mom asked.

"Oh, sorry. I was just checking messages. I must have butt-dialed you."

"Butt-dialed?"

"You know, a pocket dial—when the phone calls someone by accident."

I didn't say anything else, knowing that she'd ask more questions and fill in the gaps. She always did.

"Why were you checking messages at this time in the morning?"

Bingo. "I woke up before my alarm. Weird dreams. Anxiety, I guess, about exams. I checked messages to see if Robbie had texted me yet."

"Why would Robbie text you so early?"

"He's supposed to pick me up later and drive me home for Húsl. Didn't Tyr tell you?"

"No, I haven't seen him. I haven't seen either of them since yesterday."

"Okay, well, can you contact Robbie and ask him to call me? I have to know whether I should pack now or later. I'm planning to go to the studio early and work on my choreography."

My mom made that little sound she always made when she disagreed with me. "Svassa, you should go back to sleep. You can't burn the candle at both ends."

"I tried, Mom. But I'm already losing study time with Húsl. You know how it is at this time of year. The world doesn't stop for us to celebrate Odin's great creation. Anyway, can you get Robbie to call me?" That lump started to form in my throat again. I swallowed hard to get rid of it. "You know he doesn't sleep in."

Silence rained down the line. Crap. She knew something was up. She always did. I swear, it was part of her magic. She could ferret out anything and wouldn't let it go until every corner was uncovered—like a wolf with a bone.

"Okay...are you sure you're all right?" she asked.

"I'm fine. Just tired and overwhelmed, I guess." All true. I forced out a laugh. "Nothing your Húsl pudding won't fix."

"I'll give you an extra helping with lots of cranberries on top, *kaer dottir.*"

Dear daughter. The endearment made me smile. As did the thought of her Húsl pudding.

"But Britta, you won't need it," she continued. "You're strong—stronger than I ever was. You went your own way. Forged your own path. And the creative energy you expel every day would leave me flat on my back. You're a beautiful miracle, ulf-ungr. I'll call you as soon as I hear from Robbie."

She hung up without saying goodbye, as she always did, and I stared in bewilderment at the phone. She thought *I* was strong?

My whole life, I'd been tossed around like a boat on the waves of my emotion, confusing the heck out of my warrior family. I'd been like that weird neighbor kid you watched through the front window, who was always doing strange things outside.

My dad, Tyr, and my mom didn't know what to do with me half the time—didn't understand me—and it had taken *me* a long time to understand *them.*

Sometimes I felt like we'd just called a truce. We had learned what to say and what not to say to avoid setting off the other person. Except with Tyr, of course. He and I still fought—a lot. And he triggered me as much as I triggered him.

But in a strange way, that almost felt more honest than the whitewashed communication I sometimes had with my mom and dad. I knew they loved me and wanted me to be happy; they just couldn't always understand what *made* me happy or unhappy.

If I felt a certain way...I just felt that way. And trying to change it never helped. All it did was make me feel worse—I'd learned that I didn't always have to act on my feelings, but I had to acknowledge them and try to understand them if I could. Then let them go.

Otherwise, they would eat me up.

I felt calmer after letting myself wallow for a bit. I was still worried about Robbie, but I knew my mom would get back to me as soon as possible—probably with the news that he'd crashed on a cot at Savage or had bunked down at Wolf Tower.

Safely.

I returned to my room, grabbed my stuff, and headed to the bathroom, trying to be as quiet as possible. Esme and Benni had also had a late night—and they'd probably have the hangovers to prove it.

As for me, waking up early was a good thing. I wasn't lying when I told my mom I was losing precious study time during Húsl. Why in hel hadn't Odin created the Valdyr during Spring Break? That timing would have worked better for me.

I looked in the mirror and stuck out my tongue at my reflection. *Not everything revolves around you, Britta.*

Wow. That definitely came out in my brother's voice.

Like Odin gives a shit about you, anyway. And *that* was definitely my voice.

I sighed, stripped down, and stepped into the shower, taking extra long to wash my hair and let the water run over my face, which felt hot and puffy from crying. At the end, I turned the water to cold, waking myself all the way up, and then stepped briskly onto the mat a few seconds later, rechecking my phone as soon as I could—nothing yet from either my mom or Robbie.

After getting dressed and drying my hair, I packed my overnight bag, including the Húsl gifts I'd bought for my family, Robbie, Dahlia, and Erik: extra-large, NASA-made oven mitts for my dad, who was always burning his hands cooking dinner, a funky T-shirt with a bright yellow sunflower on it for Dahlia, some scary-looking hair accessories for my brother, a navy blue, leather-bound planner for my mom that made me drool, a book for Erik that I'd heard him talking about—if he ever got the chance to read, and for Robbie, a photo of the two of us when we were kids, set in a frame I'd designed and painted myself.

I stared at the photo for a minute before placing it in my bag. It really brought home to me how things were about to change— this may be the last time I spent Húsl with my family and my pack. And as much as they drove me crazy sometimes, I knew I would miss them desperately.

I grabbed the letter from Complexions as I walked past my desk and shoved it into my dance bag. I felt the need to keep it close, like I required a constant reminder that my path was out in the big, wide world—not here where I wasn't wanted or needed.

Although that wasn't true now, was it? Erik wanted me, and according to him, the pups needed me.

I took the letter out again, reread it, folded it neatly this time, and tucked it in the bag's front pocket. Like my mom said, I would forge my own path—wherever that took me.

The campus was relatively quiet when I got there. I'd been obsessively checking my phone since I'd left and had started to worry again. Why hadn't my mom contacted me yet? Had she forgotten?

No. She never forgot.

I was almost at the Arts building when I heard helicopters in the distance—several of them—and froze in my tracks. My eyes traced the sky, but too many trees soared above me, blocking my view. When I heard a third helicopter, blind panic took over, and I started running toward the sound, which was crazy. And dangerous—people would see me and marvel at my speed.

But I knew that sound. I'd ridden one of those helicopters almost every day for years—to and from Missoula for dance classes.

Something was wrong for there to be three together!

And then my phone beeped. I stopped abruptly, the breath sawing through my lungs, and pulled it out. It was my mom, and

I let out a shaky sob. The message read: *R will pick u up as soon as ur done. His phone is broken. Time and place?*

I stepped to the side of the path and collapsed on a bench with relief. It took me a few minutes to type because my fingers kept hitting the wrong letters.

Studio B. 2 p.m. I can meet him in the parking lot.

OK. Love, Mom.

The "Love, Mom" made me smile—like she was signing a letter.

I started laughing and couldn't stop as the twisted, frightened emotions inside me let go—it was either that or cry again. And I'd cried enough for today.

Thank you, I typed back. *Love, Britta.*

CHAPTER 8

Robbie

"G ET HUMONGOUS DUDE SOME FUCKING PANTS. M Y MOTHER IS here," Tyr said to a junior rekkr, who was passing by the parked Range Rover in which I sat—wrapped in a blanket and staring in disbelief at the empty space that used to be the Dverg warehouse.

A pair of jeans came flying back seconds later, hitting Tyr square in the face, and I snorted. He grumbled and then tossed them to me. I caught them one-handed and set them on top of the open car door…for now. Not that I wanted Britta's mom to see my junk, but I was still too wobbly to put the pants on. If anyone knew just *how* wobbly, they'd ship me back to medical.

And I wanted to pick up Britta from rehearsal today. I told her I'd be there.

Besides, Magna Larssen was old school. She didn't care whose junk she saw when we were wolfing in and out after a fight.

Or who saw hers.

Tyr and I were deeply scarred.

According to Erik, I'd been unconscious for at least an hour. By the time they found me in that scrubby field, Skoll had absconded with the blown-up warehouse. It had disappeared as they approached—however the fuck that was possible—just before Skoll grabbed a sunbeam out. Three helicopters full of rekkrs had landed minutes later and started a search for me and the fleeing Dvergar.

Tyr had caught my scent right away and led the medical team directly to me. They got there just in time. Erik was able to rouse my wolf and hold us to this plane while the medics did their magic and started my body healing on its own.

Tyr *still* looked a little pale, but maybe that was because he'd colored his hair again—half red, half white. For Húsl, he'd said.

I looked back at the missing warehouse and shook my head again in disbelief. Tyr followed my gaze. "It's a good thing you got pictures," he said. "No one would have believed it otherwise."

I nodded, too exhausted to use words.

The hazard bag that carried the crystal, silver vials, and my phone had been sent back to Wolf Ridge immediately on one of the helicopters—along with the magical gun that shot green bullets. Freyja had warded the compound years ago, and neither Hati nor Skoll could breach it, so the magic the twins wanted was out of reach. Although, I had no idea what they could do with the blown-up bits and pieces of the warehouse.

I raised a shaky hand to my face and rubbed at some orangey-colored dust on my skin and hair. It was all over me, actually, which was weird, because it wasn't in the field where I'd landed or anywhere around the warehouse.

And if it came from inside the warehouse when the building blew, it should have fallen off my wolf when he shifted into the helmingr—that energized state between our solidified bodies.

"Get a test tube or envelope or something," I told Tyr, forcing myself to talk. "We should scrape some of this dust off of me and send it back to the lab."

"*You* should get back to the lab," he said. "They need to test you out. I don't know why the Fyrstr let you stay—you can barely talk. That dust could be what's stopping your connection to the rest of us."

"I'm okay. Most of it's been wiped off."

"You're not okay. Don't think I haven't noticed you're still buck-naked beneath that blanket. You've got all the strength of a fucking puppy."

He wasn't wrong. To ease his worry a little, I grabbed the jeans from the door frame, hung them down, and stepped into them. They were a bit snug.

But I was stronger than even a few minutes ago. "No permanent damage. I'm sure it's just a matter of time before I'm connected to the pack again."

"You better hope so, brother. Who the fuck am I going to grouse to when my sister's ticking me off."

"Hopefully, not me. In fact, maybe I'll keep this dust on me a little while longer."

"Ha, ha."

"Tyr!" Magna called, heading towards us with Erik.

"Yeah?" he answered.

"Go help Gunn search the tunnels we found."

"On it," Tyr said, then turned to me. "They need my amazo-sniffer. Glad you're not dead."

"Me too."

Tyr had an incredible sense of smell. Better than any Valdyr I'd met. If some of the Dvergs were still around, he'd find them.

"Yo, Mama!" he said as he approached Magna. "Send Rob back home. He almost fell over putting his pants on."

Fucker. "I did not. I'm not going back yet. I'm picking up Britta after her rehearsal." I stood up from the passenger seat and took my hand off the door to prove I was okay. It just about killed me.

Erik started to say something, but Magna hit his arm. Huh. No one else I knew would dare do that to the Fyrstr. Well... maybe Dahlia would.

And Britta.

If I whacked him, no matter how lightly, I'd end up on the ground—humongous dude or not. Which is exactly what I wanted in my Alpha.

"Sit down, ulf-ungr," Magna said when they reached me—ordered, really.

Erik's lips twitched…because Magna was ordering me around or because she'd called me ulf-ungr?

Young wolf. A term of endearment—for the pups, usually.

Magna caught his smile. "He's mine too," she said. "I'm allowed."

Erik just nodded. Smart wolf. Then he pointed to the seat.

I gave in easily—too easily—and sat down.

"I heard from Dane," Erik said. "He found the twins' hide-out. He said Skoll arrived with something hovering between his palms—he was using magic to carry it. It glowed with a red line around it. The energy coming off it made his hair stand up."

"How big?" I asked.

He held his hands apart. "About a foot long and half a foot wide. Like a rectangular cube."

"A cuboid," Magna said.

Of course, she would know that.

Erik nodded and continued. "Skoll was spitting mad to see him there, but he couldn't release the object to fight him."

"Maybe it was the warehouse," I mused. "A shrunken version of it. It was shaped like a rectangle, and a red line marked the shield around it."

"Maybe."

Magna's hands planted on her hips. "It's a good thing he didn't find you in that field. You'd be dead by now." She said it matter-of-factly, but her eyes sparked at me. She'd already given me hel for going in alone.

"What did your wolf say?" Erik asked.

"About what?"

"Your injuries."

I wanted to downplay the seriousness of being caught in that magical blast, but I also knew the information was important. "He's not worried about recovering, but he doesn't like this dust. It's…unnatural. It's like it's coming out of my pores."

"From inside of you?" Magna asked.

I nodded, then closed my eyes and tried to get a sense of what was happening in my body.

Is there anything else they need to know? I asked my wolf.

He was in a deep state of rest, the same as I should be, but he was also listening to our conversation. *Our magic—Odin's magic—is strong. We are purging the lesser magic.*

That's what I think too.

I opened my eyes. "The blast forced the other magic inside of us, but our magic is stronger and pushing it out. It's only a matter of time before it's all gone."

"Days?" Erik asked.

"No, hours." I stretched the truth just a little. At the rate I was healing, I'd be about sixty-five percent by the time I picked up Britta—healthy enough for a spring drive through the mountains.

"Does your wolf know the magic's intent?" Magna asked.

"To cut me off from the pack. It's working…but only temporarily." I turned to Erik. "Do you have the pictures I sent you?"

He nodded and brought the photos up on his phone. I scrolled through them until I found a wide shot of the warehouse floor, showing the concentric circles of the "battery".

"What does that remind you of?" I asked.

Magna crowded in beside Erik so she could see. "A battery—the kind you kids made in science class."

"Yeah. That's what I thought too."

"A magical amplifier," Erik said.

"The residue from the blast isn't enough to affect me much—I'm getting better quickly—but maybe *this* configuration," I pointed to the photo, "could have overpowered my magic permanently. And if Skoll can transport the entire building, he or Hati could have activated the magic wherever and whenever they wanted—like during Húsl when we were all together."

Erik's jaw clenched. I suspected he was holding back a string of curses for Magna's sake. "A magical bomb. Do you think he could repair it?"

"I doubt it. The magic was volatile, and the explosion on a magnitude I've never seen before. How far was I from the blast site?"

"A quarter mile at least."

That sounded about right. "It hit me just as my wolf was crossing the barrier and blew me all the way there. I landed hard."

"No shit," Erik said.

I rolled my shoulders and stretched my neck, testing my injuries. The blast had almost completely broken me, but I was healing quickly. I always did.

"Even without the explosion, this powder could hinder us." Magna raised her hand to my forehead and swiped her fingers across it, examining the residue on her fingertips. "Does it hurt?"

She sounded concerned, but in a different way than my mother or Britta would have been concerned. Magna sympathized with the pain I felt, but she also thought like a warrior and wanted to know how we'd be affected on the battlefield.

Britta, on the other hand, would *feel* what I was feeling deep down in her bones—like my mother had. Every part of her would empathize with my pain.

Her boundaries were porous with people she cared about, and she would take on their distress—physical or emotional—which was the last thing I wanted her to do. I knew how drained she would feel—my mom had felt the same way, even though she'd tried to hide it.

"No. I'm just tired. Does Britta know I was injured?"

"Not from me." An intent look crossed Magna's face. "She

called me this morning shortly after sunrise. She was trying to reach you." Her eyes met mine. "She'd had a weird dream—said it was exam stress. I contacted Erik when I couldn't feel you through the bond."

Magna handed me a piece of paper. "I told her your phone was broken, and that's why you'd been out of touch."

I glanced down and read the note—Britta's rehearsal time and location—then pocketed it. "Okay, thanks. I'm sure it *is* broken."

They'd left the hazard bag sealed because they didn't want to contaminate what was inside it or have the contents poison us if the vial had been damaged.

My phone was still in there, and I'm sure it was cracked—how could it not have been when my body was so broken from the blast?

Surprisingly, the gun was fine—it had landed on top of me. Tyr had taken a liking to it, pretending to be every badass in every movie he'd ever watched before Magna had retrieved it from him—her recalcitrant child.

I snorted again, just thinking about it.

"You take care of her, Robbie," she said suddenly.

My gaze jumped to hers, and I caught my breath—shocked—at the glimmer of tears in her eyes. "I will, Magna. I promise. We'll get home safely."

She leaned forward and hugged me hard enough that it hurt a little—but a good kind of hurt. The kind that let me know she'd been worried about me. I returned the hug despite the pain. In the distance, the second helicopter started up, the rotors spinning slowly before picking up speed.

She pulled back from me and said brusquely, "I'm heading home now. I still have presents to wrap. Trust in the Allfather— this will sort itself out."

I nodded. She turned and took a few steps toward the helicopter before looking back at me and raised her voice to be heard over the rotors. "She called me, Robbie, whether it was a butt-dial or not. She called me just after sunrise—to find you. And she was scared."

Then she ran for the helicopter, which had just started to lift off. It hovered close to the ground until she jumped on.

I stared after her, stunned, my heart banging in my chest and my thoughts spinning in a million different directions. Was she implying that Britta knew I'd been hurt?

"A butt-dial?" I asked Erik. For some reason, that phrase had stuck in my head.

Erik shrugged. "Apparently, she didn't mean to call Magna—her finger slipped."

"After the bad dream?"

"Yes…I think. I don't know exactly."

Neither did I, and I was too exhausted to figure it out. Still, I couldn't let it go.

"Is she saying that Britta knew I was hurt? That she dreamed about it?"

"Maybe, but I think she's wondering if…Look, Britta's wolf is coming through, and Magna is worried her daughter won't be accepted into the pack. I think she's hoping…" His words drifted away again—uncomfortable.

My brows raised incredulously as the pieces fell into place. "That she dreamed about me because we're fated mates?"

Erik sighed. "She just wants to keep her daughter close, Rob. We all do."

I laughed, but it was a hollow sound. "Too late for that. She's going to New York to dance. She's been accepted into a prestigious company. And if not there, she'll go to Europe or Australia. I heard her and her friends talking about it. They're excited for her."

"Those aren't her only options. She may stay here."

"For what? So she can live close to the pack but not be a part of the pack? Rejected by Odin?"

"She'll have a place. And she won't be rejected by Odin. None of us are. Her purpose will be outside of the pack. Unless..."

"Unless what? I kyss her?"

Erik shoved his hand through his hair. "No...Maybe...Look, I don't know, and neither do you. The point is, when her wolf rises, *then* you'll know. And it'll be out of your hands. Out of her hands too. Your wolves will want whatever is in their hearts—whatever the Norns have woven there."

That didn't sit right with me—the idea that Britta and I had no choice.

"I disagree. Britta wants to be out on her own, exploring the world and pursuing her dreams. That's what I want for her too. She's meant for bigger things than this endless fight against Hati and Skoll—against Fenrir. Just like my mom was meant for bigger things."

Erik's eyes widened in surprise. "Rob, your mom was happy. She loved your dad very much, and he loved her. She didn't want to be anywhere else but here with you and him. I used to envy their closeness because my parents weren't like that. They couldn't be. The curse affected them in a terrible way...you know that. It affected all of us."

I shook my head in denial, making my head swim. "She was an incredible musician, and she gave that up for him. She died here in these mountains, her songs and music unheard outside the pack." My voice broke, and I swallowed hard. "He brought her here, and then he couldn't protect her. I couldn't protect her."

I dropped my head, unable to hold it up any longer. I couldn't deal with this kind of emotion right now—I could barely deal with it when I was healthy.

Erik's hand fell on my shoulder and squeezed. "I'm sorry, Rob. We lost so much when we lost Astra—and then almost lost you. The crash was tragic, and it broke your dad, but neither of them would have changed being mated to each other and having you. At least, that's how it appeared from my perspective."

I looked up at him. Pain was etched into every line of his face—it was a living thing between us—a shared sadness.

"I saw your parents every day, Rob. They were deeply in love and connected to each other despite the poison the curse dripped into the pack, warping things among loved ones and twisting their emotions. You know what happened. You saw how it unfolded in some families—the violence, the rage. You were a junior rekkr when I became Alpha and drew the curse from the pack. You grew up in the thick of it—years and years of corruption, of distortion.

"But your mom alleviated some of that toxicity. She spread love and joy with her songs and music, mostly just with who she was. And Britta is the same. She heals. We need her, Rob—the pack is still hurting, and I think Britta can help. I'm not saying you should talk her out of leaving, but you shouldn't let what happened with your mom and dad—or your perception of it—color your relationship with her. Or her relationship to the pack."

CHAPTER 9

Robbie

I PAUSED OUTSIDE THE STUDIO AND LEANED DOWN TO PEEK through the rectangular glass window in the door. Inside, dancers glided across the floor to modern, lyrical music, wearing an assortment of stretchy dance gear with their long hair pulled off their faces and pointe shoes on the women's feet. Mirrors lined one wall, and a barre lined the other.

I didn't know much about dance, but Britta had taught me enough that I recognized the style—contemporary ballet.

I couldn't see her in the studio, and I glanced at the clock on the wall to make sure that I wasn't late…nope, three minutes early. Where was she?

And then I smelled her. It wafted over me from behind, and I turned around.

She stood farther down the hallway in front of the washroom door, wearing sneakers with her faded jeans, a long-sleeve, hot pink T-shirt, and carrying a backpack in one hand. A small, relieved sound broke through her lips, and she ran toward me—faster than any human could have run.

I braced myself as she threw her arms around my waist—her entire body pressed against mine.

My arms wrapped around her back, and I rested my cheek on top of her head, closing my eyes and breathing her in. Her silky hair smelled like vanilla and citrus mixed with her own unique scent. It made me think of love and home and safety.

A shuddering sigh blew from her lungs as she melted against me. "You're hurt," she said, her voice muffled against my fresh, navy blue T-shirt.

I'd healed a lot in the past five hours, resting at Wolf Tower, and most Valdyr wouldn't have sensed my injuries. Britta, however, wasn't "most" Valdyr—she was incredibly sensitive to others, picking up on any changes in their physical and emotional states.

"I am. But I'm healing. By tonight, I should be back to normal...although I may need a nap when I get home."

She snorted and tipped her head back to look at me. "You? Nap? That is definitely *not* normal." And then she broke into a laugh.

It was addictive, and I laughed back. *She* was addictive.

Everything about Britta felt good, and my still-broken body buzzed with pleasure and a surge of emotional and physical repair just from being around her.

But there was something else too...

My chest tightened, and it became harder to breathe. My knees weakened. My stomach flipped. And then everything slowed—the music from the studio, my blood whooshing through my veins, the thoughts careening through my head. Every cell in my body focused entirely on her, and I realized...

I loved her. No, not just loved her...I was *in love* with her.

The awareness crashed through me like a hammer, and my heart began to pound as if I were racing in wolf form across a high mountaintop on a moonlit night—blood surging, thoughts whirling, desire rising.

Joyful chaos took hold of my body, and for a moment, I reveled in it.

I stared at her smiling lips and laughing eyes—fascinated by the sight of her pink tongue flashing between her teeth. I wanted to cup the back of her head and capture that tongue. Suck on it. Dance with it. Dominate it.

Dominate her.

Whoa. Where had that come from?

Inside me, my wolf hummed contentedly—still half asleep in that healing mode. *From you. And me. She is ours.*

I blinked and raised my gaze, focusing on a spot on the wall behind Britta's head as I controlled my urges and took a mental step backward.

No. She's not ours—you can't possibly know that. And she belongs to herself.

Yes. And to us. And we belong to her.

"Robbie…Robbie! Are you even listening to me?" she asked, bringing me back to myself.

I forced a smile and looked down into her upturned face. Her brow had furrowed quizzically, but her eyes were still laughing. I reached behind me, grasped her hands, and gently pulled them from around my waist. This time, I physically stepped backward and put distance between us.

Britta was leaving, and I was happy for her. She had her whole life ahead of her to discover—a brilliant path to forge.

"Sorry. Still caught up in my head a little. It was a long night… I can't really talk about it."

That would put a wedge between us…and maybe we needed one.

She often felt excluded by her parents, Tyr, and me when we refused to talk about our work in front of her. Sometimes it was deliberate—there were things she couldn't know—but often, it was just to protect her, and she hated that.

Her smile faded, but instead of withdrawing, she nodded.

"Okay. I was just worried about you. I had a weird dream last night, and it made me anxious. You know how I am."

"Yeah, well, don't worry, it wasn't a big deal. Just the usual." Not entirely true, but true enough. "It's a busy time of year. You're probably stressed with everything going on—and now having to decide about…you know."

She raised a brow.

"Your plans for next year," I elaborated. "You got that acceptance letter, and I'm sure more will come. I mean—you're amazing—who wouldn't want you in their company? It's everything you've ever dreamed of. I'm really happy for you, Britta. You're going to conquer the world."

Her fingers trembled within mine, and the corners of her mouth pulled down. "Ugh. Do not be nice to me. You're going to make me cry."

I leaned forward and kissed her forehead. "I don't ever want to make you cry."

Behind me, the studio door opened and pushed into my back. I stepped forward to get out of the way and somehow ended up with my arm wrapped around her as I turned to see who was there.

"Oh, my God, the giant's back!" Benni with an 'i' squealed up at me.

Esme peered over his shoulder. "Hey, it's the Big Bad Wolf. Everyone, Britta's boyfriend is here!" she called out to the other dancers.

"No, he's not my…Esme!" Britta sighed and shook her head.

My hand tightened momentarily on her waist. I was about to let go when her fingers weaved through mine and locked my hand in place.

Some of the other dancers came out, curious. Most of them were smiling. One man in particular, dressed in pressed black slacks and a button-down shirt, caught my attention. He was tall and lean with perfectly coiffed hair and a cut, almost aristocratic face—and he was not happy to see me.

I'd seen him before with Britta at one of her performances over a year ago. I'd sensed tension between them and had the feeling they might have been involved as more than just friends and colleagues.

Now I wondered who had broken off that relationship—and when.

My wolf immediately lifted his head, looked at the man through my eyes, and growled. But then he suddenly yawned noisily and flopped back down.

Wow. That showed him, killer wolf.

Human, my wolf replied.

Someone she once cared for.

No longer.

"Britta," the man said. "Can I speak to you, please? That last section still needs some work."

Britta tensed beside me. I almost stepped between her and the other man, but she would have killed me if I'd done that.

"Sorry, Paul," she said. "I have a family thing to go to. That last section feels really tight to me. You've done such an amazing job with the choreography. The ending is incredible. But we can look at it again next rehearsal if you want to."

Ahhh. She'd handled that beautifully.

Then she tugged on my hand and pulled me down the hallway, waving a farewell to her friends and roommates. "Bye, everyone. I'll see you in a few days!"

She released my hand when we turned the corner, and I almost grabbed it back, missing the feel of her warm palm pressed against mine—that tingle between us.

No, I told myself sternly. *You're going to let her go so she can live her own life—away from here.*

Inside, my wolf growled again—at me this time—but it was

half-hearted. Obviously, he wasn't worried about me thwarting his plans either.

"Sorry about that," Britta said.

I reached forward and opened the door for her, then followed her outside. The sun was bright and the air warm—much warmer than the air-conditioned hallways inside.

"Sorry about what?" I asked as I pulled my keys from my pocket. I'd nabbed a parking spot right in front of the building and headed toward the black Range Rover with the Wolf Ridge Industries logo on the side.

"About them thinking you were my boyfriend. Benni and Esme have their minds made up about you, no matter what I say."

Boyfriend. The word ricocheted in my head, making my chest feel tight again. It was hard to catch a full breath of air.

Not gonna go there even if it kills me. Whatever I thought I'd felt earlier—or had felt—I would squash it down.

I clicked the key fob, and the car doors opened with a chirp. When I started toward Britta's side of the car, she gave me a look and pointed toward my side. After a slight hesitation, I gave in and headed around the vehicle. But I kept watch, as usual, and didn't open my door until she was seated.

Safety first. Always.

I knew what was out there, and the Big Bad was no joke.

Something inside me twinged as I sat down. I winced and then reached for the seatbelt. She caught my hand as I pulled it across my body. "Here, let me help you."

I let go, and she clicked the belt into place.

"Thanks."

"No problem." She rubbed her palm up my arm and rested it on my shoulder. "Are you sure you're okay?"

I gave her the full truth this time but tried to lighten it up a little. "I'm okay to drive, and I'm okay to back that Paul guy into a corner and tell him to leave you alone, but I'm not okay to fight

Skoll if he shows up and demands my wallet." I grinned as I said it.

She did not grin back. "Again."

"What?"

"You're not okay to fight Skoll *again*."

I sighed. "No, I'm not. But I wasn't fighting him so much as running away from him last time."

"Were you alone?"

And now I was back to fudging the truth. "I was with Dane. He's okay too." Damn. That didn't feel good at all.

She sat back in her seat and shook her head. "What a crazy life we live." A group of laughing humans walked past the front of the Rover. "Wouldn't it be nice to be as oblivious as they are?"

"Maybe. But it wouldn't last long—only until Hati and Skoll freed Fenrir, and then Fenrir killed Odin. If that happened, Ragnarök would come for all of us. I'd rather know what was on the horizon and fight like hel to make sure it stayed there—and the prophecy was averted—than have the luxury of oblivion."

I turned to her, hoping in some way to reassure her. "I'm good at my job, Britta. Very good. I wouldn't be alive otherwise. And I'll do my damnedest to keep you and everyone else in the world alive too. I promise you that."

I shifted the Rover into reverse, checked my surroundings, and backed out of the parking spot. I was just about to put it into drive when a flash of light in the camera caught the corner of my eye.

I stilled and instinctively checked the doors. They were locked. My eyes jumped to the mirrors, searching for whatever had caused that glint of light.

"Is something wrong?" Britta asked.

I turned to look back over my shoulder, but I couldn't spot anything out of the ordinary.

"I thought I saw something—a flash of light—but maybe it was nothing."

Her eyes grew round. "You mean like Skoll riding a sunbeam in?"

"Yeah, maybe. Or maybe it was the sun glinting off a window or a headlight or something."

"Or somebody's phone catching the light."

"Yup. All of that." I sighed. "Sorry. I'm just being cautious. It's hard knowing that if something were to happen, I'm not one hundred percent right now."

She put her hand back on my shoulder, and I felt that buzz again. "You seem stronger than when I first saw you. Not much, but enough that I can sense it."

"I think I am. I'm not at my usual yet, but I'm stronger than I expected to be at this point."

"And by not your usual, you mean like a regular Valdyr?"

I laughed, the tension fading. "Yeah, I guess so." I did one last check around us before shifting into gear and stepping on the accelerator.

"The car is protected, right?" she asked. "Warded by Freyja like at Wolf Ridge?"

"Yes, to a certain extent. It's almost impossible for Hati or Skoll to get in. We're golden." I hated that I'd scared her.

"All right, then. Let's get this party started!" She connected her phone to the sound system, and Taylor Swift's latest song blared through the speakers. It was bouncy and fun, and I groaned inside.

"You got anything other than pop in there?"

She gasped and pressed her palm to her chest. "What are you saying? You don't like Tay Tay?"

"I didn't say that…exactly…I just asked if there was anything else."

"Not for the first hour. By hour two or three, there might be something." Then she frowned at me. "And no speeding just to get home faster. In fact, put the cruise control on so we stay under the speed limit."

"Cruise control? No self-respecting rekkr would ever use cruise control. I don't think that's even an option on the Rovers."

"Well, it should be. You guys drive like maniacs."

I merged into traffic and checked the time. We'd be home well before dinner. "I promise to stay within the speed limit and not drive like a maniac. But even then, there's no way it'll take us two hours to get to Wolf Ridge…unless I need a nap, and you have to take over. Then it'll take us three."

She pressed her palm to her chest again. "Double ouch!" Then she reached down and pulled a crinkly, cellophane bag from her backpack, holding it up for me to see. "Just for that, you don't get any."

My mouth watered when I saw the orange bag and imagined the big, puffy bites of cheesy goodness inside—my favorite.

Gunn hated them because of the orange fingerprints left behind on the steering wheel, and he'd forbidden us to eat them in the Rovers. He had a fanatical streak when it came to cleanliness. He'd get pissy if we crossed him.

But Britta had no problem crossing him. She knew that if he got grumpy with her, he was all bark and no bite. Plus, I could blame the orange prints on that orangey-colored dust still on my skin, although it was almost gone by now. I couldn't see it so much as feel it when I rubbed my fingers across my forearm.

Luckily, Gunn didn't know that.

When I'd woken from my five-hour nap at Wolf Tower earlier, I was covered in dust, and the white sheets were stained orange, so I'd chosen a dark shirt to wear after showering.

Thankfully, the dust hadn't returned much before I headed to the university. It must have been almost purged from my system by now, although I still couldn't connect to the pack. Every once in a while, I would hear something—like the crackle of a bad connection, or the odd distorted word—but nothing I could understand yet.

My wolf wasn't worried, though. When I asked how much longer, all he said was *soon*.

Britta opened the bag and inhaled the cheesy aroma. "Mmm. So good," she groaned.

I reached for a handful, but she snatched the bag away. "What was it you said about Taylor Swift? And my driving?"

Damn. "Uh, I said that Taylor is great. I love Taylor."

"And?"

"And…and your driving really sucks. Sorry, Brit. I cannot tell a lie. Even for a cheesy puff—food of the gods."

She snorted and put the bag back down, letting me have some.

Then she fiddled with her phone. I thought she was putting something else on, but another Taylor Swift song blared out.

"A gift for you," she said with a grin, "since you love Tay Tay so much. I have all of her albums. We can start at the beginning and go right to the end. You'll love it."

I took another handful of cheesy puffs and munched on them blissfully. "Worth it."

It didn't take us long to get out of the city and onto the highway heading northwest into the mountains. Our timing was perfect—just ahead of rush hour…not that there was much traffic in Missoula compared to other cities.

But the higher we ascended into the mountains, the more tense Britta became—especially when a drop-off appeared, or snow had piled up. I reached out and squeezed her hand.

She smiled at me gratefully, took a deep breath, and then released me. "I'm okay, and it'll make me feel better to see your hands on the wheel."

I repositioned my hold. "Ten and two—just for you." Cheesy, but it would make her laugh.

"Ha, ha. That's so last decade. Nine and three is the new ten and two."

I reset my hands to the nine and three positions. "Never say I'm behind the times."

"You're behind the times."

"What?"

"When was the last time you willingly listened to anything other than rock—from the previous century?"

I lifted my hand from the wheel and gestured to the speakers, my brow raised in mock astonishment. "What are you talking about? I'm a verifiable Swiftie now."

She gave me a horrified look and then snatched back the snacks. "You're cut off. You cannot just say you're a Swiftie. You have to earn it."

I put my hand back on the wheel, grinning as I wiped my orange fingers on the leather. I was full anyway. Still…

I gave her a sincere look, barely able to hold back my laugh. "You're right. It's me. Hey. I'm a problem. It's me."

Britta's eyes slowly grew round. "Oh, my gods. What are you saying? No, no, no, no, no. My ears!" She clapped her palms over her ears dramatically. "And it's 'hi,' not 'hey.'"

"Whatever."

"Whatever? There is no whatever!"

Britta grabbed her phone, scrolled through the playlist, and then blasted Anti-Hero through the speakers. "Listen and learn, rock-man."

If she could sing as well as she danced, it would have been an amazing three minutes.

She couldn't. And it wasn't. But she didn't care.

Which made me laugh and wince at the same time.

"Your mom had a beautiful voice," she said suddenly, turning down the music. "I remember her singing during Húsl. And at other celebrations and ceremonies."

I stilled as her words washed over me and sucked away my breath—typical for me when someone brought up my mom. "Yeah, she did. Unfortunately, she didn't pass it on."

"Well, maybe your pups will inherit it."

Inside, my wolf thumped his tail; my heart beat in tandem—a loud, hard drumming in my ears and through my body. I didn't think I'd ever have pups or pass down my mom's talent. Britta was leaving, doing what she was born to do, and how could there ever be anyone else?

Her talent wouldn't be hidden in the mountains like my mom's.

But Erik's words came back to me from this morning. Astra had been happy with me and my dad. I didn't doubt him; I certainly remembered her that way—singing and laughing and hugging whatever pup or Valdyr came into her presence. But she'd given up so much. Willingly, he'd said.

I sighed, knowing it was true. But had my dad even thought twice about asking her to forgo her dreams and serve Odin with him?

She hadn't been born into the Varda like most of us. She'd been raised on the East Coast in a small pack. My dad met her by chance when she was going across the country to Los Angeles in a dilapidated, old car.

She never got there. Her car had broken down in the Montana mountains, and my dad "saved" her.

That time, at least.

"Did you know I used to dance for her?" Britta asked with a laugh. "She had all those instruments, and she'd play one, then the other, as I danced around the room, or the field, or wherever we were. She was the only one who ever encouraged me in that way." She reached out and squeezed my arm. "Other than you, of course. And Erik when I was older."

I smiled back at her, but it was tinged with sadness. "I'll never stop encouraging you, Britta. I promise. I want you to be happy."

Her eyes filled with tears. "I know. I want you to be happy, too, Robbie."

I returned my gaze to the road and then found myself holding my breath—as I always did at this point in the journey. Britta slid her hand down my arm, took my hand off the wheel, and squeezed our palms together, her fingers lacing with mine.

"Are you sure?" I asked.

"Yes, I trust you. I know you don't need both hands to drive." She pointed up ahead. "Pull in when we get there."

My throat closed up, and I nodded.

I slowed as we came over the rise and maneuvered the Rover into a natural pullout. A roadside memorial dedicated to my mom was engraved into the rock in front of us—across from where her car had careened off the edge of the mountain when I was just eleven years old.

I'd been sleeping in the back seat after a long drive. Her screams, and the car yanking to the side, had woken me—just before we plunged over the cliff.

It was a horrifying memory. One I didn't think about often.

"Come on," Britta said, opening the car door.

I cut the engine and followed her. We walked to the front of the Rover, meeting in the middle in front of my mom's memorial.

Someone had done a beautiful job carving Astra's laughing face into the rock, along with a depiction of her wolf and the Norse runes for Love, Music, and Creation. In recent years, I'd asked for the sculptor's name, but nobody remembered it. Due to the curse, the pack had been in disarray at the time of my mom's death.

Her dying had only made things worse—significantly so.

On the ground beneath the carving, someone had set a bouquet of wildflowers that looked like they'd been recently gathered—probably from Astra's favorite meadow in the mountains around Wolf Ridge. She'd go there often with her guitar, saying she felt inspired to write.

"Did you pick those?" Britta asked, kneeling to straighten them.

"No. I didn't have time. She was well-loved by the pack—it could have been anyone."

She rose to stand beside me again. "She was an amazing woman. I've stopped here several times on my way home. She always gives me the strength to keep going when I want to turn around. And when I was a teen, stuck on the mountainside that time, I felt her presence, comforting me. Same as she did when I was a kid, feeling like an outcast."

"You were never an outcast."

She smiled, but I could tell she didn't believe me—the wound still festered.

I took her hand. "You are *not* an outcast, Britta. You are special to the pack. I know it, and Erik knows it. Even Tyr knows it."

She sighed. "Thank you, but—"

"No buts."

She laughed. "Anyway, it's like our connection to Asgard is strengthened by Astra's life—and her death in this spot. It feels holy to me—like a sacred place blessed by the gods." She raised my hand and kissed the back of it. "She's with your dad now, Robbie, running free in the woods outside Valhalla. Someday, you'll see them again."

"I hope so."

"You will."

I mulled over her words. Britta had always sensed the energy of the gods and magic in a way I didn't. "She had a strong connection to Bragi. Maybe that's who you feel."

"That would make sense—the god of music and poetry. I remember your mom had a shrine to him in that meadow she loved—she would go there to compose songs, and she always brought along an offering for him. Beer, usually," she said with a grin. "Although she called it mead."

"I remember."

We fell silent, staring at my mom's memorial, and I thought about what Britta and Erik had said. Astra had been happy here with her pack and family, raising me and all the other pups, living with her mate, and creating music. She was in Valhalla, now, with the love of her life. Probably singing and composing for the gods —maybe even with Bragi.

For the first time, I didn't feel that crushing weight of guilt and regret rise within me. That misplaced anger toward my father.

I let out a heavy breath. "I blamed my dad for the crash."

Britta turned to me. "Why? I thought she fell asleep at the wheel."

"Probably, but we'll never know for sure. It was a miracle I survived."

My chest loosened, and I released another deep sigh. "I was mad at him for not saving her, I guess. Mad at myself, too, even though I'd been trapped in a crushed car and a crushed body. Nobody could have saved her."

A sob broke from Britta's lips, and I looked over.

Her hand covered her mouth, and tears trickled down her face. "I remember visiting you in the infirmary and seeing him at your bedside. You were so broken. *He* was broken."

"I would be too if…" I trailed off, thinking about Britta, about how it would feel if something like that happened to her. I wouldn't survive.

She squeezed my hand. "…if what?"

"If my mate or pups were killed like that." I looked her in the eyes as I said it, and I knew the truth, then, beyond a shadow of a doubt. I loved her. I would always love her.

And I was going to let her go.

She sniffed, wiping her cheeks. "Me too. I don't know how your dad lived four more years without her. But he's with her now, thank Odin." She tapped my chest. "You, however, got me, tagging along at your heels, fighting with Tyr day in and day out, making you practice my dancing with me."

She laughed at the end. We both did.

Then she let go and trailed her hand along the hood of the Rover as she returned to her side of the car. I did the same.

"Robbie?"

"Yeah?"

"Was your mom's car warded like this one?"

"I don't know. I doubt it. And even if it was, a catastrophic fall like that would have destroyed the vehicle. The Rovers are tougher now than they were back then, but if the car's integrity was damaged, I think Freyja's ward would be damaged too."

She opened the door and sat down. I got in after her, engaging the locks as we buckled in.

"Well, it's a miracle you survived," she said. "And a tragedy that your mom didn't. We lost so much when we lost her."

"Yeah, we did."

Astra had been the glue that held us together. After her death, the pack had deteriorated even faster. But that was before Erik had contained the curse. Things were a thousand times better now. Not perfect, by any means—the pack still carried a lot of wounds—but we had hope again.

I inhaled deeply, and when I released my breath, I felt lighter, as if the burden I'd carried for so long had broken up and floated away.

I smiled and put the car into gear. "Shall we go?"

"Yes. Onward, Jeeves. Take me home."

I turned my head to check the side view mirror for oncoming traffic and caught a flash of light behind us.

It took less than a millisecond before every part of me burst into action. I slammed my foot on the accelerator, my instinct blaring at me and my wolf charging forward and growling savagely.

"It's Skoll!" I yelled to Britta as the tires squealed. "Brace yourself!"

The Rover flew forward, picking up speed, but we weren't fast enough, and the SUV came to a lurching halt.

Britta screamed in terror as the momentum threw her forward against her seatbelt. I tried to grab her phone, but it flew off the central console and slipped through my fingertips, landing on the floor next to the rest of her belongings that had spilled from her bag.

Behind us, Skoll loomed up, his face and arms strained as he held us captive by the back of the Rover.

Erik! I screamed into the bond. *Magna! We're under attack!*

Nobody responded.

Tyr! Gunn! We need help! I've got Britta with me!

"Call your mom!" I yelled at her. "I can't reach them."

I continued to floor the accelerator. The tires screeched as we weaved side to side, trying to break free from Skoll's grasp. The smell of burning rubber filled the air.

"The seatbelt's locked," she said frantically as she stretched her arm toward the phone.

And then I heard Britta's seatbelt unclip, and she leaned forward. Terror filled me. "No, Britta!"

But it was too late.

The vehicle yanked sideways—a sickeningly familiar feeling—and she slammed into the door as it flew toward the cliff.

Not again.

Because in that moment, I knew... Astra hadn't fallen asleep. It hadn't been an accident. Skoll Hróðvitnisson had attacked her while I lay sleeping in the back seat and tossed her vehicle over the cliff—the same as he was doing right now to me and Britta.

With a roar, I unclipped my belt and threw myself over her, my body protecting hers as I grabbed onto the seat and braced us in place.

We could survive this. We could make it out alive. The Rover was magically warded and reinforced. It was stronger and sturdier than my mom's vehicle had been.

If I could just cage Britta in!

I saw a flash of blue sky just before we hit the side of the mountain with a terrifying, jarring crunch. The car bounced up and then crashed again as it rolled down the mountainside.

My jaw clenched, and my muscles strained as I kept us locked in place. Britta's screams ripped through my ears.

"Hold on!" I shouted. "Hold on! I've got you, Britta. I won't let you go!"

And then I heard something more horrifying than the Rover crashing and rolling down the mountainside. I heard the rip of metal as the driver's side of the vehicle sheared right off.

And I knew the only thing left to do was pray.

CHAPTER 10

Britta

I panted in the tight, dark space, struggling to get enough air into my lungs. Robbie weighed heavily on top of me—a dead weight—and I squeezed my hands against his chest. "Robbie. Can you hear me? Robbie!"

For some reason, I'd whispered the words, which was funny/not funny after the deafening sounds of the crash. If Skoll had followed us down the mountainside, he knew where to look —the big heap of twisted metal at the bottom of the canyon.

"Robbie," I said again, louder this time.

He jerked awake and lifted his head a few inches—as far as he could. The Rover was crushed all around us.

"Britta?" He'd slurred my name.

Relief poured through me despite that. "Yes! Oh, thank Odin you're alive. Are you hurt?" Of course, he was hurt. What a stupid question.

"I'm…okay."

"No, you're not, but you're conscious. At this point, that's all that matters."

He breathed deeply and then groaned. "We have to…get out… of here." His body lifted off of mine just a smidge, making it easier for me to breathe. "Am I…crushing you?"

He sounded so guilty, and I laughed—it was either that or break into hysterical tears. "Yes, you're crushing me. How dare you do such a thing when we've just fallen off a mountaintop, and you threw your body over mine to protect me. Jerk." I closed my eyes and shuddered. "I may never drive through the mountains again."

"Me neither. That's twice now—in the same spot."

He grunted and then twisted his head to take in our situation. His face was just inches above mine. Without thinking, I pressed my mouth to his.

Soft. His lips were so soft.

He stilled for a moment and then pressed back, his fingers twining in the hair at the nape of my neck.

The gentle caress undid me, and a sob broke from my chest. "Thank you," I said against his lips. "Oh, gods, thank you. You saved my life." Tears streamed from the corners of my eyes.

"Always, Britta."

He sounded stronger now, and I knew we were going to make it. Robbie was invincible. I wriggled my arms around him until they curved across his back.

"I'm going to try and break the Rover apart, but I'll need your help. Can you do that, Brit?"

"Yes, of course. Anything."

"Good. Wrap your legs around me and then push with your hands and feet against the metal above us. I'll push with my back."

"Okay." I moved my legs slowly to avoid any jagged metal until they were on either side of his hips, cradling his big body against my pelvis. Despite our injuries and the danger we were in, it felt good. Not in an I-want-to-jump-your-bones-right-now kind of way—although that was part of it—but more of a this-feels-so-right kind of way…like connection and homecoming.

I cleared my throat. "Now?"

He bent his knees for more leverage and then nodded. "On my count. One, two, three."

I pushed as hard as I could with my hands and feet against the crushed metal above us. He grunted and shoved upward with his back, his face contorting into a determined grimace.

The metal didn't budge, and I kept pushing…and pushing… until my legs began to shake, and I felt like I might pass out.

"Keep going," he yelled at me through gritted teeth. "Do not give up. The Britta I know would never give up."

"Fucker," I grunted at him. But I found the strength somewhere and pushed as hard as I could, letting out a guttural scream until the resistance suddenly gave way, and the crushed car top shoved off of us with a wrenching screech. Blue sky and tall trees filled my view.

Robbie collapsed on top of me, and I wrapped my arms and legs around him, laughing and crying at the same time. His chest heaved against mine as his breath seesawed in and out of his lungs.

"Did you just call me a fucker?" he gasped, bringing his elbows beneath him so that he could look down at me—and not crush me.

I laughed harder. "Yeah. *The Britta you know?* What kind of mind fuck is that? Were you, like, a rekkr personal trainer in another life?"

"It worked, didn't it?"

"Only because if it didn't, I might have to hear more of that shit."

He wrapped one arm around my waist and pulled me tightly against him with a growl. My arms circled his neck as I laughed —a joyous release that we were safe. For now.

And then his teeth were at my throat. No, not my throat—farther over at the juncture between my neck and shoulder.

I stopped laughing, my breath catching in my lungs. And I found myself wanting, wanting…

"Bad language," he reprimanded me in a tone I'd never heard before—resonant and guttural like his wolf rode him hard. Something primitive responded deep within me—at the core of my being—and I tipped my head to the side, swinging my hair back and exposing my neck.

"Fuck," I said, and before I could stop myself, I added, "me." And it was just as resonant and almost as guttural.

His breath gushed over my skin, and I shivered. His mouth opened, hot and wet, and his teeth grazed over me. Then he bit down, and I groaned, my body flooding with heat, my breath stuttering in my lungs, my core dampening.

This one touch was better than any sex I'd ever had, and I wanted more. Lots more.

But his jaw released my flesh instead of biting harder, and he sat back on his heels, the air cool now against my skin where his mouth had been. His eyes glittered, and his cheeks flushed as he stared at me. Then he looked off into the distance, scanning our surroundings.

"We have to go," he said brusquely. "Skoll could be here any minute." He rose a little unsteadily to his feet and reached down for me.

I took his hand gratefully, and he helped me up. I stumbled as I straightened, my right leg shooting pain into my hip. He kept his hand on my waist until I was stable.

We may be alive, but we were more than a little worse for wear.

"Okay?" he asked.

I nodded, determined to be as stoic as he was about the pain.

We stood at the bottom of the canyon, surrounded by the

forest and the mountains that rose on either side, in the middle of a debris field.

Horror filled me as I looked at the jagged pieces of metal, bent tires, and broken glass scattered all around us. I spotted the steering wheel in a tree and clamped my hand over my mouth, my stomach twisting. And then I saw my backpack at my feet, almost completely undamaged.

I gasped and picked it up. How could that be?

Robbie stepped out of the wreckage and then reached back for me, putting his hands on my waist and lifting me right out of the debris.

The emotional high of surviving the crash was fading, and the reality of our situation sank in. Skoll could be coming for us—would be coming for us—and I began to panic. "What about the pack? Do they know what happened? Will they be here soon?"

"They know we've crashed. A beacon in the Rover will alert them to this location."

"But they don't know about Skoll?"

"No. Britta, something happened to me this morning, and I was cut off from the Alpha bond. It's getting better, but for now, we've lost direct communication with the pack."

He spotted something in the debris and reached for it. When he straightened, he had my crushed phone in his hand. He pressed the button at the bottom of the cracked screen, but it wasn't working. "Do you want to keep it? You may be able to get photos off of it or something."

I nodded, and he handed it to me. I shoved it into my back pocket.

"Can you contact your mom through your family bond? Or your dad or Tyr?"

"I don't think so. We're too far away."

"Try anyway."

"Okay." I closed my eyes and tried to connect with my family, but all I sensed was a blank void where they used to be.

Losing that direct connection to my family had been one of the hardest things about moving to Missoula. It came back whenever I was within a few miles of them, and of course, they were only a phone call away, but knowing that I couldn't just feel them whenever I wanted to had been hard—which was funny because I'd hated being so connected to them as a teenager.

If I was accepted into the pack after my wolf rose, then my range would be greater. But I didn't expect that to happen.

I opened my eyes and shook my head. "Can we just wait here for the pack?"

He grasped my shoulders, his gaze unwavering. "No. We need to move as fast as we can toward Wolf Ridge and get behind Freyja's ward. Skoll may still come after us."

"But why? Has he done this before? Thrown cars off cliffs?"

A muscle twitched in his cheek, which was bunched up, hard as a rock. "Yes. I think so. But not in many years. Maybe he thinks I have something of his. Or he's just really, really mad."

"What does he think you have?"

"Magical items from a Dvergar workshop that we raided last night, but we sent them back to Wolf Ridge on helicopters this morning. Come on." He clasped my hand and led me briskly away from the wreck. "We have to move."

I matched his pace, every bone and muscle in my body protesting. "Wouldn't he know that—about the helicopters?"

"Not for certain, but it would be a reasonable conclusion to make."

"Then why would he attack us?"

"Like I said, maybe he's just mad."

I shook my head. "He's not stupid, Robbie. Throwing our car off a mountaintop was a risky move. Anybody could have seen him."

"Which means he's motivated. Can you run?"

My hip hurt like a son of a bikkja, but I nodded anyway. If I could perform when I was injured, I could sure as hel run on a damaged leg to save my life—and Robbie's too. I knew he'd never leave me.

He broke into a jog, still holding my hand as he led the way through the trees in a north-westerly direction.

"Is that all you got?" I asked, breaking free of him and surging ahead.

He passed me in one leap. "I go first. Stay close, and let me know if my pace is too fast or too slow. And don't be a hero, Brit —we go as quickly as we can without killing ourselves. If Skoll attacks, I need to be able to fight, and you need to be able to flee. Got it?"

No. I didn't get it. If Robbie was fighting Skoll, I could help—a little.

"You know I was trained to fight, right? Over and over when I was a kid by two of the best rekkrs in the Varda."

"And they'll kill me if I let anything happen to you."

"Well, they won't get the opportunity to kill you because you'll already be dead from fighting Skoll alone."

He spun suddenly and gripped my arms hard enough to hurt —his face and eyes harsh. "You do not fight. You do not stop. You run as fast as you can. Skoll would crush you with one finger, whether you're trained or not. You do not have your wolf yet, Britta. Your strength is not even an ounce of his—or mine."

"But you'll die!" I burst out.

"And you will live. Britta, it will hinder me if I know he can get to you—hurt you. And he'll know that too. He'll use it. You run and don't look back. Promise me that, svassa."

Darling…he'd called me darling. How could I say no to that?

I couldn't, and I nodded reluctantly.

He turned and took off through the woods again, setting a hard but doable pace along a deep, swift creek that ran through Wolf Ridge. I kept up, barely. Before long, my breath was sawing through my lungs. I had good strength and stamina, but Robbie was so much stronger, and he had so much more endurance. He was still injured from this morning, and he'd been further damaged in the crash, yet he was miles ahead of me in his physical abilities, which was kind of humbling. And also reassuring.

But it also put into perspective just how strong Skoll was—a veritable monster.

"You got any more of those inspirational musings you showered me with before?" I gasped out. "Like, you got this, girl! Or pull up your big girl panties, Britta!"

"Keep fucking moving, Britta. How's that?"

"Very uninspired. Almost demotivating, actually."

A loud crash sounded behind us—metal against metal—and an enraged, frustrated roar filled the air.

Skoll.

I whipped my head around to look behind us, my heart in my throat, and almost tripped over a large tree root. Robbie grabbed my arm and kept pressing me forward along the creek bank.

"Is that motivating enough for you?" he asked, in a low whisper, kicking up the pace even more.

My adrenaline had spiked, and I had no trouble keeping up.

"Yes. Very. What is he doing?" I whispered back.

"Looking for something, maybe."

"You?"

"Could be."

"Is he going to come after us?"

Robbie paused a moment before answering. "Yes, I think so. But the pack will arrive soon. Britta, I want you to listen for the helicopters and start calling out to Tyr, your mom, and your dad through your bond as soon as you hear them."

"Okay." I tested the bond, just to be certain, but I was still too far away to connect with my family. "How much farther until we reach the boundary?"

"About five minutes at this pace. You can make it, Britta. Just keep putting one foot in front of the other. Hear the seconds tick down in your head, and we'll be there before you know it. I believe in you."

"Now *that's* inspiring. Tell me more good stuff like that."

Another pause ensued, but it seemed heavier than the last one. I glanced at him. He was still focused and battle-ready, but another emotion had risen—I could feel it—one that was all-encompassing and deeper. Much deeper.

And it was filled with sorrow.

"You mean the world to me, svassa. When my mother and then my father died, you became the light in my life that gave me hope, that made me laugh and live fully again. That made me know life was worth living. You are a treasure—Odin's treasure, the pack's treasure. My treasure—never forget that. And you will be the world's treasure, too, sharing your incredible light and talent with adoring audiences everywhere. Go out and conquer, *minn hjarta.*"

My heart.

I couldn't breathe as my chest expanded. Shock and awe swirled within me at his words, at the richness of his emotion.

And then a furious anger rose. I wanted to snap at him, snarl at him—bite him on the neck and the haunches, and thrash him in the air like prey to devour. "Gods damn it, Robbie. Are you saying goodbye to me? You are not going to die, do you hear me? You are not going to fucking die! I won't let you leave me. Ever!"

And then, a scent hit my nose that made me want to curl into a protective ball and hide in the farthest reaches of Hjarta, protected by my wolf. It smelled like the sweetest, brightest summer day with an undertone of rot. I'd never smelled it before, but I knew instantly what it was.

Robbie smelled it too because, in less time than it took for me to blink, he yelled out, "Run!" before shifting into his huge, brown wolf, lunging in front of me, and slamming his shoulder into Skoll, who was just materializing on his sunbeam.

I screamed but kept going. One foot after the other, just like he'd said. Faster and faster. I listened for Robbie, following behind me—praying to hear his hard, rapid gallop. Deep inside my body, my wolf listened too, her ears swiveling to catch any sounds.

But instead, I heard a yelp—a wolf's yelp—and I knew it wasn't Skoll.

I skidded to a stop and turned back to look in the direction I'd come, tears streaming down my face and my heart pounding so hard it felt like it would jump from my chest. Then Robbie's wolf burst onto the trail behind me, a brown rocket moving so fast I almost couldn't believe it.

I turned and ran, too, exhilaration bubbling through me. We would make it!

Freyja's ward loomed just ahead of me—I could feel it. Taking a giant leap, I crossed the boundary to Wolf Ridge and then turned, crouched over and panting as I watched Robbie in wolf form draw nearer.

He was so close, racing along the creek bank toward me. I counted down the seconds until he'd be safe—no more than ten at the speed he was running.

Nine, eight, seven—

A ball of golden flame struck his wolf in the side and sent him flying into the creek, dunking him in a deep spot. Almost instantly, he burst from the water in his Valdyr form, pulled himself onto a rock, and leapt to the other side. But before he could land, Skoll grabbed a sunbeam and swung over, a blur of light. My eyes widened as the beam of golden sunshine material-ized in his hands like a jungle vine.

But Robbie had anticipated the move. He twisted his body mid-air and hit Skoll with his feet, throwing him into the water before shifting back into his wolf and hitting the ground running, racing up the other side of the creek.

Six, five, four—

I jumped across the water on my side of the boundary, sobbing and clenching my hands. He was so close!

Please, Allfather. Let him make it!

"Come on, Robbie!" I yelled.

My palms prickled with heat, and I felt an upswelling of tingles in my solar plexus. The sensation rose into my heart and throat, then down my arms.

I clenched my hands harder, trying to contain the weird feeling, but I was just so damn scared for Robbie and couldn't control it. I couldn't control anything!

Skoll was trying to kill the wolf I loved right in front of me.

Three, two—

"Run, Robbie! Run!" I screamed again as if my voice would pull him forward even faster.

And then Skoll materialized with a flash of golden light on the other side of the boundary, blocking Robbie's path.

Robbie's huge, brown wolf didn't slow. He leapt diagonally to the right over the creek, twisting like a rotating bullet and shifting back to his Valdyr form. Skoll jumped with him, and they crashed together, chest to chest, landing in the middle of the stream.

I ran into the water on my side, getting as close to the battle as possible, sobbing and tearing at my hair and clothes. But I stayed on my side of the boundary—Robbie would be distracted if he knew Skoll could get to me.

The creek was just over my knees—deep enough for him to drown Robbie if he kept him under for too long. The water thrashed around them, and the mud churned up as they fought— so fast and so hard. Finally, Skoll forced Robbie under.

"Get up, Robbie! Get up!" I cried.

Robbie reared up as if he heard me, throwing Skoll off of him, and I gasped.

"Stay there!" he yelled at me as he lunged at his bigger, faster, stronger foe—punching, kicking, and even scratching and biting with his Valdyr teeth and nails.

Or were those his wolf's teeth and nails?

Yes, he was in Valdyr form, but he had shifted that small, deadly part of himself.

They struck back and forth, moving so quickly that the fight was almost a blur. But Robbie lost ground with every hit, slowing as his energy drained and his injuries caught up with him. Skoll was huge—at least a half foot bigger in every direction.

Suddenly Robbie turned and sprinted the other way.

"No!" I yelled. I knew what he was doing, trying to draw Skoll away from me and the boundary—to buy more time until the pack arrived.

It felt like a knife stabbing my stomach. A fierce snarl rose up my throat, and my chest rumbled ferociously. I took a step closer to the boundary, and that prickly heat inside of me seemed to merge with Freyja's magical ward.

Skoll jumped on Robbie's back, forcing him face-first beneath the water again, and I screamed.

"Let him go!"

Skoll looked back at me and smiled as Robbie thrashed beneath him. The longer he was under, the less the water churned. I dropped to my knees, unable to breathe or process what was happening. I reached out beneath the stream to him.

He was so close and yet so far away—in the hands of our greatest enemy.

"Think you can save him?" The monster asked, laughing. He was stunning to look at—as bright and radiant as the sun but with cruelty stamped into every feature. "Come on out, little she-wolf. Come and play with me. Bring your magic if you have any."

The air gushed from my lungs. I closed my eyes, feeling for my wolf, and a centering calm filled me. I slowly stood, then stepped over the boundary.

Skoll's brow raised, and delight lit up his face. He dragged

Robbie's trapped torso from the water, lifting him up by his arms and shoulders.

Robbie inhaled roughly, coughing and wheezing as his eyelids fluttered open. Fear flashed through his gaze when he saw me.

"Step…back…" he pleaded.

"She's not going anywhere," Skoll said, chortling. "She's going to fight for you. Look at her face!"

"No, Britta," Robbie said, a little louder this time. "Get back!"

He tried to tear himself from Skoll's deadly embrace, but he was like a mouse weighted down by a cat's heavy paw and sharp claws—unable to escape and knowing death could come at any moment.

I stepped forward again, and it somehow felt like Freyja's magic stretched with me—a string of taffy being pulled from the thick, sweet mass of her ward. And I sensed…the pack—every emotion within them, every joy and heartbreak, every feeling of clarity and confusion, every fear and triumph.

All the times they'd loved or despaired, laughed or cried.

The emotions welled within me—danced within me. And that tingling spread through every inch of my body until my palms roared with fire and my hands vibrated.

Skoll lifted his head and sniffed the air. "How adorable! She's going to fight for you—and no wolf yet." He sniffed again. "Maybe just a little magic to make it fun. Unfortunately, her power won't be strong enough without her wolf. She'll be haunted for the rest of her life that she couldn't save you—her fated mate. Boo hoo hoo." He broke into fake, exaggerated crying.

Then he cocked his head, listening. Helicopters sounded in the distance.

"The pack," I said. "I've called them to us."

But I hadn't. I didn't need to. I was connected to them already, swimming through every one of their emotions. They knew exactly where I was and what was happening.

"Good for you," he said to me, then looked down at Robbie, all business now. "You had something of mine—I felt it—but it's gone now. Where is it?"

"Go…fuck…yourself."

He smiled. "Maybe later. For now, I'm trying to decide whether I should hurt *you* to get you to talk." He lifted his gaze to me, "Or hurt *her* to get you to talk. I'll be on her before she can cross the line."

I took another determined step forward.

Robbie closed his eyes, despair coming off of him in waves. "I don't have anything of yours. Everything I took went immediately to Wolf Ridge."

"I sensed it on you!" he growled. "You reeked of it!"

"There was magic inside of me from the explosion, but my own magic purged it from my body—a gold dust that seeped from my pores." He laughed—a harsh, desperate sound. "You washed it off my skin when you threw me in the water. It's gone now."

I could see he was trying to rile Skoll. He had something planned, and it would kill him in the process.

He must think it was the only way to save me.

Skoll's face contorted, and I could see his wolf, half-deranged, snarling beneath his skin. He was going to rip out Robbie's throat.

I splashed my way toward them, fast and frantic, whimpering in a way that would draw the wolf's attention.

"Britta, stop!" Robbie moaned. "Let me do this."

"How sweet. She wants to die too. Maybe I'll eat her alive in front of you."

He transferred his hold on Robbie and scraped a razor-sharp claw over my arm, leaving behind a bright, red trail. The blood ran down my hand and dripped into the water.

I dropped to my knees at his feet. "Yes. Kill me, too," I begged. "I can't live without him."

"No, Britta," Robbie struggled with renewed strength, but

even one-handed, Skoll easily held him now.

I lowered my head submissively and brushed my hair away from my neck, then I reached out my hands and laid them on Skoll's thighs. "Please."

My eyes caught Robbie's. *Now*, I mouthed to him.

I released the tingling heat from my palms into Skoll, and he gasped. He let go of Robbie and stumbled back in the water, his face crumpling in sorrow as his hands fisted over his heart. A forlorn wail broke from his lips.

Robbie grabbed my waist and leapt with me into the air, flying past Freyja's barrier in one giant bound.

We landed with a splash in the water, and he collapsed on top of me, dragging me down to the creek bed. He didn't move, and I struggled under the surface to get free. Finally, I rolled his body off of me and broke through the water with a loud inhale.

"Robbie!" Grasping his back, I pulled him from the water and dragged him into my arms. He coughed, and his eyes fluttered.

"Safe?" he croaked.

I squeezed him closer, sobbing with relief and happiness. "Yes, we're safe."

He smiled but was fading fast—the healing sleep of the sótt-skáli was pulling him under. "You did it."

"We did it."

Then a terrifying roar filled the air. I jerked my head up. Skoll stood on the other side of the barrier—half humungous wolf, half savage Jotun. I scrambled backward over the rocks with a yelp, dragging Robbie with me.

"Keep going," he slurred. "Keep go—"

"What did you do to me?" Skoll thundered, his eyes burning into me.

The helicopters came into view above us, and I heard wolves landing on the forest floor.

I shrugged, shaking my head at him.

Had Freyja's powers somehow transferred to me when I

crossed her protective ward? Looking upward, I tried to see the boundary that kept Skoll at bay, tried to see Freyja's magical knots that held the ward in place.

I could only see Skoll's furious face.

"Freyja," was all I said to him. Whether that was true or not, I didn't know. But I didn't want him to think I was the one responsible for defeating him when I had no idea how to do it again.

His mouth twisted in disgust, and he spat at the invisible shield. I shied out of the way, repulsed and horrified, but the sputum suddenly sizzled in the air and turned to ash before it reached me.

Not so invisible, after all.

The rekkr wolves converged on us, splashing through the water. One stood right over our legs, snarling ferociously at Skoll, and I recognized my dad in his long, lean wolf form.

A huge gray wolf—Erik—attacked first from the other side, darting in and snapping at Skoll before twisting out of the way, clearing the way for a massive black wolf—Gunn—to dart in next. And then my brother Tyr.

More wolves attacked, and Skoll fought viciously, throwing fireballs, raking with his claws, and biting wherever he could, but there were too many of them.

He let out a final, frustrated roar, grabbed a sunbeam, and disappeared.

I held Robbie tight. It was over, and he was going to be okay. He was still unconscious, but I could feel his heart beating strongly in his chest.

I looked up, crying happy tears as warm, familiar arms wrapped around me—my dad.

"He's just sleeping!" I laughed. "He's going to be okay, Dad. He's alive!"

My dad pressed his bearded, wet cheek to mine, his chest heaving. For once, I didn't groan in protest about his coarse beard scratching my skin. "You're both alive, thank Odin. Your mother would have skinned your hides if you'd missed Húsl."

I laughed again—light and joyful. I'd never been so happy.

Robbie's hand squeezed mine, and I looked down to see his eyes open again, staring at me as if he thought I might be a dream. "I thought…you…were going…to die." He could barely get the words out; his voice was so weak—yet also filled to the brim with emotion.

"You wish. There are years of car rides filled with Taylor Swift songs in your future. Don't think you can get out of it that easily."

He reached for my hand and pressed it against his cheek. His eyelids fluttered closed. I thought he'd been dragged back into the sótt-skáli when he said, "Anything for you, svassa," his words low and slurred—barely comprehensible. "We can name our firstborn Taylor and our secondborn Swift if that makes you happy."

The world stopped spinning.

"Wha…what?" I asked, my voice shaking. "Robbie, what did you say?" But he was well and truly out this time.

I looked up at my dad, who stared back and forth from Robbie to me, then back to Robbie, his eyes wide and a little confused.

"Did you hear that?" I asked him faintly.

"I don't know. Did you want me to?" my dad hedged.

I closed my eyes and sighed but couldn't stop smiling. "I don't know. Maybe."

And then my eyes popped open. "Just don't tell Mom."

CHAPTER 11

I SAT BESIDE ROBBIE, WEAVED MY FINGERS THROUGH HIS AS THEY lay on the soft pink blanket, and squeezed his hand. My other hand supported my head, my elbow propped up on the hospital bed. The quiet beeps of the machines surrounding him pulsed hypnotically, making it harder and harder for me to keep my eyes open.

I was exhausted, and I'd considered crawling up beside him and drifting off to sleep, too, but several wires, plus a drip, were attached to him, and I was afraid I'd dislodge something.

Our doctor, Kat, had been in earlier, and she'd said he was healing remarkably fast—he'd be able to attend Húsl tonight even if they had to wheel him to the sanctified circle.

I'd almost snorted when she'd said that. No way in hel would Robbie show up to Húsl in a wheelchair. Unless, maybe, I sat in his lap and forced him down.

His heart rate monitor suddenly spiked, and I raised my head, alarmed, but he was still sleeping peacefully. Surely, he couldn't have known what I was thinking? Or had his wolf somehow known—maybe through my wolf?

"Go back to sleep," I whispered to him. I'd made it an order and frowned at him for good measure. "And don't tell him what I'm thinking," I grumpily told my wolf.

I didn't know if she was there or could even hear me, I hadn't felt her since we'd been in the creek, but just in case, I needed to establish some ground rules.

Rule number one: no telling Robbie's wolf what thoughts were running through my head. Let him figure them out on his own—with difficulty—like any other self-respecting male.

Amusement rolled through me—from her or me?

Both, maybe, because I knew that *if* we were mated, we wouldn't be able to keep our thoughts or feelings from one another any more than we'd be able to keep our hands to ourselves. Kyssed pairs were bound by Freyja and resided in each other's hearts and minds completely.

Which meant zero privacy.

I sighed, released Robbie's hand, and stretched my arms over my head. When I settled back down, I stared at him, which I'd been doing repeatedly since we'd been helicoptered back to Wolf Ridge. I lost myself again in the welcome familiarity of his face—a face I'd known and loved my entire life. I reached up and brushed my hand over his hair—so soft—then I trailed my fingers down his strong cheekbones and determined chin, feeling the tiny prick of his beard beneath my fingertips.

Had he meant what he'd said about our first and second born pups? I knew it had been a joke but come on...Taylor and Swift? Those were awesome names! Yes, he'd been out of it, but had he meant it? And if he had, how did I feel about that?

Pretty damn good.

Yup. My heart and stomach had been doing flips all day today —longer than that when I thought about it.

Hmm, was this just a crush? Same as I'd had when I was younger? Or something more?

Something more, my wolf said suddenly, startling me as her words echoed in my head. She rubbed like a silken wave beneath my skin.

You're here! I blurted out.

Yes. And you are here.

Um...yes. Uh, hi. I'm Britta. I'm glad to meet you.

She didn't respond, and I knew I was making a mess of things. She was a part of me. She never left. Not really.

So, um, about Robbie...how do you know? I asked.

We know.

But how?

Trust.

She faded away, and I knew she'd gone to him—Robbie's wolf —in Hjarta. Which confused me...I thought only kyssed pairs could be together like that. Robbie hadn't sent out the kalla for me, and Freyja certainly hadn't sanctioned the union...although I'd felt the goddess at the boundary when her wards had stretched with me.

Maybe that had done something?

Gah! It was too much for me to think about right now. The only thing that mattered at this point was Robbie's healing. Everything else could be sorted out later.

My stomach growled, and I glanced at the clock. It was just past seven—only five hours since we'd left the UM campus.

It felt like days.

Traditionally, Húsl started at midnight, but Erik had delayed it until two, giving everyone a little extra time since it had been such a trying day. Hopefully, Robbie would be awake by then.

The door swished open behind me, and my mom's scent hit my nose. I began to turn, but her arms wrapped around me from behind. "I'm sorry it took me so long."

"That's okay. It's been a crazy day. And Húsl on top of every-thing. I'm surprised your head hasn't exploded."

"Believe me, it has, several times."

She dragged a chair beside me and sat down, taking my hand, which was kind of weird. A hug, an apology, and a hand grab all in less than a minute. Who was this woman pretending to be my mother?

"What?" she asked, smiling at me.

Smiling!

"You're freaking me out."

"I'm freaking *you* out? I'm not the one who crashed over a cliff and then faced off with one of the deadliest giants in the nine worlds."

"Even more deadly than Hati?"

"I think so. He's more unpredictable, and his wolf is completely savage."

I shuddered. "He certainly looked savage, and that was with his wolf still contained. I could see it moving beneath his skin."

Magna paled. Suddenly, she hugged me again, her body trembling.

I returned her embrace, concerned. "Mom?" I had never seen her so undone.

She inhaled raggedly and tried to talk but couldn't get the words out.

"It's okay. It's okay," I soothed, rubbing my hands up and down her back. My tears flowed now, and my throat clogged. "Everything's going to be okay."

She nodded against my shoulder, sniffing loudly. "I'm sorry. I shouldn't be going on like this."

"Well, um, you kinda should. I got chased by a deadly giant, remember?"

She let out a half-sob, making me regret my words, especially when her arms began strangling me.

"Can't...breathe," I choked out.

She let up and pulled back far enough to rest her forehead against mine, cupping my cheeks and taking deep breaths to calm herself. Seeing her tear-stained face wrecked me. I don't think I'd ever seen my mom cry.

Our world had been turned upside down. I was usually the one feeling all the feels, getting lost in my emotions—too many of them, according to my brother.

My hyper-sensitivity had confounded my mom over the years, and we hadn't always been a good match for each other... but maybe most mothers and daughters could say that about their relationship.

If ever I'd doubted that she loved me, I no longer did. Same with my dad and Tyr. They were two of the first wolves coming to my defense, fighting Skoll for me, standing over me.

My dad hadn't left my side until we landed at Wolf Ridge, and I'd been checked over by Kat and given the all-clear. And Tyr had actually picked me up and spun me in a circle. Twice! I'd hold *that* over his head for a long time.

"I love you, *minn móðir*," I whispered.

"I love you, too, *minn barn*." Her hands trembled against my cheeks.

We stayed that way for a few minutes. "Do you want to talk about it?"

She shook her head briefly, but I could feel her emotions swelling within her. She released a shuddering breath and then said, "I was driving back when I heard a Rover had crashed below Astra's memorial. I knew it had to be you and Robbie...and that Skoll must be involved. Robbie would never have crashed otherwise."

"He didn't have a choice. Skoll threw the Rover over the cliff."

"I know," she squeaked, her voice ragged. "I saw the footage. We have cameras covering the entire highway in and out of Missoula. And I..." she took another deep breath, "I saw the wreck at the bottom of the mountain. I don't know how you survived."

This time I pulled her close. "I survived because of Robbie. He threw his body over mine to protect me, and then he fought Skoll for me. He could've left me behind and made a run for it, but he never did."

"Of course, he didn't. None of us would have left you." She sounded a little insulted.

"Not even Linnea?" I joked. It was no secret that our new Alpha female rubbed my mom the wrong way. Hel, Linnea rubbed everyone the wrong way.

She grunted before conceding. "Not even Linnea."

Sitting back in her seat, she wiped her wet face with her fingers. My indestructible mother looked like she'd aged ten years since I last saw her.

"What were you doing in Missoula?" I asked.

"Looking for Robbie. After you called me this morning, I couldn't reach him through the bond, and we realized he'd been cut off."

"He was at the Dvergar workshop," I said. "He told me a little about it. That's why Skoll came after us—he thought Robbie had something of his. Something magical that Robbie said had been washed away in the creek."

Magna's brow furrowed. "The dust, maybe? Oh, gods, of course! It must have been on him still, and Skoll felt the resonance of it."

I raised my brow. "Magical dust… O-kay."

She laughed. "Yes. Magical, orange dust. And I don't mean from cheesy puffs, no matter how magical you think they are."

I laughed too. It felt good to release the tension. "Why didn't you take the helicopter back?"

"I did, initially, but then I returned. I had a little shopping to do." She reached for a bag on the floor and pulled out a large square box wrapped in shiny red and white paper with a silver bow and ribbon. "For you," she said, handing it to me. "They called me at the last minute to say it was ready. I was just so happy to get it before Húsl."

"It's beautiful! Did you wrap it?" I was reluctant to rip off the paper. She'd never given me such a beautifully wrapped present before.

She snorted. "No. They did it for me."

Magna had never been one for fancy touches like bows or accessories. She was busy. She didn't have time for extras. It used to bother me, so I would always buy her things like earrings, special touches for the house, or flowers for the table. She seemed to appreciate it at the time, but she'd always lose the earrings or let the flowers die. And the parsley I bought to garnish our plates would end up wilted in the crisper.

"Well, I appreciate it anyway." I leaned forward and kissed her cheek.

"Open it," she said excitedly.

I schooled my features as I ripped the paper and opened the box, expecting to find an unwanted gift related to fighting or training, like a knife or boxing gloves—gifts she'd given me before. Or maybe something wolfy, which hadn't appealed to me since I was a kid, when I used to fill my bed with adorable wolf stuffies. Although, now that my wolf was rising, that might change. In fact, I could think of one wolf, in particular, I'd like to stuff in my bed...and other places.

I blew a breath from my lips as I dug down into layers of tissue paper and reminded myself that just because Robbie had made a joke about our future pups did not mean he'd meant it. He'd also said I had the world to conquer, which meant far away from here.

But...maybe I could have both?

My hands grasped a heavy, solid object wrapped in bubble wrap, and I groaned silently. The only thing I dreaded more than gifts related to training, fighting, and cute wolf stuffies was gifts related to the Norse gods—it was like pouring salt on a wound. Expecting to be kicked out of the pack by Odin had kind of ruined the whole idol thing for me. Any statue of him or the other gods and goddesses would go straight into the closet.

I mean, I understood why I was being kicked out—the Varda needed warriors, not contemporary ballet dancers.

I'd watched Robbie fight today and seen Skoll's ferocity first-hand. And I knew I wouldn't make the team even if I wanted to—which I didn't.

I had no desire to fight or do anything else related to saving the world.

I forced a smile as I lifted the present onto my lap and began to loosen the protective wrap. I would pretend it was a really heavy gift card for T. J. Maxx or The Dance Shop.

I pushed the plastic back…

Oh, my gods. "Mom?" I squeaked. I darted a glance at her and saw her smile stretching from ear to ear before returning my gaze to the bronze statue in my hands.

It was phenomenal.

"Is that me?"

"Yes, do you like it?"

"I don't like it. I *love* it! But…how?"

I stared at the sculpture in amazement. It was about ten inches tall and looked like me…dancing.

"How did you…I mean…how did they…" I was flabbergasted. I couldn't even form complete sentences. "It must have cost a fortune!"

She shrugged. "Consider it a graduation-slash-Húsl gift. One that I hope you'll find a place for."

"I will. I love it, Mom. I truly do. Thank you." I balanced the statue with one hand and reached out to hug her—a happy hug, this time, with grateful, excited tears. When I pulled back, I stared at the sculpture again, fascinated by the detail—the serene look on my face, the implied movement of the piece, and the perfection of the pose.

"How did the artist do all this? Did you send them a photo of me?"

She nodded. "Several. And I enlisted Esme and Benni to help. They took photos of you when you were dancing and helped me pick the final pose."

Now that she mentioned it, I remembered both of them taking a lot of pictures lately—at the house and in rehearsal.

"How did you get them to keep it a secret? They blab everything."

"I threatened them."

She said it so matter-of-factly I had to laugh. "You did not."

"I did. At first, they thought I was joking, so I took out my gun."

My jaw dropped. "Your gun? You don't have a gun. None of you do. You'd be losing them all over the place every time you shifted."

"We modified them with location devices and added sensors to the trigger so only a Valdyr can fire them. And, of course, they're not regular bullets. That wouldn't do anything against Hati and Skoll. I don't carry one often—none of us do. Honestly, they don't work well in a fight."

I shook my head. "I'll never hear the end of it. Benni will be calling you my gun-totin' mama from now on. Or maybe Annie. He loves old musicals."

Her face scrunched up. "Annie? Like Orphan Annie?"

"No, like Annie Oakley. She was a famous human sharp-shooter back in the late eighteen hundreds. They made a musical about her—Annie Get Your Gun. I'd sing, but...you know...my voice."

Magna grinned. "Annie Oakley. I like that. And I liked Benni and Esme too. They made me laugh—inside, of course."

I grinned back. "Of course."

The door swished open again, and this time I smelled Dahlia. I turned to my friend, who wore adorable baby pink overalls and tennis shoes. Her hair was pulled back in a cute, high ponytail.

"Don't get up," she said.

"I would if I could, but I'm weighted down by this incredible piece of art." I turned the statue so she could see it. "Did you know about this?"

"No. Oh, my gods, it's beautiful! Magna, did you buy this?"

My mom nodded, smiling again.

Dahlia looked at the statue closely. "Wow. Is that…?"

"Yes. C'est moi. Très beautiful. Já?"

"Sí," Dahlia replied.

We'd mixed up four different languages, and my mom gave us a strange look, which made us laugh.

Then Dahlia leaned over and hugged me tight. She was much stronger since her wolf had risen, even though she'd never trained to fight, and I wondered what role Odin had chosen for her in the Varda. Neither one of us had thought she'd be accepted.

"Don't do that again, okay Brits?" she whispered in my ear. Her words sounded strangled.

"Okay, Dahls," I whispered back.

My mom stood up. "Here, take my seat, Dahlia. I have a meeting."

"On Húsl?" Dahlia asked, surprised.

"Yes. It's been non-stop since we got that intel from Dane last night."

At the mention of Dane, Dahlia's cheeks flushed, and I rolled my eyes. "No," I said firmly, knowing exactly what she was thinking.

Magna also noticed. "No," she repeated. "That wolf is trouble."

Dahlia sighed and slouched back in her chair. "I know, I know."

"Good." My mom turned to me and stroked her fingers through my hair. It felt good, and I sighed.

"You're exhausted, *kaer dottir*. You should get some sleep. Robbie is not the only one who needs to heal."

"I'm oka—" But it was like her words brought on a wave of tiredness that threatened to pull me under, and I finished my sentence on a yawn.

Magna's brow raised. "You were saying?"

"I know. I just…"

"You don't want to leave Robbie."

"No."

She crouched down beside my chair. "I'll come back as soon as he wakes. I'll let him know you were here. Please. Get some sleep. He'll understand."

"I know he will. It's not that."

"Then what is it?" she asked.

A tremor ran through me, and I tightened my grip on the statue. "Skoll was killing him, Mom. He had him trapped under the water right in front of me. I don't know how I saved him, or if Freyja saved him through me—it felt like her magic moved with me when I passed through the ward—but I'm afraid that if I let him out of my sight, he'll…he'll…"

"Die," Magna said baldly.

"Yes," I whispered. "Like he somehow cheated fate…we cheated fate."

"He didn't. And you didn't. Nothing is going to happen to him." She took the statue from me, put it back in the bag, and handed it to Dahlia. "Dahlia is going to drive you home now."

"But—"

"No buts. You need to sleep in your own bed and recover. You'll see Robbie in a few hours."

Magna shot a look at Dahlia, who jumped up quickly. She picked up my backpack and handed it to me. "I've got the van. I can drive."

I sighed. When I rose, my body felt weighted down by cement. "Okay. How can I resist driving in Dahlia's fast, sexy wolf mobile."

"Hey, don't knock it. Alsviðr may be old and slow, unlike her namesake, but she gets me where I want to go. And quicker, I might add, than if *you* were driving one of the Range Rovers."

In retaliation, I stuck out my tongue before leaning over and rubbing my hand through Robbie's hair. "I'll see you later," I whispered, then kissed his cheek.

The heart-rate monitor beeped faster.

CHAPTER 12

<u>Britta</u>

I CRANKED DOWN THE VAN WINDOW, LEANED BACK, AND STUCK MY feet through the open space. The mountain breeze was warm for an April evening, and I enjoyed the feel of it washing over me as Dahlia drove through Wolf Ridge toward my family home.

The complex was like its own little industrial town, and a lot of care had been taken to ensure that parks and greenery filled up the areas between the buildings—for aesthetic and practical reasons. If we ever needed to shift into our wolves in a place where humans worked, we needed to be as circumspect as possible.

On the north end of the compound was the executive building, also called the den by pack members. Only Valdyr were allowed into that part of the compound—therefore, only Valdyr could hold executive positions in the company.

Nepotism for necessity's sake.

South of that was the industrial section, and humans and Valdyr were allowed to work there. We bussed all the humans into Wolf Ridge then monitored them closely, so they stayed within their designated work areas. The last thing we needed was one of Hati and Skoll's human spies infiltrating our sanctuary... or spies from anywhere. We protected our secrets from both human and non-human species alike.

Of course, we had magical help to do that.

The whole valley was about a half mile long and a quarter mile wide, and it was filled with buildings of all different shapes and sizes, including a couple that were about the size of a football field.

Wolf Ridge Industries—our official company name—was a privately owned research and development center that built and maintained satellites, high-powered telescopes, exploratory space and land transports, and specialized equipment. We also developed security systems for private, commercial, and governmental use. We didn't build human weapons, but we were involved in projects with NASA and the DOD that were strictly defense-related—as long as the project dove-tailed with our higher purpose of guarding Fenrir and preventing Ragnarök.

We looked toward the heavens—and Asgard.

The company was a billion-dollar success, owned collectively by the pack and built on land we'd settled hundreds of years ago.

Family homes, including my parents' house, were dotted on the outskirts of Wolf Ridge and rose up the mountainside—pack only. But our borders extended far beyond that into the forest and over the mountains for miles. Freyja's ward covered the entire area.

We needed space for our wolves to roam.

"It's so pretty here," I said, leaning out the van window to run my fingers over some soft, silvery-gray pussy willows when Dahlia stopped at an intersection.

"Yeah. It's like one day, spring exploded all over everything, leaving behind a riot of colors and smells. My wolf wants to roll in all the pretty things. I've let her out a few times after the human employees have gone home."

"Aww, that's so sweet. She likes flowers!"

"She does. I think growth here is a little accelerated by Freyja's magic. I noticed that the flowers in Missoula aren't as bountiful."

"Yeah, I noticed that too."

The sun had already set, and the last rays turned the sky into a sea of orange and pink. Perfect for the drive home. I was glad we hadn't used the maze of tunnels under the complex to travel—not only had I been too exhausted to walk, but I would have missed this big, beautiful sky.

I sighed tiredly, wanting to close my eyes but afraid to miss anything. It felt good to be back despite my ever-present anxiety about being kicked out of the pack. But that time hadn't arrived yet. I could still enjoy my home for a little while longer.

"You'll never guess who I found rolling around in the flowers like a mad dog on one of my nighttime wanders."

I turned to Dahlia. "Who?"

"Gunn."

"Gunn? He likes flowers?"

"He's crazy for them. His wolf can't get enough—like a lovesick pup."

I burst out laughing. Gunn's wolf was a big, black beast. Very dominant. And the mental image I got of the menacing wolf rolling around in the flowers was one I'd file away for a later date when Gunn was trying to browbeat me into doing something I didn't want to do—like working an extra shift at Savage or puppysitting his gazillion nieces and nephews that came to visit him from Canada every year.

"Did he see you?" I asked.

"Of course he did. He's a senior rekkr, and I'm...me."

I gave her a look. "And by *me*, you mean an amazingly incredible, fantastic Valdyr."

"Yes. Exactly that."

We laughed again. "Any idea, yet, what Odin wants you to do for the Varda?"

She shook her head, looking despondent. "None. Do you think he could have made a mistake? I'm hardly Varda material. I'm not a fighter or an executive type. And I'm definitely not a scientist of any kind."

"I don't think so, seeing as he's a god and all. I guess you'll find out when the time is right."

"I guess. In the meantime, Linnea will keep riding my ass, and Erik will keep prodding me with gentle, understanding questions—both equally irritating."

"Can you talk to Erik about it? Tell him to back off? Tell Linnea to back off?"

She looked at me like I was crazy. "Um…what part of me being an uber-submissive wolf and not at all suitable for the Varda did you miss?"

"Then I'll tell him. And Linnea." I rubbed my hands together gleefully. "I love getting in her face. Although now that my wolf is rising, I may be at a disadvantage. Her wolf will probably dominate mine through the bond."

Dahlia whipped her head toward me and yanked the car to the side of the road in front of a gorgeous koi pond that we had trouble keeping stocked. Not only did the wolves think the pond was there for their eating and splashing pleasure, despite Erik's wolf having warned them off, but several eagles also hunted there.

A bad combination for the koi.

"Oh, my gods. That's how you tell me your wolf is rising?" Dahlia's eyes gleamed at me with excitement and a touch of indignation.

I grinned. "Sorry. I didn't know—not really. I'd been feeling weird for a few weeks, and a part of me wondered, but…it could just as easily have been a bad burrito—like the gazillion other times I thought she was rising." I didn't need to explain my uncertainty about my wolf to Dahlia. Her wolf had risen late too. She understood.

When I first came of age, every little change in my body made me think she was about to appear...and then she didn't.

After a while, I'd forced myself to stop thinking and worrying about it and started pretending like I didn't care...because not caring felt better than being rejected time and time again—she didn't want me, I wasn't good enough.

I'd never be chosen.

Well, it turns out I was wrong. I *was* good enough, and she did want me. Right now, she just wanted Robbie's wolf more. And I understood that.

I hadn't wanted to leave Robbie's side either.

"Anyway, Erik confirmed last night that she was close. His wolf was excited to meet her, and since then, I've felt her a few times. Once, she actually spoke to me."

Dahlia let out an excited squeal. "What did she say?"

Heat suddenly filled my cheeks, and my stomach flipped. I hesitated before speaking. "She...um...she thinks Robbie is my mate."

I'd whispered the last few words as if speaking them out loud would make them true. And it couldn't be true...could it?

Dahlia's eyes grew round. She pressed her fingers to her lips as her eyes filled with tears. Then she pulled me into a tight embrace. "I knew it."

I squeezed back. "You did not. You couldn't have."

"I did. I swear, sometimes I think I'm psychic."

"Well, just because my wolf said whatever she said doesn't make it true. And she didn't exactly say it—more implied it."

Dahlia snorted in my ear and then leaned back. "It doesn't work that way—something I'm fast discovering."

"What do you mean?"

Her brow wrinkled in thought. "Well, it's hard to explain. It's more a feeling than a logical thought. Like...I'm separate from my wolf, but we're also one. We make up the same whole. But she never implies anything. She relays truth—and she doesn't have to *tell* me that truth. I just know it. And visa versa. Except sometimes I don't want to know the truth. Whether it's something she's relaying or something I just know."

"So you lie to yourself?"

"Don't we all?"

I sighed and nodded. "Yeah, probably. What about our wolves? Do they lie to themselves?"

"I don't think so. Certainly not in the way Valdyr and humans do. The wolves can misinterpret something, but only because they don't have the right information. But in something like this, something driven by instinct, they know."

I stared through the windshield at the darkening sky, twirling a strand of hair around my finger. It was all too much for me to think about right now, especially as my body kept trying to drag me into the sótt-skáli for some light healing.

Dahlia put her blinker on before she pulled back onto the road, which made me chuckle.

"What?" she asked.

"No one else is here. You don't need to signal."

She chuckled too. "Habit. My wolf likes to follow the rules."

I reached out and squeezed her arm. "*You* like to follow the rules."

"Yes. See?"

She and her wolf were one.

"I do. So does that mean my wolf likes to dance?"

"I don't know. But maybe she's a conduit for creativity in another way. Or your muse?"

"Maybe." I turned in my seat to face her. "Do you like her?"

"Who?"

"Your wolf."

Dahlia smiled and nodded. "She's sweet, and gentle, and fun. But she also wants to please others—I want to please others—and that can be good or bad. She's submissive like me and feels more settled around protective and dominant wolves like Erik and Robbie. Funny that I accept that in her, and I want to soothe her when she's scared, but I hate it in myself."

"Does *she* hate it in you when you're scared? Or hate it in herself?"

"No. Not at all. She doesn't fight who she is—total acceptance."

I let that sink in. "Wow. Wouldn't that be amazing."

"Yeah."

When we left the industrial section and started climbing the mountain, I found myself leaning forward in anticipation. We turned down a series of paved roads, Dahlia signaling with her blinker every time, before we finally turned onto my driveway. The house was lit with white and red lights on every peak and eave and around every window, and a red wreath hung on the door. A life-size wooden wolf sat on the porch with a garland of red flowers around its neck.

"Your mom went all out this year," Dahlia said as she parked her van.

"She did. I can't believe it."

"And she bought you that present. Slow week at the old Fenrir Fighting Factory?"

I snorted. That's what we'd named my parents' job when we were little. "Not today. I think they were on quadruple time, and she *still* went to pick up the statue."

I stared at my home like it was the last time I would see it— the wood and slate exterior, the dormer windows, the large porch. It was a gorgeous house, and I would miss it.

"Here," Dahlia said.

I glanced over and saw her holding a plastic, cash-filled bag in one hand and a basket filled with baked goods in the other. "Your tips from last night and the best of my Húsl goodies."

My stomach growled. "Yum! Is that an iced cranberry loaf?"

"Yup. I know it's your favorite. And there are some cookies and fudge in there, too—vanilla with cherry. It's good, but you can only eat a small piece before your teeth start to ache."

"Let me be the judge of that." I found a delicious-looking piece of fudge and bit into it. It melted in my mouth. "Mmm. Dahlia, this is incredible."

"Thanks. I can't bake many things, but I've mastered the art of fudge-making."

"Lucky me." I popped the rest of the fudge in my mouth and then took my tips and the basket from her. "You want to come in?"

"I can't. I have to stop at Erik's still and drop off a basket. And I want to set out some decorations and maybe tidy a little so it's nice for Húsl. Then Gunn's. Although Gunn has probably done some of his own baking. And his place is always spotless."

"Seriously?"

"Yup. He's like a clean freak. Have you ever seen him with his sisters' kids? They're little terrors. He constantly follows behind them, picking up the pieces. It's hilarious."

"Seen them? I've had to babysit them on several occasions."

"Yeah, me too."

I shoved the money in my backpack, slung it over my shoulder, and opened the car door. The statue was heavy, but I could easily manage it in one arm and hold the basket in the other.

"Thanks for the ride, Dahls. I'll see you later tonight. Are you wearing anything special?"

She sighed. "No. Same as last year, probably. I looked but couldn't find anything. What about you?"

"I have a dress I wore for my final performance last year. I'm going to repurpose it."

"That white one from your contemporary solo?"

"Yes. I'll dress it up a bit and add some red somewhere."

"It's gorgeous. Robbie will love it."

I stilled, and my heart beat a little faster. "*I'll* love it."

She lowered her head. "Right. Sorry."

I made an exasperated sound—mad at myself, not her. "No, I'm sorry. I shouldn't have said that. Everything's just so new in that area, and…it may not lead anywhere. For all I know, I'll be kicked out of the pack by tomorrow, and whatever this thing is with Robbie will just fade away. Same as my crush did when I was a teenager."

Dahlia's head popped back up. "None of that will happen."

I shrugged. "We'll see. Anyway, give me a hug; my hands are full."

She wrapped her arms around me in a tight squeeze and then whispered again in my ear, "None of that's going to happen."

I wish.

I got out of the car and walked toward the house. The door was unlocked, as it always was. Inside, more decorations had been hung—on the mantel in the living room, strung along the walls and side tables, and hanging from the doorways.

The red and white explosion brought tears to my eyes as I realized…even my mom thought I would be kicked out of the pack.

She was trying to make this the best Húsl ever because she thought it would be my last one while I was still living here—my family home.

Wow. That was a downer.

I dropped the basket of goodies on the kitchen counter, and after snagging a few cookies—okay, more than a few—and a glass of milk, I made my way upstairs, feeling despondent.

My room was an ode to dance, which is maybe why every gift my parents ever gave me, besides the bronze sculpture from today, reflected my Valdyr heritage in some way—they didn't want me to lose sight of that. And maybe I'd gone overkill on the dance and pushed everything Valdyr away because I *did* want to lose sight of it.

I'd felt like a square peg in a round hole my entire life. I didn't fit—I still didn't—but now, at least, my wolf was here. I was connected. And nobody—no pack or god—could take that away from me.

Like Dahlia said…I was whole.

Finally.

I placed the sculpture on my bedside table and stepped back to admire it. After a minute, my eyes drifted to my closet on the other side of the room. Propelled by a feeling I couldn't quite understand, I walked across the rug and pulled back the double doors. Pushing some of my old clothes to the side, I spotted a large, framed print of a wolf.

She was gorgeous—regal-looking, and yet curious at the same time. I lifted the picture and stared at it. The wolf was amazingly life-like. I walked to my desk and set the picture down so it leaned against the wall.

I returned to my closet, reached for a cardboard box on the top shelf, and carried it to my bed. Sitting cross-legged beside the box, I opened it.

A pair of red boxing gloves lay on the top, making me laugh. "Oh, wow." I pulled them on and pretended to spar with an invisible opponent.

"Saturday night at the old Fenrir Fighting Factory where Unbreakable Britta faces off with Lousy Linnea, the Unholy Fyrsta of the Varda. Britta darts in fast and gets off two quick jabs to Linnea's body, but Linnea comes on strong, forcing Britta back against the ropes. The crowd boos, but then Britta ducks and weaves and comes back at Linnea with a one-two combination that leaves the Fyrsta shaking her head. The crowd roars in approval! Britta comes in hard again with a surprise overhead punch and a quick uppercut to the chin, taking Linnea down. One, two, three, she's out! And the crowd goes wild." I held my gloved hands in the air and made the sound of the roaring crowd.

Linnea lay in an ungainly puddle in front of me. It turns out she had a glass chin.

After a minute, I grinned and took off the gloves. Why had I never tried boxing before? It was fun!

Because I'd resented the gift.

My grin faded.

Holding the gloves close, I examined them, feeling the smooth leather outside and the soft foam inside, running my fingertips over the tiny bumps of the stitching. My name was even embossed on the cuff.

Which made me feel like shit.

I'd rejected a gift that someone had put thought and care into, even personalized for me. I didn't have to train to fight a savage wolf or get in the ring with Lousy Linnea, who would probably pummel me bloody in real life. I could just train for myself.

Robbie could teach me, or my mom or dad. Even Tyr—although that might turn into a real boxing match.

My brother was nothing if not annoying.

I sighed, determined to do better by my family if they ever gave me another gift I didn't care for. At least give it a fighting chance.

Ha!

Laying the gloves aside, I delved further into the box. I found so many other amazing gifts I'd rejected—a stunning, hand-forged dagger with a wolf's head pommel, a necklace made of smoky quartz in the shape of a howling wolf, two small crystal wolves playing together on a mirrored base, and a beautiful hardcover book on wolves.

Okay, there was definitely a theme, but I was fine with that now.

I opened the book and flipped through the pages, wondering if my wolf would look like any of the wolves in the pictures. My gaze fell on a photo of a big male with lots of brown fur mixed into his greyish coat. He stood protectively next to a smaller she-wolf whose coat was more a mix of brown and tan.

It made me think of Robbie...and me.

I shivered, set the book aside, and then dived back into the box. All that remained were two figurines and my favorite wolf stuffie from childhood—Fang.

I pulled him out first and gave him a tight squeeze. He was a typical gray wolf and had seen better days—one ear hung raggedly to the side, he was stained, and his torso lacked any stuffing from being bent in half so much.

Still, I kissed him. "Hey, buddy. I missed you. I'm sorry I put you in a box and shut you away for so long." I placed him on my pillows. "You'll stay right there from now on. A place of honor for getting me through those tough teenage years."

I looked back in the box, seeing the two figurines. I already knew what, or rather, who the bigger figurine was meant to be—Odin, the all-seeing one. I stuck out my tongue, then thought better of it and glanced around nervously.

"Sorry," I muttered, just in case I'd offended him.

Odin wasn't a myth to us. It used to be that most Valdyr could travel across Bifrost to Asgard, but that was before Earth's polar shift happened thousands of years ago. It took the Varda centuries to find it again—at Wolf Ridge.

But then the curse infiltrated the pack, like a cobra in the night, and we lost our ability to sift into Asgard—again. Everybody but Erik that is.

Now he was training the pups to do it—and anyone else who wanted to learn—but it was almost impossible to pick up the skill when you were older.

I hefted out the stone statue of Odin. In the myths, he had several different guises, but the artist had depicted this Odin in battle armor with a horned helmet and a big bushy beard like my dad. One eye was missing, and he held his spear, Gungnir, aloft as he rode his massive, eight-legged steed, Sleipnir.

I'm sure my parents bought it for me thinking I'd like the horse—what young girl wouldn't?—but I'd already felt out of sync with my family and pack by then and wanted nothing to do with it.

Honestly, I still didn't.

I put it back in the box and pulled out the last object curiously, expecting to repack it after a cursory glance, but my eyes fell on a figure of Freyja carved in white stone about half the size of Odin's statue.

My breath caught in my throat.

It was beautiful—she was beautiful. Her hair flowed past her waist, and she sprawled on a throne, cuddling two mischievous-looking cats. At her feet sat a boar, looking up at her adoringly. The animal had gold-tipped bristles.

In the Norse myths, Freyja had two modes of transportation —a chariot pulled by her cats and a boar that she rode like a horse.

It had always struck me as odd and kind of funny. But after experiencing her protection today, my only thought was about her power. It was a good reminder that she wasn't just the goddess of love and beauty. She was also the goddess of war and magic.

And she had skills.

I reached forward and placed the statue on the bedside table next to the one of me dancing. Then I found spots around my room for the other objects too—even the dagger.

The only one I kept in the box was the statue of Odin, and I quickly closed the lid and put him back on the shelf in my closet. When I shut the doors, soft laughter whispered through my head.

I whipped around, my heart pounding, and looked for the source of the sound.

Was that you? I asked my wolf.

She didn't answer, but I sensed an eye roll. Weird.

So, I'm being stupid? I just imagined it?

I held my breath, hoping she'd answer, but instead, I felt an overwhelming urge to sleep.

Deep. Restorative. Sleep.

I sighed and gave in, stumbling as I turned off the light, stripped away my clothes, and crawled under the covers. With Fang.

The last thing I remembered thinking about was my leftover cookies. I may have even reached for one.

But something rubbed my forehead, soothing me, and I slowly started to drift.

Crazy, I know.

No one was here. Were they?

CHAPTER 13

Robbie

"Robbie, wake up...wake up, Robbie."

The female voice, soft and calm, came from the periphery of my mind, but I paid it no heed. I couldn't. Skoll was also there—right there—and he was stalking Britta. I lunged into the darkness, putting my strong, powerful wolf form between him and Britta's wolf, but Skoll was gone.

I sniffed, caught his scent, and spun around. There he was, back where he'd started—huge and savage.

But where was Britta?

My heart raced as I caught her scent—barely. Was she behind me? Or in front of me?

I charged toward Skoll, trying to draw him away from her—from where I'd last seen her—but I went right through him. My wolf growled ferociously, his eyes darting around, searching for the enemy, searching for his mate.

I spun in the dark to face the threat. Nothing but blackness rushed toward me, suffocating me, drowning me.

Britta!

"Rob! Wake up!" A new voice boomed through me, loud and male. It reverberated all around me. Commanded me. "Open your eyes. Now!"

I couldn't resist. I opened my eyes, the lids weighted down by what felt like cement, and looked into the overwhelming gaze of my Alpha. His eyes shone golden with his wolf, boring into me, dominating me.

Inside, his wolf did the same.

I dropped my gaze and huffed out a shuddering breath, then frantically darted my eyes upward again, looking for Britta. Where was she?

The steady beeping sound beside me sped up—fast and insistent.

"It's too high!" the female voice said urgently.

"Rob! Focus on me," Erik commanded.

My gaze swerved to his. I tried to look away, to find Britta and keep her safe, but he held me like fucking Svengali.

"You're in the infirmary," he said. "Stay with me."

Suddenly my wolf snarled up at him, pushing against my skin, and he snarled back just as ferociously.

My wolf retreated, and I eased back against the bed. The beeping beside me settled and calmed as my heart rate slowed.

"Are you with us?" Erik asked.

I couldn't answer. My jaw felt achy and swollen, and my throat felt parched. I rubbed my eyes.

"Kat?" Erik asked, still tense and dominant.

The name seeped into my brain—Kat. Our doctor. My friend.

I looked around again, this time seeing the hospital room and the various monitors. Tyr and Magna crowded around the bed.

Kat reached over me and flashed a light into my eyes, making me blink. I saw her face—fair and delicate with her pixie-cut brown hair and bright blue eyes. I saw the ever-present sadness in them.

"He's back," she said, and the pressure from Erik and his wolf subsided.

I could breathe again. "Someone die?" I croaked. "You all look like you've seen a ghost."

Magna leaned forward and gave me a stern look. "Do not do that again. That's twice today."

I met her eyes—the same color as Britta's. "Yes, ma'am."

Her lips pressed together. Was she mad? And then the bottom one trembled before she firmed it up again.

Holy shit. "I'm okay, Magna. Really."

Magna squeezed my hand. "You are now." She pushed between Erik and the side of the bed to get closer to me. "What happened?" she asked Kat. "He was fine when I was here earlier."

"Sometimes, if the injury, or the events surrounding it, have been particularly traumatic, the re-emergence from the sótt-skáli can be difficult."

"Traumatic? He's been in lots of fights with Hati and Skoll before," Tyr said skeptically. "Including this morning."

"Yes, but not with Britta there." Magna gave her son an admonishing look.

"She's okay?" I asked, and the heart rate monitor picked up again—stupid thing. I reached under the soft, pink blanket that covered me, found some wires, and yanked them off my skin. I winced as the tape tore out some of my chest hair.

Kat made an exasperated sound. "Serves you right."

Tyr grinned. "He's okay, just having a bad dream like a widdle, tubby puppy." He grabbed a pudding cup sitting on a table beside me. "Can I have this? Thanks. I'm starving. I've been tracking down Dvergar all day and most of the night." He ripped off the foil top and dumped the whole thing into his mouth.

Fucker. I hadn't said yes. My stomach growled on cue. The healing sleep took a lot out of a Valdyr.

Kat shook her head and grabbed a cup with a straw from the table. "Here, this will help. In the meantime, I'll try and scrounge up a meal. We have some Húsl loaf out front that Dahlia made, if nothing else."

"Uh, not anymore," Tyr said.

Magna glared at him and pointed to the door. "Go. You have less than an hour to get ready for the ceremony."

"Yes, Mother." On his way out, Tyr dunked the empty pudding cup in the trash can. I noticed his hair was back to its regular color and wondered if he would dye it again before Húsl.

"Run!" Magna said sternly. He shot her a jaunty grin before taking off. Kat followed him out the door—to find food, I hoped.

I reached for the cup as I surreptitiously scented the air. I could smell Britta. How long ago had she left?

Magna caught me and knew exactly what I was doing. "I sent her home hours ago. She's safe now, Robbie." Her voice broke at the end, and she clamped her hand over her mouth. Erik stepped closer and bumped his shoulder gently against hers in support.

"Sorry," she squeaked and took a deep, shuddering breath. "I can't seem to hold it together." When she calmed down, she laid her hand on my arm. "Thank you for saving her."

I closed my eyes, filled with regret and anger. "No, I'm the one who's sorry. Skoll attacked us because of me. *I* put her in danger." In my mind, I saw Britta kneeling before Skoll, her neck exposed and her hands on his legs—ready to die for me. If I'd still been attached to those wires, the monitor beside me would have been going crazy.

"It wasn't your fault," Erik said. "We all knew you were picking her up, and none of us anticipated what Skoll would do. I saw the footage. It was extreme."

"Why would he do that?" Magna asked. "He's never done that before."

"He has," I said.

Erik frowned. "When?"

"My mom."

"Your mom?" Magna exclaimed.

I had to clear my throat before speaking. "When Skoll threw the Rover over the edge today, the car lurched in a way that was familiar to me—a way I'll never forget. It was the same motion I felt just before my mom crashed over the edge. It woke me up."

Erik's eyes widened, a muscle ticking in his jaw. "You're sure?"

"Yes." Then I sighed. "Okay, not totally—I mean, I was eleven, and I'd been sleeping. How sure can I really be? But…it feels true to me…to my wolf." My eyes met Erik's, wanting answers. "Why would he attack my mom? She wasn't a fighter or part of the day-to-day management of Wolf Ridge Industries, and she didn't have powerful magic that I was aware of. It makes no sense."

Erik let out a long, slow breath. "Maybe it does."

"What do you mean?"

He rubbed his fingers along his forehead. "I've thought about this for a while, trying to pinpoint when the curse started, and I think it was before I was born. My first memory is being afraid of my dad—afraid of what he would do to my mom, which is unheard of for fated mates. It should be impossible—Freyja binds their hearts together. When one hurts, the other feels it too."

Magna nodded. "This is how it is between me and Kirk, but early on, we struggled unnaturally."

"It was the same for my family—until Astra died," Erik said. "Things worsened significantly in the pack after that. The last ten years before I contained the curse almost saw the end of the Varda. So many good wolves were corrupted, so many were lost or destroyed."

"I remember," Magna said with a sigh.

"But some families—some Valdyr—did better than others," Erik said. "It was almost as if they were able to counteract the curse. Certain wolves brought light and joy to others. Uplifted them."

"And you think my mom did that?" I asked.

"Maybe. Did you ever see her use her gift? I've often wondered if her music was magical. It was incredible how she could lift a room, lift a mood, with her love and energy, talent and laughter. Kind of like…"

"Like…?" I prompted, but a part of me knew what he was going to say.

"Like Britta can."

My heart pounded again, feeling like it might burst through my chest. "So you think Skoll came after Britta the same as he did my mom? Will he try for her again? He was questioning me about the magic from the Dvergar lab. I thought it was the dust that drew him to us!" I pushed myself up from the bed, but Erik and Magna strong-armed me back down.

"No, Rob. Calm down!" Erik commanded me in that dominant way again, but I wasn't listening. Neither was my wolf. "He's not after Britta. Hati and Skoll know the curse is locked away inside of me. Britta can't affect it. It *was* the dust Skoll came after. Your female is safe. He's not after her."

The fight seeped out of me, and I rested against the bed, exhausted again. Fuck.

And then his words sank in. My female?

I peered at him. "My friend, you mean. She's like a sister to me." If ever I'd contemplated being with Britta, this whole incident had kiboshed that. I needed her gone from Wolf Ridge, safe from fucking psychopaths who wanted to destroy the world. No, she was leaving to conquer the dance world—starting in New York.

It's what she'd wanted since she was a kid—what I wanted for her.

"Sure, whatever," Erik said as he released me.

Magna gave me a look, and then glanced at the clock. "You both need to get ready. So do I. And I need to check that Tyr isn't wasting time dying his hair." Then she kissed my cheek. "You are Astra's son, Robbie, and you couldn't have asked for a better mother, but I consider you my son too. Things may seem complicated now, but let your wolf guide you. He will never lead you wrong."

Then she left the room. I knew what she meant and frowned. My wolf wanted what was best for Britta too. He would happily see her safe in the city rather than here.

But the big male sniffed dismissively inside of me and stalked away into the forest.

I took a sip of juice. When I looked up at Erik, he raised his brow.

"What?" I asked, almost belligerently.

"Nothing."

"That wasn't a nothing look, Fyrstr."

He shrugged, and I could see a hint of a grin. Great.

"Glad to know I'm amusing you."

Erik laughed. "You are. I'm just so damn happy you're alive." He grabbed my hand and yanked me into a bear hug, pounding on my back.

"Which part of me being in the hospital have you forgotten about?" I asked, wincing with every hit.

"All of it. Now get your ass out of bed and hit the showers." He glanced at the clock. "We have thirty minutes. I'll talk as you shower. And if you're too slow, I'm gonna sit your ass down in the wheelchair and push you to the den for Húsl."

Fucker knew that would get me moving.

"I don't have any clothes."

"Magna brought you some. She brought me some too. I don't know what we'd do without her." He reached behind him and tossed me a folded pair of white linen pants and a white button-down shirt.

I caught them reflexively and stood. It did feel good to get up and moving. Then I took a step and groaned.

"Get over it," Erik said, guiding me toward the bathroom. "You're the big ass rekkr who fought Skoll twice today *and* survived a crash down a mountain. You're a fucking superhero. You'll be lifting Thor's hammer next."

The patient monitor behind us suddenly beeped, going crazy. We both looked at it—Kat had laid the leads on top of the machine before she'd left.

"Sorry," Erik said loudly into the empty space. "He definitely cannot lift Thor's hammer."

"Way to go," I muttered.

Erik nudged me through the door. I ditched my boxer briefs and stepped directly into the shower. The hot water poured over my head. Gods, it felt good.

And then Erik's voice boomed at me from the bathroom door, making me jump. "We nabbed a couple of top-level scientists from the Dvergar lab as well as several guards and an administrator of some kind. We got lucky. It *was* a magical bomb, and Hati *did* intend to drop it over us tonight, just like we suspected. I never thought I'd say this, but thank Odin for Dane. If he hadn't shared his intel, I don't know what would've happened."

I grabbed the soap and rubbed it over myself, still achy in places. "Is it destroyed, then? I thought Skoll had a shrunken version of the warehouse or something."

"He did, but one of the scientists said the magic is too volatile to use now. It would've imploded within a few hours and snuffed itself out. The other scientist confirmed. And if Skoll had tried to re-enlarge the warehouse to go in and fix things, he wouldn't have survived."

"Which is why he came after me." I rubbed some shampoo through my hair and then rinsed it off.

"Yeah. You had the magic in you for a few hours. That's what he was picking up on."

I let out a huff of laughter. "Then he threw me in the creek, and all the dust rinsed away."

"I hope you told him that."

"I did." I closed my eyes and let the water run over me,

releasing the tension from the day—less than a day, actually. It felt like a week. "I was trying to draw his attention away from Britta. She'd crossed back through the ward to try and save me. Skoll practically salivated when he saw her."

And now I'd completely tensed up again.

Silence came from the other side of the shower door, then I heard a long, huffed breath. "What happened?"

The terrifying scene flashed behind my eyes. I had to clear my throat before speaking. "We were in the creek, and Skoll was wearing me down. I knew I couldn't beat him. My wolf did too. Britta was in the creek on the other side of the boundary, watching. I tried to draw Skoll away because I didn't want her to see..."

"...to see him kill you," Erik said.

"Yeah."

"What happened?"

I found it hard to breathe. The panic I felt when Britta stepped through the ward refilled me.

She's going away. She will never be in danger again. I chanted it to myself like a mantra—over and over.

"Rob?" Erik prompted.

"I ran down the creek away from the ward, but I didn't get very far. He was on me in seconds, pushing me beneath the water. I saw Britta—" I stopped abruptly and had to think about it. "No, I couldn't have seen her. I was face down in the water, but...somehow I knew that she'd stepped over the boundary." I frowned. "How is that possible?"

"Freyja."

"You think?"

"Yeah. She's been known to help, especially when the fight occurs close to her wards. She feels it through her magic. Britta must have connected to her and to you when she stepped through the boundary."

I nodded. That made sense. "Well, when Skoll saw her, he pulled me from the water so that I could see too. He was gleeful."

"Piece of shit," Erik said with contempt.

"Yeah."

"You must have been frantic."

"I was. I tried to get him to focus on me—to kill or torture me —thinking she might retreat, but she just kept coming."

"She would. Britta never backs down from anything. How did you survive?"

"She knelt at his feet, her head bowed and her neck exposed, begging him to kill her too, but she had that look in her eye. I don't know if it was her magic rising or Freyja's magic working through her, but she touched his leg and…did something."

"What kind of something?"

I shrugged. "But it hurt him in some way. He released me, almost whimpering, and I grabbed her and jumped back over the line. We just made it. The last thing I remember is seeing her dad standing over us."

"Odin's bloody eye," Erik cursed. "No wonder you were so traumatized coming out of the sótt-skáli."

"I was?"

"Yeah. You don't remember?"

Vague, murky dreams came back to me, filled with an elusive, psychotic Skoll and me trying to find and protect Britta.

"Is he going to come after her now? She defeated him."

"That's not how he operates—how either of them operates. They have plans cooking all the time. They avoid us unless we're in the way, which we try to be as often as possible. She's a blip on his radar, Rob. Nothing more. And if it was her magic and not Freyja acting through her, she'll be able to defend herself. Trust in the Allfather. The gifts he's given the females are powerful. They can protect themselves better than we can in many ways."

My wolf heard the truth in his words. *Safe*, he said, and my panic receded.

Then the shower door opened just far enough for a hand to

enter, and the water suddenly turned cold. "Time to get out," Erik said before retreating.

I cursed as the freezing stream hit my skin, and I slammed off the water. "Assault and fucking battery."

"Time's a-wasting. You can take it out on me in the ring."

"Count on it, Fyrstr." I stepped out, and a towel hit me in the face. "Thanks," I muttered.

"You're welcome." The door banged shut behind him as he left.

"Now you're giving me some privacy?" I yelled.

"I gotta change!" he yelled back.

I shook my head, then rubbed the towel over my hair and down my body. When I was dry, I used my fingers as a comb before slipping on fresh boxers, the white linen pants, and shirt. All that was missing was the red stole that males wore around their necks during the ceremony. We'd been dressing that way during Húsl for thousands of years.

It was tradition.

I found a sealed toothbrush in the medicine cabinet, ripped it open, and added toothpaste.

When I was done, I walked out and found Erik dressed like me, checking his phone in one hand and fastening the buttons on his shirt with his other hand. Two red stoles lay on the bed. I scooped one up and hung it around my neck.

"Ready?" I asked.

He looked up. "One sec. I'm just making a note to extend the Rovers' wards. A foot or two around the vehicles would stop Hati and Skoll from being able to grab them like Skoll did today. And it would also give us a safe space if we didn't have time to get inside."

"And it'll piss them off royally."

He grinned. "Yeah, there's that. You okay to walk? I can get you the wheelchair." He saw my frowning face and nodded. "Okay, didn't think so. Let's go."

I tossed him the second stole, and he wrapped it around his neck, then pocketed his phone. I felt naked without mine. I'd have to stop by tech and pick up a new one tomorrow.

We exited my room and entered the main part of the infirmary. It looked like a modern-day hospital. I saw Kat heading toward us, wearing a long, flowing white dress with a red choker around her neck. Unlike us, she wore flip-flops. It was strange to see her without her lab coat.

In her hands, she carried a couple of sandwiches and a carton of milk.

She handed them to me. "Try not to spill."

"Yes, Mom."

"You're wearing white," she said. "I always spill on myself when I'm wearing white."

"Yeah, me too. Keep that food away from me," Erik said.

"Is there ketchup in it?" I asked as I tore the plastic wrap from the first sandwich and bit into it. "I could dribble it down my front. That would be Húsl-appropriate."

Kat snorted. "Then you wouldn't need a stole to represent the wolves' bloody stomachs after we burst out of them. Very grisly. As a doctor, I wouldn't recommend it."

"Did the women used to wear stoles?" I asked.

"Yes, but fashion won out. Now I choose to wear a choker to represent a slashed throat. Nice, don't you think?"

"Yes, you look lovely," Erik said.

She gave him a sideways glance. "I wasn't fishing for a compliment, Fyrstr."

"I know, but I chose to give you one."

She did look nice—tall and willowy with surprising strength. I'd seen her doing different forms of meditative exercise at the gym, like yoga and tai chi. And running. She told me once that she liked to run as therapy.

Kat was mated but without her mate. She joined the pack alone several years ago and became our previous healer's apprentice. I couldn't imagine how being separated from her mate was even possible. Hence the therapy.

We exited into a well-lit, empty tunnel. The floor was packed earth, and the walls were carved from rock. The tunnels were for Valdyr only and ran for miles under Wolf Ridge, connecting to the den, the hospital, the barracks for unmated rekkrs, the training and command center, and every Valdyr home.

Usually, the halls were busy, but by now, everyone would be waiting for us in the den. They couldn't start Húsl without their Alpha.

"Fyrstr," Kat said respectfully, and I knew she was going to request something from Erik that he wouldn't like. "I heard rumors that several Dvergar prisoners are being contained and questioned in the lower cells."

Erik let out a short grunt, neither confirming it nor denying it.

"I would like to see them after the ceremony, please."

"Why?"

"They may be hurt. I want to tend to them."

Erik let out an exasperated huff. "Kat, they were building a bomb to drop on us during Húsl. It was magical. It would have destroyed our pack and family bonds. Can you even imagine that? Or the advantage that would have given Hati and Skoll over us?"

"No, I can't imagine it. I also can't imagine leaving someone in pain no matter what species they are or what they've done."

Erik sighed. "Fine. Tomorrow, not tonight. You need to rest. For the most part, they were happy to talk. Actually, the administrator guy was raging. We couldn't get him to *stop* talking. Hati and Skoll were supposed to provide extra security. Lucky for us, they didn't. Plus, they're millions of brokkrs behind in payment. This isn't the first time they've reneged on a deal."

"So you'll let that guy go?" I asked.

"Yup. The news will spread like wildfire through Nidavellir

that Hati and Skoll squelched on a deal. Nobody will work with them for a while. We're going to hold onto the scientists, though. See what we can learn from them."

"For how long?" Kat asked, her brow pinching together.

"For as long as it's beneficial to us." Erik's tone brooked no argument.

Kat quickly lowered her head. "Yes, Fyrstr."

If you hadn't grown up in the Varda, it was easy to forget that we were at war with Hati and Skoll and that those who chose to help them were also our enemies.

The passageway began to ascend. At the top, we rounded a corner and saw numerous pairs of shoes—sandals and flip-flops —placed alongside the wall. Kat quickly added hers to the pile.

The tunnel ended abruptly in an impenetrable-looking stone wall, but Erik simply raised his hand, placed it against the rock, and pushed it open.

Chaos bombarded us when we stepped through the door.

CHAPTER 14

Robbie

THE NOISE OF A HUNDRED-PLUS VALDYR JAMMED INTO THE DEN—talking, laughing, and shouting greetings to one another—assaulted my ears as I followed Erik and Kat through the swinging rock door. We stepped out from the side of the mountain into the back of a shallow, eight-foot-high "cave" that opened onto a large, two-tiered sunken rotunda. It became the pack's sacred circle when sanctified. The floor was copper slate, and the ceiling was a domed glass structure that opened and allowed the heavens to shine down during special ceremonies like Húsl.

Pups of all ages, barefoot and dressed in white with red accents like their parents, played on the steps, yelling and shrieking as they jumped and danced around, darted across the circle, and chased each other—all on too little sleep.

It was adrenaline-filled pandemonium.

In the open space beyond the rotunda and on the spiral staircases and balconies that overlooked the sacred circle, older Valdyr chatted with one another, waiting for Húsl to begin. A hush fell over the crowd when they caught sight of Kat, me, and Erik entering through the back of the cave.

I spotted Britta immediately. She stood with her family on the rotunda level near the front. They crowded around her, just like I wanted to do. Magna had wrapped her arm around Britta's waist, and Tyr had draped his arm over her shoulder. He leaned on her heavily as if he was too tired to stand and needed her to hold him up, but I knew my friend...he wanted to keep his sister close. Britta's dad, Kirk, loomed behind her with his hands on the shoulders of his wife and son, enfolding them all in his big embrace.

Her crash over the mountainside, and the subsequent attack by Skoll, had shaken the family.

And me too. I knew without a doubt that I loved her, but I was more determined than ever to see her living the life of her dreams away from Wolf Ridge and the dangers of further attacks.

Her face lit up when she saw me, and she waved. Then she jerked her head surreptitiously at Tyr and gave me a 'what the hel?' look.

A laugh welled up inside of me. Gods, I was going to miss her.

From the other side of the rotunda, someone called my name. "Wobbie!"

I glanced over and saw the sweetest, funniest little pup running toward me across the sunken circle. She wore a white princess dress with a big, red flower pinned at her waist and a red, flowered headband in her hair. Even her tiny toenails were painted red.

When she reached me, she held out her arms to be picked up.

"Hi, Shelby," I said as I leaned down to get her. "Don't you look beautiful."

"I'm Mewida," she said, flinging her arms out behind her in some kind of pose.

I had no idea what she was doing or who she was talking about, but I played along. "Well, hello, Merida."

Then she roared at me, curling her fingers like claws and exposing her teeth. "Hello," she growled.

"Is that your wolf?" I asked.

"No. I'm a beaw. Like my mommy."

"Your mommy's a bear?"

"Uh huh."

"Lucky her, being a wolf and a bear."

"No, my pwincess mommy."

"Oh, okay. So you're Princess Merida?"

"Uh huh."

Gunn appeared beside us, and Shelby growled at him too. He kissed her cheek, then covered her ears and whistled to get everyone's attention.

I winced as the sound continued to ring loudly in my head. "Thor's balls! You could have given me a little warning."

"Thow's balls! Thow's balls!" Shelby yelled, laughing.

Gunn grinned. "Now you're in for it."

I looked guiltily around the rotunda and saw Shelby's mom standing on the opposite side, watching us, her hands on her hips. "Uh, maybe we should go see your mom."

My long strides took us there in seconds, and I put Shelby down, intending to go back and find a place near my adopted family, but the tiny Valdyr held onto my hand and tugged until I sat next to her on the steps.

I glanced up and saw Britta smiling at us. I grinned back and shrugged.

The steps were usually reserved for pups, but I was still tired, and it would be good to sit for the ceremony. Odin's presence, felt but not seen, could warp time, and you never knew how long the ritual would last. What may feel like fifteen minutes could be two minutes or two hours in real time.

Shelby crawled onto my lap and rested her head on my shoulder. The weight and warmth of her solid little body warmed my heart, and I kissed the top of her head. My gaze drifted up again. Met Britta's.

Suddenly, it was hard to breathe.

The sound faded into the background, and I couldn't look away. All I could see was her like we were in our own little world. Then something poked my cheek—several times—and the spell was broken. I looked down to see Shelby with her finger sticking straight out and about to poke me again.

"Pay attention," she whispered.

"Okay. Sorry," I whispered back. I grasped her hand gently and lowered it to her lap.

The pups had crowded onto the steps, clearing the rotunda, and anticipation rose through the pack like a living entity. Erik approached a stone altar that stood at the front of the cave where Linnea waited. She looked nervous, and I remembered this was her first Húsl as Alpha female.

When our previous Alpha female had died, and no one had challenged to replace her, Erik had asked Linnea to assume that role. She'd agreed—reluctantly—and so had Odin. Unfortunately, she'd been determined to lead with a show of strength, but she didn't seem to understand that power and command didn't have to be paired with force and intimidation. Little by little, she was losing the pack's confidence and trust.

Usually, the Alpha male and female were mated, and maybe that would have helped to soften Linnea a bit, but Erik had sworn never to take a mate due to the curse he carried. Plus, I had never sensed any attraction between the two Alphas. Their wolves would refuse to mate even if Erik and Linnea decided they should kyss for the sake of the pack.

But maybe that was a good thing. The last fated mates to be Alphas had been Erik's parents, and their kyss—like so many others during that time—had turned out horribly. I couldn't imagine how Erik had dealt with such heartache.

Not to mention the weighty responsibility he'd taken on as

leader of the Varda—the first pack and greatest defense against Hati and Skoll, who wanted nothing more than to free their father Fenrir and bring on Ragnarök.

"Happy Húsl, everyone," Erik said as he rested his palms on the altar. In front of him sat a small ceremonial knife, a white candle, a bowl depicting a grisly scene of the Valdyr bursting from the bodies of Odin's chosen wolves, and a pitcher of water.

"Happy Húsl, Fyrstr," I replied with the rest of my pack.

"Thank you for allowing us to delay our start tonight. It's been a day."

A murmur of laughter ran through the crowd.

"But we count our blessings—all of our pack family alive and well, disaster averted, and the sons of Fenrir thwarted. Not to mention, I got some of Dahlia's vanilla and cherry fudge for Húsl. A great day all around, I'd say!"

Hoots of laughter erupted, along with cheers and whistles. I looked across and saw that Magna had laid her head on Britta's shoulder, and Kirk had tightened his embrace around his family. Unashamed tears ran down his cheeks.

I felt a hand on my head and saw Shelby's mom smiling at me. Someone else patted my shoulder. My chest tightened with emotion, knowing my pack was happy and grateful I'd survived.

When I glanced again at Britta, she smiled at me too. *Thank you*, she mouthed and then placed her hands over her heart. I felt a tug on my own heart like she'd stolen a piece of it.

Forever.

"We share in a time of great joy and celebration," Erik continued, "and we give thanks to Odin, our creator, as we welcome him among us tonight. We welcome his trusted friends and allies, and our ancestors who live as heroes in the woods outside Valhalla. All are welcome here."

"Welcome, Odin," I replied with my pack—words my mother had taught me so many years ago. "Welcome, Freyja and the other gods and goddesses of the Aesir. Welcome our beloved family, who've passed before us. Drink and sup with us at our tables tonight and find warmth and fellowship before our hearths." I closed my eyes, searching in my heart for my mom and dad. Tears pricked the back of my eyelids when I felt their presence.

The veil between worlds was thinned during Húsl.

Then Erik tilted back his head and released a joyful howl. I joined in with the rest of the pack, including the littlest pups. Shelby's bright curls tumbled over my arm as she tilted back her head.

When the howl ended, Erik lit the candle with a match, held his palms over the flame as he muttered something in Old Norse, pricked his thumbs with the knife, and then poured water into the bowl and washed his hands. The scorching of his palms represented sacrifice for the pack, the bloodied thumbs represented his sworn duty, and the washing represented a cleansed soul to greet the gods.

After Linnea did the same, the Alphas lifted their gazes past the retracted glass ceiling to the heavens beyond and called on the magic of Asgard and the gods. In unbelievable tones and hues, a beautiful, softly-colored light shone down from the stars upon the rotunda, flooding the den and sanctifying the circle. It was no longer a play area for our pups, but a sacred hringr where we celebrated special holidays and rituals.

The pack basked in the magic that sang to their souls as they communed with their gods and loved ones. I couldn't see my parents, but I knew they were there. I felt the touch of my mom's hand in mine and my dad's arm around my shoulder. I sensed their love, pride, and joy. And beyond them, I sensed my ancestors all the way back to the beginning, when Odin first created the Valdyr.

When his favorite wolf pack sacrificed itself for us.

And I gave thanks to them—we all did. As did our wolves.

I ran with my pack and all of my ancestors in Hjarta—back to when we were still just animals. My four legs galloped hard against pine-needle-covered ground, through tall grasses, and across soft moss that grew on the rocks and fallen trees. The wind riffled through my fur and up my nose, bringing me the exciting scents of prey darting through the underbrush, the sweet smell of spring flowers, and the musty odor of decaying leaves and twigs that would give way to new life.

Time passed—or maybe it didn't—as I connected with the wolves who came before me. We moved in coordination, running, hunting, playing. A female bumped against me, then darted away.

Britta in wolf form!

I joyfully gave chase. She'd never run with the great pack before. Did that mean…

I opened my eyes and looked at her across the circle. She opened hers, too, laughing, her face filled with joy.

Other Valdyr were stirring, some even yawning and stretching.

Then Erik called out her name. "Britta."

I glanced at my Alpha. He'd moved to the front of the altar and held his hand toward her.

"Will you dance for us?" he asked. His voice still resonated deeply with the power and magic of Asgard.

I rose, Shelby a sleepy weight in my arms. What was happening? Usually, at this point in the ceremony, Valdyr returned to themselves at their own pace as the magic receded—quickly for some, slowly for others—but it was still thick and heady in the den, the colors brighter and more luminous.

I could hear music…or maybe that was the sound of the magic. Like crystals singing. It pealed harmoniously in my head with intricate rhythms and beats, the tempo rising and falling, the tone so pure my throat tightened, and my teeth ached.

Britta smiled at Erik, still caught up in the beauty and magic of Asgard, and moved forward as if in a dream. When she reached the Fyrstr, he gently grasped her head and spoke to her. I tried to hear, but the music filled my ears.

She nodded, and he kissed her forehead before stepping back. Britta moved to the center of the circle. Around me, more and more Valdyr stirred and focused on her.

Shelby's mom reached for her daughter and took her from my arms. I barely noticed, I was so intent on Britta.

Eyes closed, she swayed side to side in tiny movements, her hair a silken sheath that flowed halfway down her back. Her white, spaghetti-strap dress stretched over her curves, and a red scarf knotted around her waist, falling to a point along one side of her thigh.

She looked so beautiful that my chest ached. I pressed my palm over my heart to ease the feeling, then sank back down to the steps, waiting with anticipation for her to begin.

In my head, the music swelled, and I gasped as Britta moved with it, her arm rising to the side and sweeping over her head as she bent at the waist and then spun in the opposite direction, gliding across the floor. She hit every note perfectly as if she were one of the instruments, and the magic played her—a marionette attached to musical strings, her timing flawlessly coordinated with every beat, every note, and the rising and falling crescendos.

She leapt in the air, arms floating up, toes pointed down, legs strong and graceful, before landing as softly as a feather. She stood completely still for a few beats before running backward and transitioning into a series of endless spins that took her around the circumference of the circle.

When she reached me, she stopped and smiled, her heart in her eyes, her body vibrating with the music and magic. She raised her hand and traced her fingertips across my forehead and down my cheek. Her other hand pressed over my heart, and I gasped as tingles exploded within me, swirling like little tornadoes that moved through my body and soul, making me feel lighter, freer.

More whole.

On some level, I knew she was healing me. Not physically—Odin's magic had already done that—this was healing on a heart level, curing my emotional wounds and scars from as far back as I could remember. Even past that to when I was barely crawling and still in my mother's womb.

The curse had tried to disconnect the pack from one another, to corrupt us—and it had—but we'd survived and triumphed over it through Erik. Still, we carried those old hurts and regrets deep down, those feelings of guilt and shame, fear and confusion.

A weight I didn't know I carried released from me as the tingles spread to every cell, uplifting, fortifying, and scrubbing me clean from the inside out.

Britta laughed joyously, and then turned and fell backward, knowing I would catch her. I did, and she sprang forward again, leaping and twirling across the sacred circle, moving so fast my eyes could barely track her. The luminous, magical colors that filled the air moved with her as if they were partners dancing in perfect timing.

She reached Erik and leapt right at him, twisting at the last moment to twirl around him, her hands drifting over his shoulders and sending out sparks of color and light that coalesced around him, grew brighter, and sank inside him. He stiffened, his eyes closed, and his face tormented, then he sagged forward. What had she done to him? Was it the same thing that had happened to me?

Whoa, did that mean she'd affected the curse too?

No, my wolf said. *The curse is guarded in Hjarta.*

Britta's magic can't reach there?

Her touch eases only Valdyr burdens.

So this experience was mine alone. Not my wolf's. He experienced emotions differently and more simply than I did.

Is this how she hurt Skoll? Did she do something with his emotions?

Silence fell as my wolf pondered the question. *Same but different. Ask her.*

I can't ask a female about her magic.

You can. Mate.

No. Not mate.

A bark of laughter rose within me from my wolf—a pure, clear sound like the pealing of bells, affected by the music in my head and the magic still whirling in my cells.

Obviously, he found my resistance amusing. That should worry me, but I was too blissful and filled with love and joy to care.

I took a deep, cleansing breath. It felt like a layer of grime had been cleared away.

Britta was still dancing, and I realized I had never seen her dance like this before—every leap was higher, spin tighter, run faster, contraction sharper.

She was dancing to her full ability rather than holding herself back for her human audience and the other dancers. How incredible must that feel? But also sad that all these years, she'd had to hide her true talent...and would have to keep doing so.

She jumped toward the heavens, her legs scissoring, and the pack gasped in delight and amazement. When she landed, she swept to the floor in a series of rolls and poses, her body bending and flexing, her legs and arms tucking and stretching.

Rising in one fluid motion, she spun in a widening circle, like the earth orbiting the sun. Her hair swung around her, sparks of color and magic shooting into the crowd from the end of each strand—tiny magical bombs that landed and exploded, bursting more color into the air and burrowing deeply into each Valdyr, young and old alike.

She beckoned to the children, and many of them, including Shelby, ran forward to dance with her, laughing and squealing. The magic built among them and floated like a sparkling cloud throughout the den.

More laughter erupted—tears as well—as the Valdyr were set

free from the remnants of the curse and the emotional damage that had been left behind after Erik had sucked it into himself.

Even Linnea was smiling, but I sensed she was affected by the magic second-hand, from the joy that flooded the pack. She had joined the Varda after Erik had contained the curse.

And Kat? She was dancing with the pups on the rotunda floor, filled with happiness, too. But her joy was also second-hand from the pack's bliss and exhilaration.

The magic seemed to target only those affected by the curse.

Still, what a blessing Britta had bestowed upon us.

I searched for her and then stopped breathing when I spotted her. My wolf let out an excited bark and raced forward. He pushed against my skin, trying to get out, but I shoved him back.

Hold on! I yelled, but I knew why he wanted to shift and fought so hard against me.

I'd seen it, too, and my heart pounded like I'd raced up Mt. Everest.

Britta's arm had shifted into the hazy blur of the helmingr.

Her wolf was coming.

CHAPTER 15

THE MUSIC IN MY HEAD CHANGED, AND I CHANGED WITH IT.

I danced heavier. My movements became stronger, more powerful. My center of gravity lowered.

I charged rather than ran. I bound rather than leapt. I twisted rather than spun.

I danced from the heart of my wolf.

I was my wolf.

I slowed and dropped to my knees, swaying with the deep, pounding rhythm inside me. Raising my hands, I marveled at the hazy blur overtaking them. I'd seen it all my life, of course, every time a Valdyr shifted in front of me, but I'd never seen it on me before. Or rather, I'd never seen that part of me before, that magical space that existed between me and my wolf.

Some speculated that the helmingr was Hjarta manifesting in the physical world; others thought that it was the magic within reforming us.

Whatever it was, it felt strange and familiar all at once, and a burst of exhilaration exploded within me like a popping soap bubble.

She was coming!

Are you there? I asked, barely able to contain my excitement.

I'm here, she replied. *I'm always here.*

Are you scared to rise into my world?

No.

I laughed. *Of course, you're not. You're fearless.*

I fear. But not this.

Well, I'm a little scared. Excited too. Will I go to Hjarta when you rise?

Hjarta is within. You will go within.

Oh, that was odd. I'd always thought of Hjarta as a different place, like an alien planet or something. *Has it always been within?*

Yes.

Have you always been within?

Yes. And no. I have always been within you, and you have always been within me.

Then how come I couldn't feel or hear you before? Why can I finally talk to you?

Now, we know.

I wanted to ask a bazillion more questions but knew I would always get the same answer. For my wolf, it was simple—*now, we know.*

Will it hurt? I asked.

We go slow. Fast will hurt.

Okay, slow. I can definitely do slow.

She cocked her head as if listening to something—or someone—and I realized I sensed her movements and emotions. And I could see her within my mind's eye!

She was beautiful!

My gaze ran over her eagerly, my fears dissipating under the wonder of what was happening. My wolf was with me. Finally!

She was a gorgeous mix of brown, tan, and gray fur, her body long and lean, her tail fluffy. Her ears looked soft with tufts of fur at the tip. I could actually feel them in my hands when I thought about them. I had a sense of stroking the sensitive skin and silky fur.

I can see you. Feel you. You're stunning. Can you see me?

Yes.

And everything around me?

Yes.

I waited for her to say more, to acknowledge me in the way I'd acknowledged her. When she didn't, I felt a moment of insecurity. My wolf cocked her head again, but this time she was trying to understand what I was thinking and feeling.

Sorry, I'm just...are you happy with me? Instantly, I regretted my words. She didn't think about things the same way I did.

Yes. Happy.

Okay, good. I'm happy with you too, and I'm excited for you to experience my world. Would you like to see it now? I'm ready. Our mother and father will be overjoyed to meet you. And our brother, too, although he'll probably natter on in the most annoying way and pull on your tail.

She yipped in agreement, and then a feeling swept over me that was part pleasure, part pain. No, not pain, exactly, more like an uncomfortable pressure. Like I was being filled to the brim—and then some—from the inside out.

My mouth felt weird, and I started to salivate. The tips of my fingers and toes tingled. Then the pressure faded, and I looked out through my wolf's eyes at my pack. The sea of pups around me swarmed, shrieking with excitement and hugging and petting me. A few tried to ride me, making me laugh.

I licked, nuzzled, and playfully nipped a few, especially the ones trying to climb on top.

Careful, I said. *Even playful little nips can hurt. The pups in this form are more fragile.*

She began to weave her way through the crowd, sniffing the

air, and then she made a bee-line for the edge of the rotunda. I couldn't see where she was going, but I assumed it was toward our family.

When she stopped, I was looking directly at Robbie sitting on the rotunda steps.

Of course...Robbie.

I inhaled, and the scent she'd been sniffing filled me too. So familiar, yet...more. Sweeter, wilder, sexier. More dominant.

Mate, she said, her voice brimming with pride.

You're sure? I asked, but I knew. I'd always known.

My throat tightened, and it felt like my heart would burst through my ribs. I pressed my hand to my chest, where it ached. *He's definitely ours?*

Yes.

Robbie reached up, a wide, wondrous smile on his face, and stroked his hands along my wolf's muzzle and over her head. His fingers curled around our ears and dug in. We both moaned at the incredible sensation—like a deep massage with perfect pressure.

My wolf leaned forward and touched her nose to his. He closed his eyes—she did too—and we stayed that way for a while before she rubbed her muzzle across his cheek to the back of his ear where his scent was strongest.

You marked him? I asked.

Ours, she replied, same as I had moments ago.

Then she sprang into the air—a happy little jump—and raced around the edge of the rotunda. The Valdyr moved out of her way, everyone laughing and smiling. Some of the pups gave chase.

Careful, I urged again.

She shushed me—shushed me! It didn't sound like a hushing sound I would make, but I knew what it was, and I burst out laughing.

I was a strong, agile, fast Valdyr, and she was even more so. She didn't bump one pup—unless she wanted to.

Suddenly, she leapt up the steps and landed in my dad's outstretched arms. As always, he caught me, his strong embrace surrounding my huge wolf's body and holding me tight. He laughed joyously as I licked his face. My mom hugged me close, sinking into my fur and sobbing, and Tyr patted and petted me, nattering non-stop nonsense like he would to a silly puppy—of the canine variety.

I nipped him, and he yanked on my tail.

Annoying, my wolf said, making me fall over laughing.

She jumped down after licking my mom, and yes, even Tyr, and then headed to Erik next, twining around him, keeping her head slightly lowered and her shoulder tilted down.

A sign of respect.

He grasped her head, smiling, and this time he did the marking, sliding the side of his face back to her ear. "Welcome, Britta-wolf," he said. "Your pack is happy to meet you."

She barked excitedly, spun in a tight circle, then raced around again, looking for one more Valdyr. Dahlia's sweet scent hit us, and I spotted her up on the first balcony, leaning over the railing, her face wet and her mouth stretched into a big, soppy grin. My wolf barked at her, and Dahlia waved and blew me a kiss.

Love you, she mouthed.

I blew her a kiss back. I knew she couldn't see me, I wasn't actually there, but I hoped she could feel my love and appreciation.

She does, my wolf said.

Then she lifted her nose toward the clear night sky, the colorful magic from before having dissipated, and let loose a long, loud howl.

And panic ripped through me.

Wait, what are you doing?

Oh, my gods, she was calling to join the pack. This was the

beginning of the Handsal ceremony. She was petitioning Odin, seeking his acceptance.

I'd seen it many times in my life, often during Húsl. The last time I'd seen it was when Dahlia's wolf had howled to join the pack last fall, shocking all of us.

Stop! I'm a dancer. I don't belong here.

We belong.

No, you don't understand. The only thing I want to fight is frickin' gingivitis.

My wolf didn't get it—of course, she didn't—so I tried to think of another way to tell her, but all I could envision was a cartoon image of a scary-looking bacteria I'd seen at the dentist when I was a kid.

She picked up on it, and her ruff rose. *I will help you kill it.*

Great. Thank you. But—

The tone of her howl changed, and Erik immediately added his deep, commanding timbre to the call—a call to Odin.

Oh, crap. *Please, stop! He's not going to want us, okay? I'm not that kind of Valdyr. I'm really sorry to disappoint you, but that's the truth of it.*

Truth, yes. Disappoint, no. We are wanted.

Then the rest of the pack joined in one by one—some in wolf form, some in Valdyr form—until a beautiful chorus filled the air, the sounds harmonizing. The song swirled around me, building in intensity and pace.

I listened to every note with bated breath and watched the sky with tears in my eyes, afraid but also a tiny bit hopeful. The feeling grew little by little as my wolf kept singing.

Would her song—our song—reach its crescendo? Would the colors appear? Or would Odin shatter my song across the sky?

Would the Allfather hear the notes he wanted and join me to the pack? Or cut me off from them forever?

I told myself it wouldn't happen—I wouldn't be accepted—and that was okay because I didn't want it to happen. My destiny was out in the big, wide world. But my wolf knew better, and she kept calling to her maker with such beauty and clarity that I realized…I wanted to be part of Odin's plan. In whatever way I could. I wanted to reach that musical peak and be bonded to the Varda.

I clamped my hand over my mouth as sobs erupted from my chest and tears overflowed onto my cheeks.

Please, I don't want to leave. I want to be here—with my family, with Robbie, with my pack. To help in whatever way I can. To serve.

The music continued to swell, to rise in intensity and vibration.

Please!

And then colors burst across the sky above us. The same colors that had surrounded me in the circle—like paint across the heavens. Bright, beautiful, radiant.

As one, the wolves stopped singing and watched the sky, enraptured with the incredible light show.

I gasped for breath, tears coursing down my face. *Are we…?*

Yes, my wolf said. *Pack.*

Slowly, the colors faded above us. Happy yips and cheers loosed in the den. My wolf yipped, too, and spun in a circle, nudging and nipping the pups around her excitedly. I didn't say anything this time—I couldn't. I was too shocked, too overwhelmed. Odin had accepted me into the Varda.

Me!

A cacophony of voices burst into my head.

The pack!

I'd always been able to hear my family, but now I could hear the pack too. Oh, my gods. It was so loud! But I knew how to focus on who I wanted to connect to…and I found him.

Robbie?

Britta?

And I burst out laughing, overwhelmed with joy, excitement, and enthusiasm. I'd been chosen!

Then my wolf leapt onto the altar. She looked back over her shoulder at Robbie and barked. I gazed at him through her eyes. Robbie was flashing in and out of the helmingr like he was fighting his wolf for control.

What's wrong? I asked him, my laughter fading. He didn't answer. *Robbie?*

Then his huge brown wolf formed and lunged toward us.

Run! he yelled.

CHAPTER 16

Britta

My wolf turned with an excited yip and leapt toward the back wall of the cave—for the door that didn't look like a door. It swung open automatically, and she darted into the tunnels, racing as fast as she could toward the nearest exit. Her claws dug into the hard-packed earth, and her ears swiveled back, listening for Robbie's wolf in pursuit.

When I heard the swoosh of the door opening behind us and then big padded feet hitting the ground fast, my heart rate jumped. So did hers, and her pleasure surged through me, saturating every inch of my body—our body.

Her muscles bunched as she ran faster, her ears plastered against her head—as streamlined as possible.

I knew these tunnels like the back of my hand, which meant my wolf did too, and she zigged and zagged, knowing exactly where to go. At first, we descended and then dashed upward at the end on a sharp incline. At the top, we ran straight toward what looked like a dirt wall.

I braced myself, thinking she was going too fast and she'd hit the hard surface, but suddenly, the door was open, and she was leaping into the star-lit, cool night.

She barked exuberantly as she ran, her legs stretching and her paws pushing off as far and hard as they could with each gallop.

The debris on the forest floor crunched beneath her padded toes, and the night air ruffled her fur, bringing divine smells on the breeze.

Different, she said, her sides expanding as she inhaled. *Earthy.*

What does Hjarta smell like?

Different, she said again, and I laughed. Then, she suddenly veered to the left. I saw the bobbing, white tail of a rabbit and slapped my hand over my eyes. Was she going to kill the adorable, soft bunny and eat it right in front of me? I loved a good steak or shish kabob, but I preferred it sizzling hot from the barbeque—and wrapped in plastic before that.

Then her excitement escalated, and she darted in the other direction—just before I smelled Robbie. He was close! So close I could hear him.

I don't get it, I said, feeling like I was on the edge of my metaphorical seat. *Why are you running from Robbie?*

Chase. Catch us.

But you said he's our mate. Why can't he catch us?

He will.

He will?

Yes.

Then why run?

Chase. Catch us.

Now, I was totally confused. We were in some kind of logic circle that lacked any logic. To me, at least.

So...you want him to catch us, but only after you've run from him? Kind of like when I was little and loved being chased?

I'd always been fast and agile, and even the grown-ups had had a hard time catching me. I'd felt the same thrill my wolf was feeling now.

Yes. But mate. Prove himself.

Prove himself? He saved us multiple times today. He held us as we went over the mountain and fought Skoll for us. He almost died. Why would he have to prove himself any more than that?

To mate, she said again, sounding exasperated this time.

And then it twigged. *Oh, my gods...you mean maaate.* Suddenly, my heart was racing as fast as hers.

Just you and wolf Robbie mating? Or do me and my Robbie get to...you know?

A wave of confusion washed over me, but it didn't come from me. It came from her. It was like Dahlia had said—my wolf and I were not separate. We were one. Which meant...

Robbie and I were going to have sex.

My breath caught in my throat as I saw us together in my mind's eye—his big, naked body looming over me, rubbing against me, those humungous hands cupping my breasts and thighs, stroking over my skin. Heat formed in my belly and spread outward to the tips of my toes and ears, pooling in my groin and swelling my breasts.

He was dominant enough to position me however he wanted —however *I* wanted. Strong enough to hold me down or lift me up, to go fast or slow, hard or soft.

Deep. Shallow.

I shivered and had to squeeze my thighs together. Robbie did everything perfectly, and I had no doubt I would soon be thoroughly fucked.

I bit my lip and groaned. And my wolf responded with her own huff. I wasn't the only one consumed with thoughts of sex.

No, not sex. It was waaay more than that between us. I loved Robbie—was in love with him—and we were fated by Freyja to be together.

Would she appear tonight and join us in the Kyssa?

Yes. Mates, my wolf said simply.

And then a thought hit me, and my chest squeezed. *But only if Robbie calls for me first.*

Yes. Mates, she said again.

Easy for you to say. You know that his wolf is chasing you; he wants to be with you. But my Robbie told me to run. What if he doesn't want his wolf to catch us?

She didn't actually roll her eyes, but that's the feeling that came through the bond.

Great, now my wolf thought I was being ridiculous.

One, she said.

One what? I asked, but I knew what she meant—just like Dahlia had said.

We are one. They are one.

I huffed out an emotion-filled breath, not feeling very reassured.

Trust. Our mate wants us.

And we want him.

Yes.

I inhaled as deeply as I could, trying to release the tightness in my chest. I did want him. More than anything else in the world. More than dancing in New York or traveling the world. Seeing him on the edge of death had driven that home to me in a way nothing else could have done. And being accepted by the pack, being joined to them, and feeling their elation that Odin had chosen me, had driven home that I wanted to belong.

To fight this fight however my maker wanted me to.

I didn't know what my future would look like, but I knew that Robbie would be by my side. My chosen mate. My friend. My lover.

Okay then. Let's give this tough Valdyr a run for his money. Let's make him work for it!

My wolf dug her paws in, re-energized, and I laughed. She loved being chased as much as I did.

And she relished being caught, too, just like I did.

I settled into the space I existed—wherever that was. Hjarta, I assumed. And as I did so, it was as if I became more of my wolf, like I was her—we shared a heartbeat, we shared breath, we shared our thoughts and feelings. I didn't just feel her body running—I ran. I didn't just see her dart through the forest—I darted…and listened, smelled, and tasted the air on my tongue.

Ulf-mynd, she said.

Yes, that's exactly what I'd been thinking.

The ulf-mynd was a perfect joining of the wolf and the Valdyr —a merging of the two souls. We were one—together—a unified whole.

He'll never be able to catch us now, we said, yipping it to the sky.

And then Robbie's wolf burst from the underbrush beside us.

We let out a startled, excited yelp and changed direction on a dime. Robbie narrowly missed us. Dashing up an incline, we leapt as hard and far as we could across a deep gulley. We felt like we were performing our grandest jeté ever—toes pointed, legs stretched, power and momentum propelling us across.

Our paws barely made the other side, and we dug our claws into the bank for purchase, pushing us forward.

Robbie wasn't so lucky. He'd been right behind us, his teeth snapping at the tip of our tail, but he'd been too intent on the chase—on catching us—and hadn't anticipated the gulley.

We heard a yelp and then a crash as he missed the edge— which normally he could have leapt over with no problem.

Is he okay? I asked, separating from my wolf a little. *Maybe we should go back and check?*

No. He comes.

I closed my eyes and listened as hard as I could. There…to my left. *Oh, my gods. He's beside us again! How did he get there so fast?*

Our mate is strong. Dominant.

I shivered at the way she said dominant, and I thought about those big, strong hands on my body again. *Maybe we should let him catch us?*

No.

But—

No!

She suddenly veered in the opposite direction, leaping over a downed tree just as Robbie tried to cut us off, but this time, there was no gulley to jump across, and Robbie stayed with us, flanking us, edging us farther and farther in the direction he wanted us to go.

But to where? What location did he have in mind?

You've got to get behind him somehow. Go back in the opposite direction.

Yes. Try.

There's a big tree up ahead that was struck by lightning a few years ago. Rebound off of it and redirect us, then head to the stream. We can lose him in the reeds. He won't be able to smell us there.

He will hear us.

True, but if we shift, I can throw something in the other direction and distract him.

She did not like that idea.

Trust me, I said. *You can shift back as soon as we start moving again.*

The half-burned tree loomed ahead of us, and I sensed her uncertainty. I could also feel Robbie's teeth nipping at her heels. *He's herding us. Show him that we are not sheep!*

Indignation rising, she veered slightly to the right, looking like she intended to go around the tree. Robbie's wolf turned to the left, and I knew exactly what he intended... he would speed up and get ahead of us so that when we came around on the other side, he could force us even farther in the direction he wanted.

And then suddenly, like the best parkour athlete on YouTube, my wolf jumped straight at the half-burnt, branchless tree, rebounded off it, and leapt back in the direction we'd come. We hit the ground running, our adrenaline surging with renewed exhilaration as we streaked through the woods like lightning away from Robbie.

Behind us, he howled in frustration. The sound echoed loudly through the forest, and I laughed gleefully. I'd forgotten how fun it was to be chased when my pursuer wasn't a psychotic killer.

To the stream! I yelled.

She galloped full out, her tongue lolling from the side of her mouth, her ears plastered against her head, her tail pointed backward in a perfectly streamlined shape.

She couldn't go any faster, be any more agile, be any stronger, and I was so damn proud of her.

We were almost there. I could smell the water, hear the stream gurgling over the rocks and swirling in the deeper areas. We could hide in one of those pools or the reeds lining the edges. He wouldn't be able to hear, smell, or see us unless he loomed right over us.

Just a little farther.

The bank's edge appeared in the moonlight, highlighted against the forest on the other side. The rushing water splashed louder now and drowned out the sound of my galloping feet.

Stay near the edge in the reeds. I can grab some rocks or mud and throw it into the—

We were hit from the side, knocking us off course. We stumbled sideways and almost crashed to the ground, but huge arms wrapped around us.

Robbie—and no longer in wolf form.

We are caught! my wolf said excitedly, and suddenly, she was gone.

I gasped as my body formed in an instant, fully pressed against Robbie—both of us buck naked. He twisted us in the air and took the brunt of the fall on his back and shoulders, sliding along the ground.

We came to a stop in a small, grassy area. I was lying face-down on top of him, and his arms were squeezed around me, one hand over my shoulder, the other covering my butt.

He was hot and hard all over—which spiked my temperature and softened every inch of me. My body welcomed his, happy to be conquered by him and excited to be taken—finally!

I raised my head from his chest to find him staring at me.

His eyes burned as hot as his body.

My lids dropped to half-mast, and I slowly smiled. "Took you long enough."

CHAPTER 17

Britta

ROBBIE GRUNTED IN REPLY AS IF HE DIDN'T TRUST HIMSELF TO speak. Or maybe he couldn't speak.

I decided to test that theory and slowly spread my thighs over his pelvis, building the anticipation until my knees hit the ground.

He groaned at the increased intimacy as I settled over him, and his body tightened even more, his hips bucking. The breath shuddered from my lungs as I slipped along that stiff ridge.

He squeezed my ass in a death grip and pressed me harder against him.

"Britta," he growled.

"Uh huh?" My heart was beating so damn fast like I'd just danced two performances back-to-back.

Freyja's kiss, he was big down there. I'd had a few lovers—all human—and every one of them had left me wanting. Now, I knew why.

I needed a Valdyr—I needed Robbie.

I was so wet for him, ready for him. My outer lips had parted, drenching his shaft and creating a slick, swollen runway for him to slide along. I wriggled against him despite his hold, and he pulsed beneath me.

What I wouldn't give to just sit up and impale myself on him.

But I wanted him all in—literally and figuratively—and I wanted him to do the taking.

This time.

But first, he had to get with the program.

"Robbie?" I asked, still breathless.

He grunted again.

"My wolf tells me you're mine. And I'm yours. What does your wolf tell you?" My fingers caressed along the dips of his collarbone as I waited for his answer.

He stilled for a few seconds before raising his hands to clasp my head and hold my gaze. "That there's no going back from this. If we have sex, Britta—"

"Sex? This is about more than sex, isn't it? We're fated mates, Robbie. Even if my wolf hadn't told me that, I would have known. I've always known."

The silence grew between us, and my heart began to pound. But not from desire this time. From fear.

Didn't he want me?

"Yes," he said finally. "My wolf tells me we're fated mates. I love you, Britta. I always have, and I always will. But—"

I clamped my hand over his mouth. He was about to say something noble. I didn't want noble right now. I wanted him— my mate—to claim me in the way of our kind—all-consuming, uncontrollably, driven by passion and instinct. I wanted him inside me, his body bearing down on me, his teeth piercing my shoulder.

As I came all over him.

And now that I knew he loved me—loved me!—that my wolf was right, all of my uncertainties disappeared—replaced by desire, excitement, confidence, and sass.

This wolf was mine. He knew it, and I knew it.

More than that, he wanted it—forever.

If I could just stop him from overthinking.

"I'm going to remove my hand, and I don't want you to say another word. Understand?"

His brow wrinkled as he frowned at me, making me laugh. I felt giddy. Robbie loved me—in *that* way. I wriggled my hips again just to confirm, and he closed his eyes and groaned, his pelvis jutting upward.

Yup. He definitely wanted me as much as I wanted him.

Placing my index finger on my lips to remind him not to talk, I pushed myself upward from his chest, delving my fingers through the crisp hair that covered his pecs until I leaned over him at an angle. My breasts swayed with the movement, and he dropped his gaze to stare at them.

He looked hungry, almost feral, and I loved it.

His chest rose and fell in sharp, quick breaths as I settled over his loins. He wasn't inside me yet, but he was *right there.*

His hands had fallen to my thighs, and his fingers trembled against my skin, alternately squeezing and caressing.

Slowly, his gaze shifted upward, and he focused on my neck and shoulders. I knew what he was thinking, what his instinct was driving him to do. He wanted to bite me there, to claim me. I watched in fascination as the shape of his jaw changed slightly, and then the points of his canines lengthened and gleamed almost imperceptibly from beneath his lips.

Heart pounding with excitement, I reached behind my neck and pulled my hair back over one shoulder, my head canting slightly to the side—an invitation.

The neck and shoulders were highly erogenous zones for female Valdyr, and just knowing that he was about to clamp his teeth around me sent another wave of deep heat through my body.

I rocked on top of him, trying to find some kind of relief from my burgeoning arousal, and he thrust against me, sliding his cock upward and nudging my sensitive clit.

I gasped at the contact, my entire body clenching with need.

He was more endowed than I could have ever imagined, and I couldn't wait to be filled by him, my muscles softening and stretching to accommodate his size.

Suddenly, he sat up, one big hand wrapping around my waist and the other digging into my hair and clasping the back of my head.

I cupped his cheeks and pulled his face to mine, tilting my head slightly and pressing our lips together. Time stopped for a moment as we kissed—our first real kiss—not driven by adrenaline or gratitude this time.

Driven by need and desire.

His lips were soft and warm, his breath sweet. The tip of his tongue touched mine, and an explosion of sensation coursed through my body, making me shiver. My mouth opened wider, and his tongue slipped inside, caressing the sensitive skin as he delved deeper.

I wanted to be consumed by him; every inch of my body connected to him. I squeezed my arms tighter around his neck.

His embrace grounded me, yet at the same time, I felt like I was flying apart. I couldn't think anymore, just feel—my heart pounding, my blood surging, my breasts swelling, and nipples tightening. I rubbed them against the crisp hair on his chest, shuddering at the contact. Mind-blowing desire spread like lightning and pooled low in my belly and groin.

My sex felt ready to burst—like an overripe peach begging to be eaten—its juices sweet and plentiful.

And I wanted Robbie to feast on it.

Suddenly, he shifted to his knees before lowering me to the forest floor. My ankles hooked around his waist.

The grass beneath my back was soft, but it wouldn't have mattered if it had been rocky and hard. I wanted this desperately.

When he straightened, my legs fell to either side of his knees —my thighs splayed.

I was completely exposed to him, and I reveled in it.

I reveled in him, too, his body heavy with roped and rippling muscles, his shoulders massive, his broad chest covered in a sprinkling of crisp brown hair. His nipples peeked out at me from beneath the fine covering, and I greedily reached for them with both hands, grazing my fingertips over the hard nubs. He let out a deep, throaty growl.

Gods, I loved that sound.

I continued downward, scraping my nails over his abdomen. His muscles contracted and released with every touch, causing his breath to shudder raggedly from his lungs. I smiled wickedly as I drew out the sweet agony—for him *and* me.

"Have you dreamed of this, Robbie?" I whispered. "Have you lain in bed at night, thinking about my hands on you?"

I dipped lower.

His cock was as large as I thought it would be. Now, the bulbous head pointed upward. The slit was topped with a bead of clear liquid, and the shaft was long, smooth, and thick.

I couldn't wait to taste him. My mouth watered just thinking about it.

Dragging my fingers through the soft hair that grew in a vee down his stomach, I reached the base of his cock, intending to stroke my palm up the length of him, but he captured my hands and held them tight. My gaze jumped to his.

"I thought you said no talking?" He looked and sounded almost feral.

Lust surged through me, and I grinned wickedly, thrilled that I'd done that to him. But I was also overflowing with joy and anticipation about what was to come.

"For you, not me," I said sassily. "Unless you're saying words like hot and wet or pussy and fuck. Those words are allowed. Me? I may get a little chatty. And loud."

"No surprise there. And I would never say pussy. I hate that word."

"You just did."

He lifted my hands and bit one of my palms in retaliation. I let out a little squeak. Then he kissed and nuzzled it, his eyes closed and his nostrils flaring as he savored me with all his senses.

My heart melted, and deep down, I felt my wolf's approval.

Are you happy? I asked her as I tried to catch my breath. Robbie's tongue on my palm was way more arousing than I could have ever imagined.

Yes. Happy, she said. *We are complete.*

He pulled back and blew on my wet skin, making me shiver. "Hot," he said.

Then he lifted my other hand and did the same to that palm, this time nibbling and tasting my fingers, too. When he finished with that hand, he said, "Wet."

I giggled, then I realized what words came next, and my breath caught.

He transferred my hands to one of his and pressed them over my head, trapping the backs of my wrists against the ground.

I tugged on my arms, but he didn't let go. I was well and truly caught. A thrill shot through me as I met his eyes—he could do whatever he wanted to me.

And he took his own damn time, his gaze hot and heavy-lidded as it pored over my body.

He started with my breasts, which jutted up at him, my nipples hard and distended in arousal. He licked his lips, and I moaned, but he didn't lean down to suck on the hard nubs like I wanted. Instead, he continued his leisurely perusal.

I was long and lean with an hourglass shape at my waist and hips, and gentle dips and swells over my ribcage and belly.

His eyes trailed every curve until they fell to the trimmed, light brown curls that covered my mound. A low grumble rose from his belly.

"Pussy," he said. Then he dropped his hand to the back of my knee, ran his palm along my calf to my ankle, and pushed my leg up until it rested against his shoulder, raising my pelvis and curling it upward. I lifted my other leg and wrapped it around his hips, praying he would touch me soon.

I was completely open to him, completely exposed. And the look on his face as he stared at me almost made me come right then and there.

But still, he didn't touch me. The seconds ticked down, and my need ratcheted up.

Then, *finally*, he laid his palm on my stomach just above my mound and rubbed his thumb in one slow motion through my inner lips to my aching clit and stroked it in a hard circle.

I groaned and threw back my head, my eyes closing and my hips rocking, begging for more. But the weight of his hand disappeared.

I opened my eyes, a protest on my lips, to find him licking his thumb. He was scenting me, tasting me. When he sucked it into his mouth, a deep, aroused moan escaped my throat.

"You know, you can go straight to the source."

He grunted, then leaned down and nuzzled behind my ear. "Patience, svassa."

His forward motion pressed my leg against my body—an easy stretch for me—and lifted my pelvis higher. He rocked against it with his hips. The pressure felt good, and we groaned in unison.

I turned my head and hungrily opened my mouth beneath his. We kissed deeply, carnally, our tongues rubbing, our teeth nipping and lips sucking, our bodies rocking together. He leaned on me heavily, and I hooked my other leg around his waist.

When I lifted my mouth to draw in much-needed air, he kissed across my cheek, then sucked my earlobe into his mouth. The rhythmic pulling drove me wild.

I dug my nails into his back. "Baby, can we *please* proceed to the fucking now?"

He nipped my ear and whispered, "You and I, Britta, will *not* be fucking. We're making love."

I groaned. "You hate the word pussy; I hate the term making love. But I'm down with it, so long as you *get down*. The sooner, the better."

He snorted, catching my double entendre. "So demanding." Then he dipped his tongue inside my ear and traced the delicate whorls before kissing his way down my throat. At the crook of my neck, he paused, his mouth opening over my skin.

When I felt the protrusion of his canines, I froze, my breath sawing through my lungs as I waited desperately for him to bite me.

Claim me.

If I thought I was aroused before, it was nothing compared to how I felt now as I anticipated his teeth piercing my skin and holding me in place as we mated. My hormones went wild, and my hips loosened, my knees splaying wide.

Liquid heat flooded my channel, perfuming the air, and he inhaled sharply through his nose. A deep, possessive growl rumbled from his chest and vibrated against me, making my head fall back in complete and utter submission.

I was his for the taking.

But then his teeth retracted, and he withdrew his mouth, leaving my skin cool in the night air. "Robbie?" I asked, confused.

Quickly, he moved down my body, his hand lifting my breast to his mouth. He sucked the soft mound deep inside and bathed it with the flat of his tongue. I whimpered, the pulling sensation traveling straight to my groin.

My concern flitted away under a sea of desire.

Then he circled the nipple with just the tip before crossing to my other breast and sucking on it.

His hand palmed the wet one while his mouth gorged on the other, making me moan long and loud—just like I'd promised. I rocked against him rhythmically, and when he pinched my nipple, I jerked on the brink of orgasm.

Inside, my wolf howled, but…it wasn't in pleasure.

I sensed her dissatisfaction on the periphery of my mind, but I was too caught up in the maelstrom of my approaching climax and blocked her out.

Robbie's mouth and hands followed the same path his gaze had taken earlier as he continued to move lower, playing my body like a master musician, leaving me unable to think—only feel—and on the perpetual edge of release.

"You have to let me come!" I begged.

"Soon," he promised. He continued to stroke and strum my skin. I gasped and sighed as he touched me, my body undulating, and my knees alternately tightening around his body, then falling wide.

I wanted him *down there*. Heavy and hard. Taking me. Or feasting on me. Something!

"Robbie," I groaned again.

He slid all the way down this time, his shoulders spreading my knees and his hands sliding beneath my cheeks, lifting me as he inhaled my scent. His eyes devoured me from beneath half-lowered lids—the way I wanted his mouth to.

Silence fell, broken only by my uneven breathing.

Finally, he released the air from his lungs in a slow *whoosh*. "I have never seen, felt, tasted, or smelled anything as beautiful as you in my entire life." Then he closed his mouth over me, hot and insistent, making me lose my mind.

He didn't tease me this time. He supped on me like a starving man, lapping all the way up with broad, heavy strokes to my clit —again and again. Then he drew my inner lips into his mouth and sucked on them—first one, then the other.

I was utterly mindless, squirming and bucking my hips—or trying to. He held me tight—a prisoner—lifted to his mouth for his possession.

"Oh, Gods, Robbie. Please. Please!"

Raising me higher, he slid his tongue all the way inside me. I was filled up like I'd been begging for, but this was just an appetizer, and I wanted the main course.

Although, it felt good, too, and I moaned. He seemed to spend hours down there, in and out, up and down, as I floated in a state of ever-increasing arousal.

Then he withdrew his tongue from that hot, wet part of me, and I suddenly felt his teeth nipping my inner thighs, before soothing the spot with his tongue.

I twined my fingers in his hair and pulled—hard. He growled against my skin, which vibrated all the sensitive nerve endings through my loins, making me moan again. I didn't know if it was a protest or a plea.

All I knew was that I needed more. Now.

He slid one hand from beneath my ass and then pushed his finger where his tongue had been—first one, then two. Stretching me.

Priming me.

He massaged from the inside, and I let out a high-pitched squeak as he hit that spot, my back arching, my body stiffening. From beneath lowered lids, I watched him watching me, his fingers pumping in and out of my body, his cheeks flushed, his lips wet, and his eyes feral.

Then he lifted his gaze to mine. I panted hard and fast, my orgasm hovering just out of reach. My hands dug into the grass beside me as I tried to anchor myself.

His eyes blazed with heat. With possession.

"I love you, Britta. Come for me, baby."

Then he lowered his head, finding my clitoris and closing his lips over it, sucking on it as he flicked it with his tongue—all while he continued to stroke the pads of his fingers against my swollen flesh.

I screamed at the intensity of the sensations, the enormity of them.

Finally, the damn broke, and my orgasm roared through me in great waves. I bucked beneath his mouth, my body undulating as he held me in place and drew out the contractions. When I finally caught my breath, he changed the pressure of his tongue and the rhythm of his fingers and took me right back up to that peak.

"I can't," I gasped, my hands fisted in his hair. "Really. I can—oh, my gods, I'm coming again!"

In an instant, his fingers and mouth withdrew, leaving me hanging on a precipice as he moved up my body, sandwiching between my thighs and tilting up my hips. I lifted my legs and impatiently hooked them at the small of his back.

His body leaned on mine, supported on his elbow so he didn't crush me—pelvis to pelvis, chest to breast.

I pulled him closer, my arms wrapped around his neck as I licked and kissed his throat, releasing a stream of tiny growls.

He found my mouth, biting and sucking my lips in a way that drove me wild, and then—finally—I felt him *there*, pushing at my opening. He slid inside me slowly, and my body gave way, inch by inch. It was a tight fit, and when he was fully sheathed within me, we both let out a satisfied groan.

"Britta," he panted.

"Yes," I squeaked.

"Are you…okay?"

"You mean, has that huge cock of yours split me in half?"

He snorted and dropped his head down into the crook of my neck. "You say such beautiful things."

"I do. And no, it hasn't. You can carry on. *Please*, carry on."

"Your wish…is…" He had to stop to catch his breath, and I continued for him.

"My command."

"That's for damn sure."

"Didn't you hear me say please? I did, several times, but you were too busy torturing me to—*aaahh!*" I groaned as he pulled back out and slid his hips forward again, filling me.

My body had completely relaxed and molded around him—made room for him. As I always would.

My fated mate. Forever.

"Robbie."

"Mmm?" he groaned as he withdrew again.

I caressed my fingertips across his temples and over his hair, turning his face to mine and meeting his eyes. "I love you so much."

He stilled, just the tip of him lodged within me, twitching and pulsing. Then his hand cupped the back of my head, and he dropped his mouth to mine.

"Me too, Britta. So much."

We kissed gently at first, then his hand tightened on my hip, and he surged inside me, our kiss deepening as our bodies met.

I held on for the ride, his body covering mine, inside of mine—his tongue in my mouth, his arms holding me tight.

Still, I strained to get closer to him, to be consumed by him.

We moved together, rocking in unison as he stroked in and out of my body. The hard ridge of his pelvis rubbed over my clit every time.

He moved more powerfully now, his breath coming in short bursts, his heavy sack smacking my cheeks. Gods, it felt incredible, adding to all the other sensations rioting through my body.

I ripped my mouth from his, my neck arching as I panted his name over and over. "Robbie, Robbie! Oh gods, don't stop, Robbie. Don't stop. Oh, my gods, Robbie!"

His mouth opened over my neck as his rhythm began to fracture, and the points of his teeth grazed my skin. The pressure increased, and I moaned. It was happening—I was his for the taking—and my head fell to the side in complete and utter surrender. I longed to be claimed by him in the way of fated mates—his wolf riding him hard to make me his, and my wolf accepting the claim.

Then his hand moved to my breast, and he suddenly shifted his mouth and bit down on my earlobe instead of my shoulder as he squeezed my nipple.

I felt the pinch all the way down to my swollen center, and I screamed as my release struck hard, catching me unaware. It washed over me like a hurricane, my hips bucking wildly beneath him and my body contracting on waves of pleasure.

He climaxed after me, roaring into the night—his muscles rigid, his teeth clenched, his eyes squeezed shut—before collapsing on top of me.

I held him close as I gasped for breath. He did, too, his body still shuddering.

Then he rolled onto his back, taking me with him so I fit in the crook of his arm, my head on his chest and my top leg thrown over his.

"Sorry," he croaked, kissing my hair. "I didn't mean to crush you."

"S'okay. I like being under you." I was so spent my words slurred together.

Then something niggled at me, a splinter of glass that pierced my post-sex haze, and my orgasm-induced high quickly faded.

I raised my hand to my neck and pressed my palm against it, trying to feel a difference. Had he...? Are we...?

No, my wolf said, suddenly fully with me and brimming with displeasure. *Our mate did not claim us.*

Tears pricked my eyes, and my throat tightened. *But why? I felt him there. Twice.*

We will leave, my wolf said, and she scraped the earth with her back feet in disgust, dirt and debris flinging behind her.

No. I don't want to leave. Not yet.

He does not deserve us.

That's not true! He saved us today, saved the entire pack. I get why you're mad and hurt—I am too—but no one is more deserving.

She grunted and sat down with her back to me.

Her emotions rioted within me. Mine did, too—more complex than hers but no less deep. I squeezed my hand over my mouth to stop a sob from escaping.

Let's just...see what he has to say. And then if you don't like it, we can leave. I crossed my fingers over my heart. *I promise.*

She didn't look at me, but her tail thumped once.

Whatever Robbie had to say, it better be good because my wolf was ready to bolt and never look back.

CHAPTER 18

I COULDN'T THINK, LET ALONE MOVE. I HAD NEVER EXPERIENCED such intense arousal or so powerful a release before, or been filled with such overwhelming joy. But then, I'd never been with a female who lived in my heart the way Britta did.

Then why didn't you claim her?

The question came from deep within me—not from my wolf—and it startled me. My eyes popped open, and my heart began to pound. A cold sweat broke out on my skin.

The feeling was vaguely familiar and not in a good way. I'd been battling evil twin one and two for eight years now, and I knew the signs of an adrenaline rush.

But this was different. This felt like flight—not fight.

I inhaled deeply, trying to soothe myself, and Britta's scent, mixed with mine, filled my lungs. It was all over our skin and deep within her body. That pleased me down to my core. Yet it also made my chest tighten and my stomach twist, adding to the other things I was feeling, and I realized why it was so familiar— I'd felt it for years after my mom died.

I still did, but I pushed it down—not even realizing it.

Constant, low-level anxiety that had somehow blown up over Britta.

I closed my eyes, confused. What was wrong with me? What did I have to be anxious about—other than fighting Hati and Skoll?

Although, I never felt anxious during a fight. I felt hyper-alert and focused. Except for yesterday when Britta had been with me. Then, I'd been filled with panic and fear for her.

Gods, was that only one day ago?

A low, deadly growl started within me, and the tiny hairs on my skin rose. I searched for my wolf, but I couldn't see him in my mind's eye. Suddenly, his fury-filled gaze dominated the unusually dark, empty space. He nipped at me angrily—more of a bite —and my eyes snapped open.

My arm tightened around Britta, and I noticed her body was stiff. She sat up, keeping her back to me. My hand trailed across her shoulder and down her spine.

And I knew—I'd fucked up.

I tightened my hand on her hip and sat up behind her, desperate to make things right.

I kissed her shoulder. "I just realized I forgot to say fuck." I was trying to be amusing—and to remind her of our time together—but it came out forced. Still, she would know what I meant, wouldn't she? Fuck was the last of the four words I was "allowed" to say when we were making love. She would know I was teasing.

Please, laugh. Please, laugh.

But her shoulders hunched, and her arms wrapped around the front of her body.

I recognized that posture. I'd seen it a lot when we were younger, and our lives had been so unstable—sometimes unsafe —due to the curse. She was hurt and feeling vulnerable, protecting herself.

And I knew why. Because of me.

I shoved my hand through my hair and blew out a breath. "Britta?"

She made a muffled sound like she'd pressed her hand over her mouth. It broke me.

My wolf barked at me ferociously, pacing back and forth in a grassy field. Then he raised his muzzle and let out a mournful howl. The sky above him turned dark and turbulent.

"I'm sorry. I shouldn't have said that." Regret filled my voice. "I didn't mean to cheapen our first time together. I didn't mean to...to..." To what? Reject my fated mate?

She turned toward me, her eyes blazing with her wolf as tears rolled down her face. "Your *words* didn't cheapen anything, Robbie. You did. It has nothing to do with what you did or didn't say. It has to do with my fated mate not wanting to claim me! Twice, you were at my shoulder, my neck. Twice, you refused to bite me. You don't want to be with me, Robbie."

"That's not true. I love you, Britta."

She rose to her feet, and I rose with her. I tried to hold her hand, but she pulled it out of my grasp. She walked a few steps away and then turned to me, her body morphing into the hazy blur of the helmingr.

It bothered me that she wanted to hide her nakedness from me, especially after what we'd shared.

"I believe you, Robbie. I know you love me. I just don't know why you want to stay separate from me."

"I don't—"

"Yes, you do. Deep down. Or you would have done what your wolf was driving you to do, what my wolf wanted you to do. The bite is more for them than for us. They need it. But you fought him over it, didn't you?"

A shiver ran through me. She was right. My wolf had been riding me hard, and I'd refused. He was furious with me—Britta's wolf was too.

She let out a humorless laugh. "The ironic thing is that if you had sent out the kalla, and I'd answered you, Freyja would have joined us in the Kyssa, and I would know exactly what you were thinking and feeling—even if *you* didn't. I wouldn't be standing here hurt and confused. I'd be able to help you."

The thought of Britta being so tied to me, so close to me through the Kyssa, sent a fresh wave of panic through my body, and I swayed on my feet, my fear driving my pulse upward.

She saw it and pressed her hand over her heart. "What is it, Robbie? What are you so afraid will happen?"

I stepped back, but inside, my wolf was urging me forward.

No! I yelled.

Mate! he snarled in response.

I turned and staggered to the edge of the clearing, sat on a stump, and dropped my head in my hands. How had this happened? She was going to leave me.

Which…was good, wasn't it? I blocked out my wolf's howling as I focused on my thoughts.

I wanted her to leave—to go to New York and slay the dance world, to follow her dreams.

To set her free.

"Robbie?" Her voice came from right in front of me. Britta would never leave someone she loved in pain.

I massaged my temples to ease the pounding in my head. "What did you do to me—and to the pack—when you were dancing? It was your magic, wasn't it? I saw it and felt it. We all did."

She didn't answer, and after a moment, I glanced up.

She looked stricken—her eyes wide and her face pale. "Did I hurt you? Is that why you didn't claim me?"

I shook my head. "No, Britta. It's not that. I'm not hurt."

"Then what is it? I don't understand." She raised her hand toward me but withdrew it when colorful sparks came out of her fingertips. "I…I can help you, Robbie. That's what I did in the domr when I was dancing. My magic somehow healed the pack from the trauma endured during the cursed years. Erik restricted me to that, but I can go deeper with you. I can find out what's troubling you and fix it."

My eyes jumped to hers, and I shook my head. Her face fell.

"Later. I can't right now."

"Why not?"

"Because I can't."

"That's not good enough. Talk to me, Robbie."

I jerked upward. "Because I don't want you to stay here with me."

She gasped, and I instantly regretted my words. "Not because I don't love you, but because I want you to follow your dreams. To follow your heart."

"My heart is here. You are here."

I shook my head vehemently, denying it. "Hati and Skoll are here. You almost died yesterday. Skoll was close enough to cut you. Go and be free, Britta. Don't stay here and..."

I clamped my jaw shut, not wanting to let the words out—as if saying them would somehow make them come true.

"And what?"

When I didn't answer, she closed the space between us and placed her hand on my chest. "Answer me. *Please.*"

"Die. Don't stay here and die."

Her eyes rounded in shock.

I stepped past her and moved to the center of the glade, keeping my back to her. "Go and dance. That's your dream. Leave all of this behind. There's nothing here for you but pain and heartache."

"What are you talking about?"

"Don't be like my mother. She had dreams, too, and ended up dead because of Skoll."

The silence stretched between us. Then I felt her hand on my back. It was warm, and a tiny stream of energy leaked from her to me. Her magic was intent on me, wanting to heal me—her mate.

I tried to endure it, but a welling of grief came up. It was too much, and I stepped away again, facing her, my arms across my chest.

"I'm sorry," she said. "I don't have control of my magic yet. I'm so connected to you, and I can sense your pain so strongly. It wasn't there before—not like this. Something happened."

"You happened."

"Me?"

I nodded, not wanting to say anymore—I'd already said enough.

She studied me, her brow furrowed as she tried to figure everything out.

"You should know that Erik's bought a theater and rehearsal space in Missoula, and he asked me to head it up. Not just dance but all the arts. I'll be the artistic director, and I'll also teach and have my own dance company. I'm not losing anything by staying here. It's a dream come true for any dancer. And if I want to go to New York or Europe or Australia, I can always hop on a plane and do that."

I froze, my panic spiraling upward. She was staying here.

"I'll be teaching classes for Valdyr and humans," she continued. "Erik wants to encourage the arts within the pack. He doesn't want any pups to feel unsupported like I was. He wants us all to feel worthy whether Odin chooses us or not—or whether *we* choose Odin."

"And do you?" I asked, my voice flat.

"Yes."

She'd said it emphatically, and I took a deep breath, trying to steady my nerves.

"I'll serve in whatever way I can," she continued, "while still pursuing my dreams and being a part of my pack."

Her body lost the hazy blur of the helmingr as she solidified into her Valdyr form, all long legs, soft skin, and sensual curves, and she stepped toward me—so beautiful my heart hurt, and so damn sexy my loins ached.

"And I'll have a mate and pups because I dream of that too. I dream of you, Robbie."

I shook my head. "No. You're leaving. Far from here."

She shook her head. "No. I'm staying. Right here next to you."

I knew she would do it, and I couldn't hold in my distress or terror any longer.

"And what if I lose you the way I lost my mom? The way I lost my dad?" I shoved a shaking hand through my hair. "He was broken after my mom died. Hati killing him was a blessing—he got to go to her in the woods outside Valhalla… And he left me behind. What if I do that to you, Britta? To our pups? In no scenario does this end well for you—or me."

I turned, walking erratically across the glade, but suddenly, she was right in front of me, tears back in her eyes, sorrow etched deep upon her face.

I grabbed her upper arms hard—too hard. "I would die all over again if I did that to you. You have to go!"

She winced, and I forced my hands to relax, but she grasped my waist and dug her nails in. I welcomed the pain.

"I'm not going anywhere, Robbie. Yes, I may die, and you will have lost someone you loved again. And you may die, leaving me heartbroken and our pups without a father. But that will be nothing compared to the pain of being separated. We were made for each other, Robbie, whether our joining lasts one minute or one hundred years. Claim me."

I shook my head, closing my eyes. "No."

"Yes."

"I want you to leave." But I was pulling her toward me as I said it.

Her body melted against mine, and I groaned. She wrapped her arms around my neck, a sob shaking her slender form.

I tightened my arms around her, needing her as close as possible, and a warmth spread between us, tingling over my skin.

"Let me help you, Robbie," she cried. "Please, *minn hjarta*. Let me ease your pain. I won't take your parents away from you, I promise, but I will help you to grieve them, release them. They loved you so much, and they would hate to see you hurting for so long."

My pulse pounded in my ears, and my breath sawed anxiously in and out of my lungs.

"You're not alone anymore, svassr," she whispered. "I'm right here. Focus on me, not on something that hasn't happened yet. I've got you, Robbie. We're going to be okay."

Her words resonated through me—words I'd chanted to myself over and over after my mom, and then my dad, had died... *you're going to be okay.*

For the first time, I believed them. It wasn't just me this time—it was us. *We're going to be okay.*

I nodded my head, unable to speak, and felt the tingling energy seep through my skin. My wolf was right there with me—quiet and supportive.

A wave of anguish overcame me, and my knees weakened, but Britta held me up.

The energy was different from what I'd experienced earlier in the den when she healed the pack. This healing went deeper and slower, to the very core of me, and it was imbued with love—not just Britta's love, but my parents' and the Allfather's, too. I could even feel her drawing on the pack's love for me.

Still, my heart felt like it was being crushed, and a broken wail—my wolf and I howling together—erupted from my throat. The sound continued, long and mournful, and when it finally faded away, I dropped my head, my cheeks wet, into the crook of Britta's neck and released a shuddering breath.

Slowly, the pain in my heart eased, and the knots in my stomach unraveled. I inhaled deeply, and Britta's scent filled me again, strengthening me. My shoulders loosened as the last of the healing energy curled up my spine and dissipated through the top of my head.

I became aware that Britta was shaking under my weight, and I quickly straightened, feeling stronger and more powerful than ever.

She sagged against me, sighing in relief. "Has anyone ever told you that you weigh a ton?"

I scooped my hands beneath her butt and lifted her into my arms. She quickly hooked her legs around my waist and her arms around my shoulders.

"Yes. My doctor," I replied.

"No way," she gasped, her eyes wide and her mouth rounding into a surprised 'o'.

I took advantage and leaned in for a kiss. My tongue slipped between her lips to stroke the warm skin inside. She softened against me, tasting even better than before—although how that was possible, I had no idea.

When the kiss ended, she rested her forehead against mine as we caught our breath. "Seriously," she said between inhales. "You cannot weigh a ton. That's like…thousands of pounds."

I snorted. "I've just given you the best kiss of your life, and you're still thinking about how much I weigh?"

"You can't just say something like that and expect me to drop it!"

"You mean like a normal Valdyr?" I grinned so hard at the look on her face that it felt like my cheeks would crack.

She smacked my shoulder, and I spun us in a circle, laughing. I felt lighter than I had in years—rejuvenated and carefree. All because of this amazing, incredible female. My beloved mate. It was exactly as she'd said—I hadn't lost my parents; I'd just released all those negative emotions surrounding their deaths.

"I think you've been healing me your whole life, even if your magic wasn't involved. You've been healing all of us."

"Even when I was a pup?"

"Especially when you were a pup. All pudgy and cute. You got all of us through the tough times, even if you weren't aware of it."

"I'm pretty sure Tyr would disagree."

I laughed. "Yeah, he would. But deep down, he knows it's true. He'd never actually say it, but he loves you a ton."

"There's that word again," she said, giving me the stink eye.

"That is literally how much he loves you—a ton. And your mom and dad, too. You know that, right?"

"I do. More now than I did before. My mom cried in the hospital when she first saw me. I'd never seen her so upset. And my dad and Tyr were so fierce protecting me when they finally got to us at the creek."

I shuddered and held her even closer. "Are you happy to be part of the pack? Truly happy? I'll leave with you, Britta, if you change your mind. I'll go anywhere with you."

Her face lit up. "Fantastic! I haven't been to the mall in ages. Will you go with me? Please, please."

I groaned. Mall flu. "I walked right into that one, didn't I?"

"Yup. Just like you'll walk right through the mall with me, carrying my bags. Do you have any money, by the way? I'm kinda broke."

I started laughing and couldn't stop. Britta joined in.

"Baby, look," she said, her voice filled with wonder as she pointed upward.

The sky had lightened, and the sun was cresting the top of the mountains—a golden ball of fire sending gilded rays of light through the heavens. I caught my breath at the stunning sight.

A new day… A new beginning.

We watched quietly, filled with awe, as the colors danced across the sky.

When Britta shivered, I rubbed my hand up and down her back and arms, trying to warm her. Her skin glowed in the dawn light.

"You're cold," I said, pulling her tighter into my embrace.

"So make me burn, bad boy."

"Bad boy?"

"Uh-huh. Very bad."

I lifted her hips and positioned her over my rigid cock. She gasped in pleasure as I nudged her entrance, and then she slid down my length. We both groaned when I was fully enveloped within her.

"Is that bad enough for you?" I growled.

She raised herself up and rode me again…and again. "Yes. Astro…nomi…cally…bad." Her words came out choppy as she punctuated the strokes of her hips with the syllables.

I widened my stance, my muscles contracting to hold us upright, then lifted my hand to her cheek. "Britta, do you still want…I mean, can I…" I huffed out a breath. "I need to know if you still want me to claim you."

She stopped moving. "You have to ask?"

"I *want* to ask."

Her bottom lip trembled, and then she held my face and kissed me, soft and sweet. "Yes, svassr, I want you to claim me. And then I want you to fuck me to heaven and back. Absolutely no lovemaking. Afterward, well…follow your heart. If you call for me, I promise I'll answer. And Odin willing, Freyja will join us in the Kyssa. I want it all, Robbie. Do you want that, too?"

"Yes, *minn hjarta*. I want that, too."

"Forever?" she asked.

"Forever."

Our gentle kiss soon took a carnal turn, and she started up again, riding me in a steady rhythm that left me aching. I grasped her hips and increased our pace, surging upward as she slid down on me, then found her clit with my thumb. She whimpered as I circled it, and my wolf's teeth extended through my gums. Moving quickly, I clamped down on the crook of her neck, claiming her in the way of our kind.

My bite released hormones that flooded her bloodstream, increasing her pleasure tenfold as she capitulated to my dominance. Her body yielded to mine—her wolf to my wolf—and she moaned ecstatically, her breath coming in short, excited pants as I thrust inside her, taking her to the heavens and back. Then she screamed my name, her neck arching, her channel clenching and releasing around my cock as she climaxed.

I followed right behind.

We held each other afterward, catching our breath, and I bathed her skin with my tongue, healing the bite. I lowered her to the ground until she stood steadily, our bodies pressed together.

My wolf resided under my skin, and watched her through my eyes. He radiated satisfaction, adoration, and a little possessiveness.

No, that wasn't right. It was more like ownership. She was his female—his mate—and he was hers. They were one together.

Britta's eyes glowed with her wolf, too, and she looked content, secure, and satiated.

I didn't know how exactly to call for my mate, so I followed my instinct. I kissed her hands and then tilted my head back and along with my wolf, released a low, melodic howl. It resonated within me and extended outward to swirl in the air around us—I couldn't see it, but I could feel it.

Britta cocked her head and listened, a beatific smile on her face. Then she threw back her head and answered my call. The purity of the emotions between us—love, desire, joy—were evident in the purity of our combined howls.

Our kallas harmonized, creating a rich symphony of sounds.

I had no idea how long we sang to one another—lost in the magic of the Kyssa—but when I felt a gentle yet powerful presence, I knew Freyja was here.

Slowly, I drifted back to earth and opened my eyes just as Britta opened hers.

The goddess of love stood next to us, strong and stunning

with lush curves and a mane of shining brown curls the color of a newborn fawn. She wore a peasant-style dress in a luxuriant green covered by a cloak of falcon feathers, and she shone with a radiant glow.

Even so, I could barely take my eyes off Britta.

"It is as it should be during the Kyssa," Freyja said, her voice like wind chimes in my ears.

I dipped my head in acknowledgment, and Britta did the same.

"Thank you, goddess. We appreciate your service to us."

"We are blessed by your presence, Freyja Njördsdottir," I added.

"It is my joy and my duty to judge your union," she replied.

Then she raised her hand, and suddenly, we were both fully dressed in the white outfits we'd worn during Húsl.

Britta gasped and then laughed delightedly, as luminous as the goddess that graced our presence.

Her love and happiness radiated out to me and enveloped me.

I dug my hands into her hair and kissed her. "I love you, Britta."

"Even though I make you listen to Tay Tay in the car?"

I grinned. "Even though."

"Perfect." She snuggled into me, her head resting against my heart.

"Britta has one more question for you," the goddess said.

"I do?" Britta asked, swinging her gaze back to Freyja.

"Yes."

"What's that?" I asked, concern whispering through my heart. "You can ask me anything, svassa."

She gnawed on her lip, and my trepidation increased.

"By any chance, do you remember suggesting we name our pups Taylor and Swift?"

My eyes widened, and I wracked my brain for the memory—it was blank. "Uh...Taylor and Swift? Are you sure?"

"Yes. And I wholeheartedly agree. Best names ever, babe."

I glanced up and saw Freyja smiling at me, her eyes twinkling with amusement. Her gaze caught mine, and she nodded.

I smiled back at her and then kissed the top of Britta's head. "Agreed. Best names ever, babe. Are you ready?"

She stood back, still holding my hands, and stared at me with her heart shining through her eyes. "Always, Robbie."

I caught my breath and sent my love back to her. "Me too, Britta. Always"

Then we reached out for Freyja, and she grasped our hands in hers, forming a circle.

"Let's begin."

EPILOGUE

Odin

ODIN, THE ALL-FATHER, STOOD ON THE MOUNTAIN'S EDGE, watching the sun rise over the horizon. He clutched his spear Gungnir with one hand and stroked his other hand over his resplendent ginger-colored beard, striving to enjoy the last moment of peace he would have for the next few years—possibly forever if he failed.

Behind him, his eight-legged steed, Sleipnir, grazed in a dew-filled glade. Odin had arrived early, and the wind blew through his long red hair and billowed his plum-colored robes—even when the breeze died down. His favorite horned helmet perched on his head, and a silk patch that matched his robes covered the empty socket of his right eye.

Today, he'd chosen the visage of a leader rather than the old, grey wanderer he preferred. King of the Gods seemed like a more appropriate form to take when leading the nine worlds to the brink of destruction.

In the valley below, his Valdyr children, the Varda—descendants of the first pack—had built their compound. For eons, he'd been watching over them and experiencing every one of their heartbreaks and triumphs as his own. He'd taught them, led them, molded them, and yes, sometimes even hindered them.

More than anything, he'd loved them.

And now it came down to this.

"Odin."

Odin didn't need to turn around. He knew who was there, and he waved his friend forward. Freyja stepped up beside him, wearing her cloak of falcon feathers and carrying a purring, blue-grey cat in her arms. A loud rumbling came from Odin's other side, and he held out his hand to another cat, smiling. The larger feline pressed his head into the god's palm. The cats had been a gift to Freyja from Thor, and they could change size to fit into Freyja's arms or pull her chariot.

Odin was a favorite of theirs.

The silky fur glided through his fingertips, and he felt more certain about his decision. He had faith in his Valdyr children, and he believed in the magical power of love. He just hoped that his children would continue to have faith in him.

"You've done something," Freyja said. "I feel a shift. It's troubling."

"Yes," he replied solemnly. "It is indeed."

When he didn't elaborate, her lips tightened, then she lifted her hand, closed her eyes, and sensed the energy. "There," she said finally. "I can feel the change. It's just beginning."

He didn't answer, knowing she would soon see clearly. Among other things, Freyja was the goddess of seiðr, a form of magic that could both divine and shape the future—she'd been his teacher many eons ago. And she was, after all, the goddess of love…and war. She would see the new patterns being weaved.

When she let out a shocked gasp, he sighed, knowing what was coming.

She rounded on him, her eyes wide and agitated. "How could you not consult with me on this?"

The cat in her arms jumped down, disturbed by her sudden, jerky movements. He grew in size, and then both cats slunk off toward Sleipnir, stalking him. Naturally, Sleipnir would know they were coming, and he'd escape just in time.

It was a game they played.

But today, Sleipnir was also disturbed. He was waiting for the return of his mother, and he was…conflicted. Not that that was surprising. All the gods were conflicted about Loki.

"I did not want you to be burdened," Odin replied to Freyja, and he meant it. This choice was on him, and him alone.

And Fenris-Wolf, of course. Another of Loki's children.

"I am the Goddess of Love," she admonished him, and the sky began to darken. "It is my duty to match the hearts of your Valdyr children, to bind them together in the Kyssa as I did with Robert Helvig and Britta Larssen just moments ago—two of your favorites. I could have told you if the nine matches you were considering were compatible or not."

He deliberately ignored her reprimand. "I have no favorites. I love all my children equally."

"You should have told me! I could have chosen couples whose hearts were aligned and would call for each other. Now you've put our lives, your children's lives, the entire cosmos at risk. All Fenrir needs is for one couple to fail!"

Rain began to pelt down, and Odin flicked his fingers toward the heavens. The sky cleared, and the sun shone bright once more.

He turned to Freyja, one of his dearest and oldest friends, and grasped her hand. "The choices I made could not be determined with logic or reason. Love blooms from emotion and intuition—not calculation or deduction. You know that."

"But I could have made sure—"

"No, Freyja. Rationality has no place when it comes to the magic of love."

Freyja turned away from him, her jaw set, and looked over the valley. He saw a glimmer of tears in her eyes before she blinked them away.

"Did you choose her?" she asked.

Odin knew of whom she spoke. "Yes," he said quietly.

She nodded, her hands clenching tightly together. "The magic will require more than just the Kyssas to avert Ragnarök. True love is interwoven with sacrifice—to have one, you must have the other."

"Which is why I didn't choose the mates whose paths would be easy. I chose them for that elusive spark between them. Each pairing will have to fight for their love—make sacrifices for their love."

Freyja held herself stiffly...before she finally sighed and let her shoulders droop. He spoke truth, and she knew it.

"When will you know if Fenrir's accepted the wager—for it is a wager, yes?" she asked.

Odin tilted his head in assent. "Heimdall returns shortly with Loki. He will have an answer from his son."

As if his words had summoned them, a glimmer of bright, rainbow colors appeared in the air before the god and goddess—suspended over the valley. Slowly, the colors solidified into a walkway that extended toward Odin. A fair-skinned god with long, white-blond hair and a penchant for white leather stepped out of the colorful, flaming mist. Heimdall, the guardian of the rainbow bridge, carried the horn of Gjall over one shoulder and a gleaming sword strapped across his body. The horn traveled everywhere with Heimdall. One day, he would use it to summon the rest of the gods to battle during Ragnarök.

Now, he wore a scowl upon his face—directed at Odin.

"He nattered the entire way there and sniggered all the way back," he said, referring to Loki, of course, a hunched, piteous figure who had just stepped out of the mist behind him. "Weevils have taken root in my brain from listening to his drivel. Someday, I swear, I'll drive my sword straight through his heart—if he has one. How Sigyn puts up with him, I have no idea. The goddess is a saint."

Heimdall had never—would never—stop blaming Loki for Baldur's death. And rightly so. Some crimes couldn't be forgiven.

But Loki had once been dear to the Allfather. Nobody made him laugh—or cry—as hard as his longtime friend and blood brother Loki Laufeyjarson did.

Still, his punishment had been long and agonizing. Would this be the end of it? Odin still didn't know—Baldur had been his son, and emotion had superseded Odin's wisdom.

"Goddess!" Heimdall greeted Freyja, his face breaking into a smile. "Your beauty and grace are a boon to my senses after witnessing the ugliness of Loki's progeny. Fenrir is more loathsome a monster than you could ever imagine."

"I've heard," Freyja murmured. "You were brave to embark on such a journey, especially with the Wizard of Lies in tow."

Her eyes flicked to Loki, who stood alone on the edge of the Rainbow Bridge. His clothes were ripped and dirty, his body gaunt, and terrible wounds—raw and pustulous—covered his face.

It hurt Odin's heart to see him so injured, murderer or not.

The trickster bowed deeply and gracefully to Freyja, despite her contempt, his long hair, still jet black, sweeping his feet. "Greetings to you, too, Goddess. As you can see, I've been well. Thanks for asking."

Freyja's lips tightened, and she turned her face away from Loki. She, too, would never forgive him for Baldur's murder.

Loki stepped off the bridge, closing the distance between him and the other gods. He looked like he'd aged a millennium, making Odin want to weep. The punishment for Baldur's murder had been harsh—Loki had been strapped to a rock with the entrails of his son while a serpent dripped venom down upon him—but so had the crime. Sigyn had stayed with her husband and done what she could to spare Loki the agony of his skin melting and burning with every drop, but she could only do so much.

Odin imagined the pain had been unbearable—as his pain had been.

Behind him, Sleipnir approached, his eight hoofs heavy on the grassy field. The horse stopped at Odin's shoulder and nickered, then reached his head toward his mother. Loki's face softened, and he slowly stretched his hand toward his son, murmuring to him and stroking the stallion's nose.

Sleipnir closed his eyes and snorted softly.

Odin allowed the family reunion to continue—for Sleipnir's sake, if not for Loki's. But Loki's emotions seemed genuine—and Odin knew what it was like to be deprived of his son. Although, he had never mothered a child the way Loki had.

Sleipnir suddenly swung away and raced across the field, jumping over the tree tops and leaping from mountain peak to mountain peak. Freyja's cats excitedly gave chase.

Loki watched his child's display of strength and speed with wonder in his eyes and a smile upon his face.

Then he brought his attention back to Odin, lowered himself to the ground, and kneeled at the god's feet. "Allfather. I have done as you requested. I have my son's answer."

Odin knew the outcome already, but he waved his hand and allowed Loki to continue.

"Fenrir has some conditions before he accepts the wager."

"As expected, Trickster. But know that I have seen your meeting with Fenris-Wolf. Do not twist his demands to your own end."

Loki lowered his head in submission. "Never, Allfather." Then he looked up again, his eyes sharp. "His demands are as follows: Freyja cannot interfere to ensure the Kyssa."

"Done," Odin said. His voice intoned across the mountains, and lightning struck down from the clouds, landing beside Loki.

The Trickster god jumped. He cowered for a moment, then

straightened. "None of the other gods, including you, can interfere in the Kyssa either. The mated pairs must reach that point on their own, and when Freya checks their hearts, she must not join them if it is not a true love match."

"Done," Odin said, and another strike of lightning landed beside Loki, closer this time.

The Wizard of Lies hesitated, and his voice trembled when he continued. "If one of the nine couples fail—if they choose not to join with their fated mate—then Fenrir will be released from his prison immediately and delivered without hindrance to Jotunheim, free to proceed as he desires."

"Done," Odin said, "But if all nine couples find true love and join together in the Kyssa, Fenris-wolf will cease to exist, and Ragnarök, the end of the worlds, will be averted."

Loki blanched, although it was hard to tell because his skin was so pale. Then he closed his eyes and nodded. Immediately, the clouds rumbled, and a massive lightning strike hit the mountain beside Loki with a deafening crack, making the earth shake.

"We are agreed!" Odin boomed. Then his head fell back, and his eye rolled upward until just the white was visible in the socket. He raised his arms, and the lightning hit Gungnir, flashing along the metal and setting Odin aglow. "The wager between Odin the Allfather and Fenrir, son of Loki, has been set. All are bound to this agreement, and none can interfere. It is as I proclaim: the fate of the nine worlds rests upon Love's shoulders. Forevermore."

THE GODS HAVE GAMBLED.
NINE TIMES SHALL THE WAGER BE ANSWERED.
NINE TIMES MUST LOVE PREVAIL...
OR THE END COMES.

In Missoula, Montana, Odin's wølves fight to save the world from *Ragnarök*.
One Kyss at a time...

Thank you for reading **Wolf's Kiss**!

Want more Wølves Of Odin?
Wolf's Reign is available for purchase and features Erik and his fated mate Kristin as they battle the curse, the sons of Fenrir, and their own true love!

READ AN EXCERPT:

<u>WOLF'S REIGN</u>—Chapter 1 (Sneak Peek!)

Kristin

Missoula County, Montana

Leave it to Gina to kill me before I even got to the compound.

I stared into the grill of the black Range Rover as it barreled toward us, sure this was it. I tossed the gods a quick prayer, and for the second time in my life, I waited to die.

Gina swerved left, long red nails flashing on the wheel, and I slammed against the passenger door. Eyes closed, I braced myself for impact.

When the Mini came to an abrupt halt without the death blow I'd expected, I unclenched my teeth and took a deep breath. "I said pull over, not kill us now."

My foster sister cut the engine. "Technicalities."

Opening my eyes to a bright summer day and a gorgeous mountain view, I sighed with relief. Then I noticed the Mini convertible was parked sideways, a foot away from the drop-off—and there was no guard rail. "Not funny."

"Consider it behavioral therapy. I'm helping you face your fears."

"Uh-huh. Cause that's what you're all about. The helping."

Gina stepped out of the car and sauntered to the edge of the cliff.

Her gauzy white skirt revealed shapely legs, and her crocheted pink halter top exposed way too much boob. She looked back, her dark hair blowing in the breeze, and smirked.

I gritted my teeth. I would not give my sister the satisfaction of seeing me climb out of the driver's seat. Instead, I opened the car door, planted my boots on the tiny ledge between the car and the drop-off, and forced myself to stand.

Do not look down. Do not look down.

Closing my eyes, I side-stepped toward the trunk of the car. My fear of cliffs was not real. It's not like I could fall, being supernatural and all. I was like Supergirl. Or, even better, Hawkgirl—my favorite comic book character when I was a kid.

When my right foot hit the back wheel, my lids opened just a smidge…and I stilled. Below, nestled in a wide, rocky valley, lay Wolf Ridge Industries. A thrill shot through me despite my fear, and if I hadn't been afraid of falling to my death, I would have started happy dancing.

This must be it.

I had no doubt the complex—hel, the entire valley—was guarded. Even if a pack didn't live in this range of mountains northwest of Missoula, Montana, the nature of the company dictated heavy security.

"Maybe you shouldn't go," Gina said. "It's a long way down. It could set your cliff-therapy thingy back years."

Her sarcasm grated, but I could hear the worry festering beneath the words, and I sighed. We'd been over this. I needed to get close enough to discover if Valdyr lived in the valley—close enough to scent them.

More importantly, to scent Hans. I'd been hunting him for years.

Still, every once in a while, it was nice to know my foster sister cared—which, right about now, as I stared into the jaws of death, was doubtful.

"They can't smell me, Gina, not unless I shift. And no way in hel is that happening with a bunch of unkyssed males around. When I met Dahlia in Denver, she didn't realize I was Valdyr, even though I scented her as soon as she entered the gallery. We don't even know if a pack lives here or not."

Closing my eyes again, I jumped over the back of the car instead of going around. I'd had about all that I could handle of my phobia right now.

When I landed on the other side, the jolt woke my wolf, who huffed before rolling over to go back to sleep. The pique that rose through me made me smile.

Lazy dog.

Inside, my wolf growled.

Where exactly "inside" was, only Odin knew. A Valdyr resided on two planes: the physical plane of Earth and a spiritual plane called Hjarta—or *heart*. Years ago, when my wolf tried to explain the supernatural realm to me, she relayed the image of a rock—a spherical geode—with thousands of crystals inside. I interpreted each crystal to be an individual cell or dimension within the spiritual plane.

Bonded wolves, whether kyssed pairs, family, or packmates, shared these special cells, and a wolf could exist in one or all of them, all at once. But since I had no mate, no pack, and no family, me and my wolf were alone.

Pinching the bridge of my nose, I made my way toward my sister. Thinking about things like higher dimensions made my head hurt. I was an artist, not a cosmologist or astrophysicist.

The only thing I knew for certain was that my wolf was always with me and ready to shift at a moment's notice if I needed her. Or just to natter in my ear.

Another growl. *Natter?*

Sorry. I meant "give advice and express opinions...frequently."

When I reached Gina, I grabbed her hand and pulled her a safe distance away from the precipice.

"Maybe Dahlia did smell you, and this is a trap," Gina said. "You were locked up before. They might try it again."

"I was locked up by a psychopath who may or may not have been Valdyr. Hans had magic—only female Valdyr are magical. Anyway, if it is a pack, I'll look around and report back. If not, I'll sell a bunch of art for outrageous prices. Either way, I win."

"It is a pack—or something non-human."

I glanced at her sharply. "How do you know?"

"The entire valley is warded." Gina lifted her hands as if feeling the air. "The fortifications are strong...and old. I could break them for you, but…" She frowned, and I could see her fingers glowing. "It'll take me a few days."

"No. Keep your itchy-witchy fingers to yourself. We'll be gone before then."

A vehicle roared up behind us, and I spun around. Instinct had me stepping in front of my sister, who poked me in the back. "Hello. Daughter of Freyja here. I could easily turn the driver into mush."

It was an exaggeration—of sorts—and I didn't move. No way would I lose another family member. Gina might not be my real sister, but she was a sister of the heart, and I wouldn't be here if not for her.

A stinging electrical shock zapped me in the ass, and my wolf jumped awake with a yelp before snapping in my sister's direction. Gina didn't sense the wolf, of course—she was a witch, not a Valdyr—but I did.

I stepped to the side with a muttered curse, resisting the urge to rub my tingling butt. To hel with sisterly love.

"Language," Gina said smugly.

The big black Range Rover we'd almost hit earlier screeched to a halt, and my gut sank. Damn…the vehicle looked official. The last thing I wanted was to piss off people at Wolf Ridge before I even made it to my appointment.

Tinted windows hid whomever was inside, but when the driver's door opened, a familiar scent hit me, and I inhaled deeply. It reminded me of my brothers—strong, dominant, protective—and brought tears to my eyes. I quickly blinked them away.

My wolf raced forward, tail high.

Easy, I said, mentally clamping down on my scent even though I knew the Valdyr couldn't smell me as anything other than human. I'd mastered the ability to conceal my scent during the tragedy of my ulf-risa when the early rising of my wolf caused the unkyssed males to go feral. Too bad I hadn't mastered any other aspect of my magic.

Since my escape from Hans, I'd barely felt a spark in my belly.

But in other ways, I was stronger and faster. I'd trained with Gina for years, honing my skills against my sister's magic. I had no doubt I could take Hans—and kill him this time.

If I could find him.

The male who exited the driver's side was tall and broad-shouldered with buzzed black hair and dusky skin. He wore jeans and a tight gray T-shirt over a flat abdomen. All Valdyr carried a colorful aura I could see when I used my super-acute second sight—my avian sight, as my dad had called it—and this male, who leaned on the Range Rover's hood with his arms crossed over his chest, shone like a rainbow. Same as my sister.

It was the magic within them. Humans didn't carry nearly the same punch.

Dark sunglasses covered the Valdyr's eyes. He looked toward Gina—who'd cocked her hip and thrust out her chest.

Who'd have guessed? A man snookered by big boobs.

But then the man frowned. "What kind of idiot crosses two lanes of oncoming traffic without looking? You almost caused an accident."

Gina flicked her hair over her shoulder. "You're alive, aren't you?"

"I'm not the one who would've eaten the pavement, sweet cheeks. What's the matter? Too much silicone seeping into your brain?"

I groaned and quickly stepped in front of Gina, facing her just as my sister raised her hand to zap the man. I let my wolf shine through my eyes. "Just say you're sorry, Gina, and let's leave."

My sister's mouth set, and we glared at each other. Finally, she lowered her hand. With a sigh of relief, my wolf subsided.

This could still end peacefully.

Then, a second scent hit my nose, and I almost dropped to my knees.

<hr>

Erik

I sat frozen in the passenger seat of the Range Rover, watching the dark-haired woman argue with Gunn. The blond had turned toward the vehicle and was staring directly at me through the tinted glass.

Can she see me?

The darkness inside of me—the curse that had ravaged me since I'd sucked it out of the pack and trapped it inside the hjarta with my wolf—surged in response, almost breaking free of its prison. My wolf forced it back down, mentally fortifying the blocks of the well that contained it and stopping its poisonous spread of suspicion and distrust. When my wolf had finished, I turned my attention back to the women.

The dark-haired one was a knockout, but it was the blond who held my attention—my wolf's too—which was unheard of for a human, or even a Valdyr.

The darkness was drawn to her too.

She was tall and slender with long legs encased in tight jeans that she'd tucked into high-heeled boots. A white T-shirt skimmed her curves, which were slight. Except for her ass. When she turned around to speak to her friend, it bowed out like an apple.

One I wanted to bite.

Compelled to see her eyes, I opened the passenger door and stepped out. Pushing my sunglasses onto my head, I stared. She met my gaze, wide-eyed, and tucked a strand of long, wavy hair behind her ear. My wolf gave an approving growl while the curse began to bubble.

Settle down, I told my wolf. *She's human, for Odin's sake.*

Mate, my wolf replied, bowing down on his front paws and tossing and tilting his head.

Damn. I'd been around wolves, natural and Valdyr, all my life. My wolf was flirting with her. No way should the big male be attracted to a human any more than I should be attracted to a natural wolf.

Gunn glanced at me, sensing my unease through the Alpha bond.

Advancing slowly, I scented the air. Had I missed something? Nothing unusual tainted her scent.

Gunn strode around the Range Rover to my side. "What's up?" he whispered.

"Maybe nothing. It's just…my wolf likes her."

"What's not to like? The woman's a living, breathing sex goddess. And a mouthy one too. Just my type."

I smiled, but it faded quickly. The arousal, whether mine or my wolf's, wasn't a laughing matter. "Not that one. The blond woman. Just be careful."

"Always." Gunn flashed me a leering grin. "But maybe your wolf just wants to get laid. The pack won't fall apart if you take a night for yourself, you know." He swung his gaze toward the women, this time checking out the blond. "She's got pretty hair and great legs. And when she turned around, her a—"

My wolf snapped at Gunn through the bond, his lips pulled back in a snarl. Gunn—and his wolf—jumped back.

"I warned you." I knew Gunn hadn't meant any disrespect. My wolf shouldn't have been so possessive. The woman was human, after all.

The dark-haired "sex goddess" tossed a pebble at us. It hit Gunn on the shoulder. "Yo, rock star. You got a problem?"

Irritation, but also admiration, crossed Gunn's face. "Nothing to concern you, Miss Silicon Valley."

The blond briefly closed her eyes and shook her head. I understood why when her friend narrowed her gaze and sauntered toward Gunn, the sway of her hips matching the natural sway of her breasts.

"Freyja's tits," Gunn murmured.

I shifted my focus back to the blond, and when our eyes met, my wolf nipped at me to get moving. As I approached her, I tried to remember why I needed to be cautious. But that was hard to do when her eyes, a golden hazel streaked with amber, tugged at something deep inside.

"Hi," I said, my voice cracking at the end.

Her lips pulled back in a smile. "Hello."

And then I couldn't get my tongue to work. Silence hung between us. *Suave, dude,* Gunn said through the bond. I resisted the urge to give him the finger.

"I'm sorry my sister nearly hit you," the woman said. "She really is a terrible driver. If it's any consolation, I almost had a heart attack."

"Me too. Maybe you should drive from now on." I wanted to touch her and found myself raising my hand to her hair. I quickly shoved it in my pocket.

"I needed to navigate. Her driving is actually better than her sense of direction."

"Hard to believe. But it's better to be lost than dead. Where are you going?"

"Wolf Ridge Industries. I saw the logo on your car. Are you with the company?"

Gunn!

I heard.

"You need an appointment to get in." I tried to keep my voice relaxed, but it was tough with the tension that had invaded my muscles.

"I have one with Dahlia Kron. She came to my gallery in Denver last week and asked me to come and see her. She's decorating the offices."

Right. The artist. Dahlia wanted to buy some of her paintings—amazing depictions of wolves and other wildlife. I'd recently put Dahlia in charge of refurbishing the pack's den, trying to find a place for her, and she'd found this woman's work.

"You're the artist she mentioned. Kristin Andersen." I held out my hand. "I'm Erik Kron. Dahlia's my cousin."

She squeezed my hand briefly before pulling away. It was enough to make my wolf howl.

Settle down.

"I read about you when I researched the company. You're the CEO."

"Yes. And that's Gunnar Lang, Head of Security. We call him Gunn. You can understand why he's a little touchy about your sister's driving."

When Kristin looked over at the still-arguing Gunn and Gina, I stared at her. This time, I noticed all the little details—the long blond-tipped eyelashes, the faint white scar on the top of her left cheek, the stone Norse rune for strength fastened on a leather cord around her neck.

Hmm. That was suspicious too. I glanced at Gunn. *You getting anything?*

Just a bunch of sass. This woman has some mouth on her. Maybe if I got her to put it on me instead, she'd shut up.

I brought my attention back to Kristin. "Gina's your sister? You don't look alike."

Pink tinged her cheeks, and she pushed a self-conscious hand through her hair. "I know. I take after my dad. We really should get going. My appointment's in twenty minutes." She signaled Gina and then held out her hand to me—firmly this time, as if she'd prepared herself. "It was nice to meet you, Mr. Kron."

"Please, call me Erik." I took her hand, and a shiver of desire rolled through both me and my wolf. That other part of me, the joy-sucking darkness I detested, boiled up to the top of the walls that contained it. I released her and quickly stepped back. "Why don't you come with me to Wolf Ridge? It'll be easier to get past security."

"Oh, well…thank you, but that's not necessary. I'm sure it won't be a problem."

"I'm afraid I insist. We don't let strangers into the compound often. I agreed last week because Dahlia said you needed to see the space." I turned to Gina, who was striding toward us with a frown on her face. "You, unfortunately, won't be allowed in without clearance. And that can take weeks."

"Do you expect me to just sit here and wait?" Gina asked, planting her hands on her hips.

"Yes. But don't worry, you won't be alone. Gunn will keep you company."

Thanks, big dog.

You're welcome. In the meantime, why don't you use that mouth of yours in a nice, non-sexual way and see what you can find out.

How does that work again?

Repressing a smile, I took the keys from Gunn and turned to Kristin. "Do you have everything?"

She reached into the back seat of the car for a large portfolio bag, swung it over her shoulder, and then one-arm hugged her sister, who was gripping her other arm. "I'll be fine," she said and then stepped away and strode ahead of me toward the Range Rover, her head held high and her rounded ass rocking my world.

I had the sudden feeling nothing would ever be the same.

WOLF'S REIGN is out now!

FREE BOOKS!

**Sign up for Madelyn Layne's
Newsletter and get access to
free books, bonus material, and
exclusive content.**

Find Madelyn's Newsletter at her website:
www.madelynlayne.com

Also, please leave a review! I greatly appreciate you taking the time to tell others why you loved Wolf's Kiss. It allows me to keep writing this wonderful series. 🩶

Interested in more of Madelyn Layne's writing?

Madelyn also writes adventure-filled historical romance set in the wilds of Scotland under the pen name Alyson McLayne. Check out her critically acclaimed series The Sons Of Gregor MacLeod and meet one of Erik's ancestors in Highland Thief!

I also have a free series sampler called First Dates With Alyson McLayne that features all five books. Happy Reading!

GLOSSARY OF TERMS

WORDS:

•**Allfather:** Odin.

•**Alsviðr:** One of two horses that pulls the Sun (Sol's chariot) across the sky in Norse mythology. Alsviðr means very quick.

•**Bikkja:** A Valdyr slur from Old Norse, meaning a female dog.

•**Blóð sausage:** Blood sausage. Often made during Húsl.

•**Brokkr:** Dvergar money.

•**Dýr pie:** Venison pie. Often made during Húsl.

•**Domr:** A sanctified circle the Valdyr use for high rituals, in which Odin and the pack's Alpha male or female bring judgment upon a Valdyr or other creature.

•**Domari:** The Valdyr who sanctifies the sacred circle.

•**Fúinn fiskr:** A childish Old Norse derogatory term for someone, which means rotten fish.

•**Fukja:** Old Norse curse word (fuck).

•**Fyrsta:** Alpha female of the pack.

•**Fyrstr:** Alpha male of the pack.

•**Handsal:** A ceremony that bonds a wolf to his or her pack.

•**Helmingr:** A magical merging of the Valdyr with his or her wolf. The helmingr happens the first time the wolf rises and the last time upon death. A strong Valdyr can enter the helmingr at will.

•**Hjarta:** A Valdyr resides on two planes: the physical plane of Earth and a spiritual plane called Hjarta—or *heart*. Kristin's wolf uses the image of a rock—a spherical geode—with thousands of crystals inside to describe the supernatural realm of Hjarta. Each crystal can be interpreted as an individual cell, or dimension, within the spiritual plane. Bonded wolves, whether they are kyssed pairs, family, or packmates, share these special cells. A wolf can exist in one or all of them, all at once.

•**Hringr:** A sanctified circle the Valdyr use for high and low celebrations or rituals.

•**Húsl:** An annual holiday that takes place on the first Wednesday in May, celebrating the creation of the Valdyr and commemorating the sacrifice of the wolf pack that died so the first Valdyr could come forth.

•**Kalla:** The howl a male Valdyr sends to his chosen female during the Kyssa. If the female responds and Freyja sanctions the union, the goddess will join them in the Kyssa.

•**Kaer dottir:** Dear daughter.

•**Kyssa (kyssed, kyss, unkyssed):** The magical bond, sanctioned by Freyja, that joins fated mates. Equivalent to human marriage.

•**Meinfretr:** An Old Norse slur, meaning stinkfart.

•**Minn barn:** My child. A term of endearment.

•**Minn hjarta:** My heart. A term of endearment.

•**Minn móðir:** My mother. A term of endearment.

•**Rekkr:** Warrior wolf.

•**Seiðr:** A form of magic that can both divine and shape the future. Freyja is the goddess of seiðr, and she taught the magical art to Odin.

•**Smalahove:** A dish made with a cooked sheep's head. Considered a delicacy.

•**Sótt-skáli:** The deep, regenerative sleep that injured and sick Valdyr go into in order to heal.

•**Svassa:** A term of endearment for females, meaning beloved.

•**Svassr:** A term of endearment for males, meaning beloved.

•**Ulf:** Wolf.

•**Ulf-einn:** Lone wolf.

•**Ulf-mynd:** When the souls of the wolf and the Valdyr merge.

•**Ulf-risa:** The rising of a female Valdyr's wolf. A rite of passage.

•**Ulf-rist:** The rising of a male Valdyr's wolf. A rite of passage.

•**Ulf-ungr:** Young wolf.

•**Ulf-verr:** Husband.

•**Ulf-vif:** Wife.

•**Valdyr:** Shape-shifting wolves created by Odin to guard Fenrir and prevent Ragnarök.

•**Varda:** The strongest Valdyr pack—descended from the original pack created by Odin.

•**Vel Finna:** A formal greeting. Also used to say goodbye.

•**Yla:** The howl a wolf sends out during the Handsal, asking to join the pack.

RACES/CHARACTERS:

•**Dverg (singular), Dvergar (plural), Dvergish (the language):** A race of magical alchemists and mountain-dwellers who live in Nidavellir. They are generally shorter than human females, very strong, and fierce.

•**Dvalinn:** A dverg who is said to have introduced the writing of runes to the Dvergar.

•**Fenrir (Fenris-Wolf):** A monstrous wolf-shifter. Son of Loki and a witch Jotuness.

•**Freyja:** Norse goddess of love, sex, marriage, fertility, and war. Also the goddess of seiðr.

•**Hati:** A wolf-shifting Jotun whose magic is tied to the moon. He is the son of Fenrir and twin brother of Skoll.

•**Heimdall:** Norse god in charge of Bifrost. He will call the gods to battle during Ragnarök.

•**Jotun:** Race of Giants. Enemies of the Norse gods.

•**Loki:** Trickster god. Blood brother of Odin and father of Fenrir. Murderer of Baldur.

•**Mimir:** The wisest of the Norse gods.

•**The Norns—Urd (past), Verdani (present), Skold (future):** The Norse Fates who weave the great tapestry of life and care for Yggdrasil at the Well of Urd.

•**Odin:** Allfather of the Norse gods and ruler of Asgard.

•**Skoll:** A wolf-shifting Jotun whose magic is tied to the sun. Son of Fenrir and twin brother of Hati.

PLACES/EVENTS:

•**Asgard:** Home of the Norse gods.

•**Bifrost:** Also called the Rainbow Bridge. Bifrost connects Earth to Asgard.

•**Hel:** Citadel of Niflheim.

•**Nidavellir:** World of the Dvergar. Interchangeable with Svartalfheim.

•**Niflheim:** World of the dead.

•**Ragnarök:** A prophesied apocalypse that is brought on when Fenrir escapes his prison and devours Odin.

•**Valhalla:** A paradise for warriors killed in battle and deemed worthy by Odin.

•**Well of Urd:** A well in Asgard that waters Yggdrasil.

•**Yggdrasil:** The World Tree at the center of the nine worlds.

SPECIAL OBJECTS/ANIMALS:

•**Gjall:** Heimdall's horn with which he'll summon the gods to battle during Ragnarök.

•**Gleipnir:** A leash of ribbon that binds Fenrir until Ragnarök.

Made by the Dvergar, it's the only fetter strong enough to hold Fenrir.

•**Gungnir:** Odin's spear. Gungnir is said to never miss its target.

•**Sleipnir:** Odin's eight-legged steed. Birthed by Loki.

ACKNOWLEDGMENTS

As aways, I'd like to acknowledge the love and support of my family and their unwavering belief in this book and Wølves Of Odin. I couldn't have done it without you.

I'd also like to thank my friend and editor Kari Cole for critiquing every chapter and Melonie Johnson for her fabulous proofing skills at the end.

And to the rest of my writing gang—Carol, Iona, Jaycee, and Layla—for being there daily to share our writing lives from wherever we are in the world.

Also, a big thanks to Brenna Aubrey for listening to my plan to write a prequel novella and then offering an alternative that worked so much better.

Hugs to all of you. 🤍

ABOUT THE AUTHOR

After earning her degree in theatre at the University of Alberta, Madelyn Layne moved to the west coast of Canada and worked in film for several years before buckling down and finishing her first published book.

She lives in Vancouver with her prop master husband, twin eleven-year-olds, a sweet, sucky chocolate lab, and two cats who are always up to something.

Madelyn loves coffee, listening to podcasts, and watching Harry Potter with her kids. In case of emergencies, she keeps a stash of chocolate in the cupboard, which she savours late at night when she's writing…and everyone else is asleep.

Visit Madelyn's website:
www.madelynlayne.com

ALSO BY MADELYN LAYNE

Wolf's Kiss

Wolf's Reign